ALOHA LOVE

ALICE WOOTSON

ALOHA LOVE

BET Publications, LLC
http://www.bet.com
http://www.arabesquebooks.com

ARABESQUE BOOKS are published by

BET Publications, LLC
c/o BET BOOKS
One BET Plaza
1900 W Place NE
Washington, DC 20018-1211

All Kensington Titles, Imprints, and Distributed Lines are available at special quantity discounts for bulk purchases for sales promotion, premiums, fund-raising, and educational or institutional use. Special book excerpts or customized printings can also be created to fit specific needs. For details, write or phone the office of the Kensington special sales manager: Kensington Publishing Corp., 850 Third Avenue, New York, NY 10022, attn: Special Sales Department, Phone: 1-800-221-2647.

First Printing: January 2005

10 9 8 7 6 5 4 3 2 1

Printed in the United States of America

ACKNOWLEDGMENTS

Thanks to my new friends in Hawaii: to Alan Olmos, CFI of the HPD Helicopter Section, who sent me a wealth of valuable information and referred my questions to the real Kalele, Janet Lee. Janet followed her dream and has been a commercial helicopter pilot and flight instructor in Hawaii for Makani Kai Tours for twenty years. She has been most helpful and patient in answering my many questions about various scenarios. Mahalo (thank you), and aloha to both of you.

Thanks again to Ike. I couldn't do this without you.

Last, but definitely not least, thanks to God for making Hawaii. It's as if He decided to gather up all of the leftover beauty from his other nature creations and used it to make Hawaii.

ONE

Jeanine Stewart sat in the pilot's seat. The flight was over and the chopper sat on the ground, but she didn't move. Normally the slowing whir of the chopper's blades helped her unwind, but not today. Today she waited for her common sense to replace the outrage and fear that filled her.

The blades quit and, without looking, Jeanine knew they slumped at rest. She took a deep breath, grabbed her papers, and climbed out of the cockpit.

As she shoved the door shut, she wished it had a more car-door-slamming thud. She shook her head. *It wouldn't have helped.*

The sun easing itself across the Hilo, Hawaii horizon didn't help her mellow, either. In fact, if it needed more heat, she had tons to spare. Jeanine wasn't angry. She was mad.

For somebody only five-feet-five, her strides were surprisingly long as her steps quickly ate up the tarmac to the hangar.

"Nate." Her voice lifted over the hum of a few active engines on the closest table, but not because she had planned it that way. "Where the devil are you?"

"Here." A short muscular man came from the small office at the rear. "What's your problem this time?"

He added more dirty oil from his hands to the already full rag that he was holding.

"It's the same problem as the last time and the time before that. And it's not just my problem. It's yours, too." Even if every engine on every one of the five long tables lining the hangar had been running, Nate would have heard her. "Something is still wrong with that chopper."

"Look, I've gone over that engine more thoroughly than any other one that we got. Nothing's wrong except that its showing it's age." He stared at her. "You must be suffering from PMS or something."

"Oh, no, no, no." Jeanine shook her head. "I know you didn't go there." She shifted her papers to one hand and pointed toward the parking lot. "Not with your midlife crisis parked out there disguised as a red Porsche convertible."

"I'm too young for a midlife crisis."

"That's not what your face says."

They held a staring standoff for a few seconds. Then Jeanine spoke again.

"Look. I know you've gone over it, but I tell you something is wrong. It stalled on me again. I thought I was going down over one of the valleys. I don't want my headstone to say, 'She Was Right.' Will you check it again, or do I have to become a mechanic and fix it myself?"

"I've forgotten more about those birds than you'll ever know. What I know didn't all come from school."

"I hope what you've forgotten isn't what you need to fix that chopper."

"All right, little lady. I'll check it again, but I think it's all in your head."

Little lady? Jeanine opened her mouth to say something, then closed it. *I'm not wasting any more time on him. He said he'd check it again. I'll quit while I'm ahead.*

She used her shoulder to push the door to the parking lot just as somebody pulled.

"Watch out!"

Jeanine stumbled but didn't go down. Instead, she watched as her top papers slid to the ground, mixing with papers that fell from the other person's hands. A sheet skittered off, pushed by the breeze blowing in.

"Sorry." She grabbed a rolled-up paper before it could get away.

"I would say no problem, but that would be a lie."

Jeanine glanced at the face of a man who looked as if he should be on a pedestal among the bronze statues in an art museum.

"Oh, I'm sorry." She forgot about the page she had been reaching for.

"You already said that." *His smile is more than any hunk of metal could capture.*

"I'll get them." She bent at the same time he did, and their heads bumped. More pages and rolls of paper slid from their hands. A sheet skipped on a wind gust.

"If we're going to do this dance, I think we'd better learn the steps first." His smile widened as they both stood straight.

"I'd say 'sorry' again, but I'm afraid of what might happen this time." Jeanine smiled up at him. *Six-foot-three if he's an inch.* Nate faded to just a name.

"Chris Harris." He held out his hand.

"Jeanine Stewart." She let his hand envelop hers. *You really* can *feel electricity from somebody,* she thought as she eased her hand from his.

"Maybe we should take turns? Or at least slow down."

"Either, or," she managed.

Neither moved.

"Hey, Chris. You looking for me?" As if he hadn't already done enough damage, Nate's voice intruded.

"Yeah. Wait a minute." Chris looked back at Jeanine. "Let's take this slowly. Less chance of getting hurt that way."

"Sounds like a plan." *Slowly is the last thing I want right now.* Jeanine took a deep breath and moved to retrieve a roll from under a table.

"How's Sarah doing?" Again Nate's yell intruded. This time Jeanine listened to the answer.

"She's fine. I'll be over there in a minute."

Chris gathered the last of the papers. Jeanine watched as he glanced through them, separated some, and handed the rest to her.

"Thanks." She took them, turned, and walked away and out of the hangar without looking back.

"What did you do to make her mad?" Chris said to Nate, but his gaze was on Jeanine as she walked away. *She looks just as good from that angle as she did up close.* When he could no longer see her, he turned his attention back to Nate. "Well?"

"I didn't do anything."

"What did you say to her, then?"

"She's got some fixation about her engine. She's always complaining about it."

"About what?"

"The engine in her chopper. She's a pilot."

"She's always complaining about the same thing?"

"Yeah."

"Did you check it?"

"No. I decided to let her crash." He shook his head. "Of course I checked it." He stared at Chris. "Hey, Big Brother, somebody make you my boss when I wasn't looking?"

"I just wouldn't want anything to happen to her." He frowned. "Or anybody else."

"Neither would I. That would be kind of hard to explain, especially with her. Being her, she probably logged each complaint with five different people and left a 'to-be-opened-if-my-chopper-crashes' envelope at her place."

"If I didn't know you better, I'd think you meant that." Chris glanced at the empty doorway. "Who is she, anyway?"

"Didn't she tell you?"

"She told me her name, but who is she?"

"A female chopper pilot with an attitude. She's been with us for about six or seven years."

"I'm sure your attitude doesn't have anything to do with her attitude."

"There you go. Taking somebody else's side again. I told her that I'll check it again. Satisfied?"

"Not really." Chris stared at his younger brother. "When are you going to call Sarah?"

"Phones work both ways." Nate concentrated on the rag in his hand as if it were a piece of broken machinery and he was trying to figure out how to repair it.

"You know you were wrong." Quiet hung in the air as heavy as a sack of wet sand.

"I guess." He shrugged. "You know me and Little Sis are always arguing."

"That's because you're always pushing her buttons."

"She makes it so easy."

"Nate."

"Okay, okay. I'll call her when I get off."

"Good. Here are the plans you asked for. We need to discuss them, but I thought you might like to look at them first. I don't know why you don't just tear down that old shack and build a new house."

"Spoken like an architect."

"Spoken like somebody who's here to tell you that little grass shacks have been out of style since way before our time."

"It's not built of grass."

"Only because the previous owner decided not to rethatch the roof and that tin ones are noisy in the rain." Chris shook his head. "It's certainly old enough for either." He held up a loose-leaf notebook. "Look at the plans and my notes." He handed him several rolls of papers and the book. "I drew up two sets for you: one for the remodeling and one for a new house that will bring you into this century. The difference in the costs will even out over time."

"That place has sentimental value."

"You're sentimental over a falling-down shack, and yet you don't care about your broken relationship with our sister?"

"Gotten philosophical, have we?" Nate frowned. "Okay, I'll call Sarah."

"When?"

"When I get leave here."

"Maybe you'd better stop by. That way she can't hang up on you. You can stick your size thirteen in the door so she can't close it."

"Jealous, are we?"

Chris laughed. "Talk to you later, Bro."

When he reached the doorway, he thought of Jeanine. *I wonder. If I find an excuse to be here tomorrow, will she be here?* He shook his head. *This feels like high school and I'm trying to get next to a female who's not interested in me.* He frowned. *I caught vibes from her at first. Then she changed. What happened?*

***

After she got into her car, Jeanine just sat staring out the windshield. *Good to find something out sooner rather than later,* she thought. She leaned back. *I think that whoever said that all the good ones were taken was right.* She shook her head. *I don't know if he's a good one or not. I never had enough time to find out.* She sighed. *Yeah. Better to find something like that out sooner rather than later.* She thought back to Barry of a year and a half ago. *Why do so many married guys think there's something better out there? Why do they feel the need to get next to some single woman who they think won't care?*

She sighed again, then popped an oldies CD into the player. In spite of her disappointment, she smiled. Trent and Angela had given it to her last Christmas. They had indulged her fixation on music from the fifties and sixties. Her smile widened as she pulled out of the lot and headed for her house. A twinge of regret poked at her when she thought of Chris Harris who was obviously taken by lucky Sarah. *He had seemed interested. Is he a player or was it my imagination? Maybe Nate is better at fixing faulty imaginations than he is with motors.*

She pushed that thought away and forced herself to sing along with Gladys Knight and the Pips even though she had never ridden any kind of train to Georgia.

TWO

Jeanine took the Bayside Highway to the other side of Hilo and turned down Manono Street, heading inland to her house in the Prince Kuhio development. Tension faded the farther she got from the airport. The canopy formed by the tree branches meeting over the road reminded her of a soft green cave. She lowered the windows and smiled. Nature's air-conditioning beat anything man-made.

The road sloped up gently into a small complex with twenty houses scattered on large lots on either side. Most hid among the tall, leafy trees marking property lines. Jeanine smiled as she drove to the end of the road and pulled into the driveway of her house.

As she got out she glanced at the sloping hills. Farther along they would climb to Mauna Kea. Her smile widened. *I wonder how far Pele's territory reaches?* Strong aromas reached her from the few coffee trees the Hans grew in their backyard next to hers. Before they sold a few acres to a builder years ago, all of this land had belonged to them. Jeanine was grateful to them. Not only had they made it possible for her to buy her own home, but they were great neighbors.

Sweet-smelling plumeria perfume reached her from the tree beside her own house and pulled her gaze to the yellow-white flowers covering the delicate tree. Its fragrance blended with the scent of other plumerias as well as that of ginger blossoms from the trees scattered among the nearby yards, adding to the coffee beans' scent. She leaned against her car for a few minutes, trying to absorb all of the beautiful smells. Then she went inside. Chris Harris was just a recent memory.

She relaxed as she stepped inside the airy hallway and placed her keys in the shallow basket on the small chest to the left. Then she picked up the phone and hit a speed-dial button.

"Hey, Lisa. I'm going to assume that you'll be home in the next fifteen minutes since this is our regular running day. Meet me at Wailoa Park at the usual place. Kalele will meet us there." She frowned. "You'd better not be at some construction site watching concrete dry."

She hung up and went into her bedroom. The cool blues and greens of the drapes and spread offset the view from the large window with its hot streaks of pink and orange and a few narrow black stripes showing at the end of another gorgeous sunset. *If I could figure out how to capture that, I'd be independently wealthy and only have to fly for my own enjoyment.*

She changed into running shorts and a sleeveless T-shirt, laced up her shoes, and drove to the park.

Fifteen minutes later Jeanine stood beside a park bench, stretching in the constant breeze blowing from the lagoon and waiting for Lisa and Kalele. She had just decided to run alone when she heard her name.

"Don't leave me. I'm here." Lisa Williams stopped beside Jeanine. "I'm sorry. I lost track of time."

"So what else is new?"

"There was a mix-up in a supply shipment." The short woman braced her hands against a tree and stretched her legs.

"I repeat: What else is new?"

"I know." She nodded. "It's always something. The

deliveryman had only two orders to deliver, but he mixed them up. Even if my business had been in operation a long time, a mistake like that could have done a lot of damage to my reliability. One of the deliveries was the materials needed to finish an office building. My biggest job so far, and the man almost blew it."

"Did you fire him?"

"Nah. He's new. I did give him a chewing out that would make his mama proud. He won't be that careless again." She looked at Jeanine. "People think the construction supply business is simple. Buy the supplies wholesale and sell them retail. If you have enough orders and hang on long enough, you make a living. Some people don't realize how many things can go wrong." She twisted from side to side.

"Are you talking about me?"

"If the sneaker fits, lace it up."

"Funny."

"You said Kay was going with us?"

"That's what Kalele told me."

"I am." A small woman dashed up to them. "Sorry. A passenger asked me to circle Mauna Loa again, just in case Pele had decided to throw rocks as soon as we passed by the first time. Then he had me circle Mauna Kea again, too. After the second circling, I told him, gently, of course, that we had to go. Both volcanoes have been erupting for years. Why should Pele throw a hissy fit now?" She began her stretching routine.

"Hissy fit? Maybe you should stop hanging out with us. You're picking up some bad slang habits." Jeanine smiled.

"You really believe that Pele stuff?" Lisa asked.

"When I walk anywhere in Volcanoes National Park, I clean my shoes off with a wet wipe just before I leave." Kalele stopped stretching and shrugged. "That story's been around as long as the islands have. My parents said that was one of the first things their grandparents learned about when they came here from China. The story still lives. There must be some truth to it." She shrugged again. "Why take a chance?"

"Do you believe in Pele, Jeanine? Do you think there's a jealous goddess living in the volcano?"

"I keep telling you that I'm not getting into that."

"I think you do believe."

"Whether she does or not is immaterial. What is the truth, is the truth."

"Wow. Is that ancient Chinese wisdom?" Lisa asked.

Kay laughed. "Could be. I read it in a fortune cookie."

She tightened the scrunchy holding her straight black hair back from her delicate face. "Okay. Ready?"

"Yeah. Let's see if we can find the zone."

"At least let me dump the day's stress," Lisa said.

"Let's go over the lagoon today." Jeanine headed toward the paved path leading to a footbridge.

"Again? I don't know why you've got a thing for those obnoxious geese."

"They just like to let you know when you're in their territory. Straightforward. I like that. Nothing sneaky about geese." She picked up the pace. "They're honest creatures." She turned her speed up a notch. "Not like some people."

"I know you're not talking about me," Lisa said.

"Me, neither," Kay added.

"So who is it?" Lisa ran alongside her.

"Nobody."

"What happened?"

"Nothing."

"Something, or is it somebody, has you running like a sprinter rather than a jogger," Kay said. "Who?"

Jeanine slowed to a jog as they crossed over the first hump of the bridge over the lagoon. Lisa and Kay dropped back to let a jogger from the opposite direction go by.

"I just got the wrong impression about somebody today, that's all," she said as she drew alongside her two friends again.

"Does this somebody have a name?" Lisa asked. The three matched strides.

"Doesn't matter. It was my fault." Their approach to the wide section of the lagoon was announced by a group of geese to the right of the bridge. Jeanine glanced at them and smiled. "Honest. See. They let you know how they feel."

"You know you got to tell us, right?" Kalele glanced over at her.

Jeanine stared straight ahead. "I got the impression that somebody was available, but I found out that I was wrong."

"You didn't tell me that you're seeing somebody."

"I'm not. I bumped into somebody and misinterpreted his reaction and his vibes." She shook her head. "Either I'm slipping or desperation has made my judgment faulty. Either way, it was a non-incident, as they say."

"I don't know why we can't find somebody." Lisa was a step ahead when they crossed the last hump and followed the path circling the lagoon.

"Must be looking for love in all the wrong places." Jeanine sang the first line of an ancient song.

"Someday my prince will come," Lisa sang back.

"Maybe mine will be with them," Kalele added. "I'd settle for a pauper, right now."

The three laughed as they followed the path past the geese and ducks on their side of the lagoon.

An hour later they left another bridge that led them back to the parking lot. They slowed to a walk.

"That was a good one, wasn't it?" All three stretched

in unison as if somebody had choreographed their movements but had forgotten to turn on the music.

"Yeah. I'll be ready to face Nate tomorrow," Jeanine said. "Pray for me."

"You got a flight?"

"Ten o'clock. A family of five."

"How about you, Kay?"

"Eleven, a mixed group." She finished and stared at Jeanine. "What's going on between you and Nate? You said he's more obnoxious than the geese."

"He is. He's also supposed to be a great mechanic, so I have to put up with him." *He also knows Chris Harris well enough to know his Sarah.* She frowned. *Let it go, girl.*

She stopped with the others to stretch.

"That chopper still giving you trouble?"

"Nate said he's checked it out and he can't find anything wrong. Maybe it just doesn't like me."

"What's not to like?" Lisa matched her stretches to Jeanine's.

Jeanine laughed. "You're good for my soul."

"I aim to please." They gave one last stretch. "See you guys at the gym tomorrow?"

"At the usual time," said Kalele. "Maybe we'll find not one, not two, but three Prince Charmings, or at least acceptable facsimiles."

"It doesn't cost a thing to keep hope alive," Jeanine smiled.

"Don't let Nate get to you." Lisa got into her car.

"Don't you let a load of concrete hold you up," Jeanine warned. "And don't forget our trip next weekend." She turned to Kalele. "And you stay out of Pele's range." Then she climbed into her car.

It was a more relaxed Jeanine who drove home. Chris Harris got her attention only twice.

THREE

Jeanine flew two flights on Wednesday and again on Thursday, and the chopper gave her no problem. On Friday afternoon Nate stopped her when she returned from her final flight of the week.

"How'd she fly?"

"Like she's supposed to."

"I told you there wasn't a problem."

"Yeah, I know. It was all in my head."

"I'm sorry about that." He shrugged. "I did check it over again, but I didn't find anything. Maybe something was loose, and me fooling with it tightened the connection."

"Maybe. I hope so."

"Yeah, me, too." He stared at her. "You off this weekend, huh?"

"Monday, too. I got to take a day or lose it."

"Where you going? Vegas?"

"Nope. I'm going over to Maui."

"Maui? You can swim to there. It ain't no different than here. You may as well go to Kona. You can drive down there and pretend to be a tourist."

"You know every island is different."

"Yeah. What are you going to do? Lie on the beach and work on your tan?" Much as she tried not to, she laughed with him.

"Between what the Lord gave me and what I get just walking around, I don't have to make an effort to add to it. I'm going with a friend. We intend to do some serious hiking."

"That's too much like work." He patted his middle. "I might lose my youthful figure."

This time her laugh came easier. Jeanine shook her head. *Maybe he's not so bad after all.* For a few seconds she just stared at him. *I will not ask him about Chris Harris. I will not.* "See you in a few."

"Yeah. Hang loose."

Jeanine raised a hand and returned his shaka "hang loose" sign. Then she went to her car and pulled out of the parking lot. She tried to center her thoughts on her days off and not on Chris Harris.

Too bad Kalele has to work, but Lisa and I will have fun. She frowned and tried to concentrate on the next couple of days. *Don't think about Chris Harris. Don't even start to imagine what it would be like to be going off with him.*

She waited at a stop sign at Baker Street for a group of kids coming from school to cross. *A whole state filled with good-looking men, and I have to focus on one that I can't have.* She frowned. The kids all crossed, and she drove the next block and turned down the narrow street that a faded sign announced as Parker.

"What do you think of the house plans? What did you decide?"

Chris settled into one of two chairs crammed on Nate's narrow deck. If he had leaned far to the right, he would have seen the sun as it filtered the last of its light through the palm fronds in the stand of trees at the end of Nate's yard. The final look at it would come from the clearing offering a wide view of the ocean.

"The lanai in the new plan would put this poor excuse to shame. It would hold a lot more furniture, and every seat would provide a view of the sunset."

"I don't get much company. This is fine for me." Nate set two beers and a glass on the wicker table, then sat on a matching chair.

"Maybe you don't get much company because this is a dump."

"Love me, love my dump."

"I think I remember Mom finding you on the front porch after somebody rang the doorbell. Maybe you take after your real parents."

"I'm going to tell Mom." Nate took a swallow from the can.

"No, you won't. You probably made her mad and she's not speaking to you, either." Chris poured some of his beer into the glass Nate had brought him.

"I called Sarah and everything is cool."

"Until the next time."

"Let me look at the plans again. Tearing down my home is a big decision to make."

"You only have to make it once."

"Give me a few more days to think about it."

"I'll meet you at the shop on Monday."

"Anybody ever tell you how pushy you are? Somebody would think you don't have enough business to keep you busy."

"I had to squeeze you in. This is a for-your-own-good-because-you're-my-brother job."

"How's the new building coming?"

"We've had a few glitches, but that's normal. We're still on schedule."

"No regrets about picking that new contractor over a more established one?"

"Everybody has to start somewhere. We've stumbled a few times, but nothing serious. We should be finished in a month as planned. By the time it's ready we should be a hundred percent leased." He looked at Nate. "We don't have to wait until then to build your house, though."

Chris took a swallow and grimaced. "I tried, Little Brother. I just don't like the taste of beer."

"That's got to be a crime."

They laughed. Then Chris leaned back and tried to act casual.

"Have you seen Jeanine Stewart lately?"

"Saw her today. Won't see her again for a while, though. She's going to Maui for a few days with a friend." Nate stared at Chris. "Want me to try to get her number for you?"

"No." Chris turned to look at the white blossoms on the plumeria tree at the edge of the yard. *No reason for me not to come here on Monday instead of going to the airport.* He frowned. *No sense in wondering if her friend is male or female. A woman like that has to have somebody.*

"Why not? You must be interested."

"I don't think she is." Chris continued to stare at the tree as if waiting for it to string a lei from its creamy blossoms. "She and her friend must be pretty tight to go off for a few days." He thought of the way she had walked away, as if, the second she turned, he had ceased to exist.

"Not like you to quit before you get started."

"We're not talking about a race or a contest. I always stop when I realize that I'm wasting time." He leaned forward. "You seeing anybody?"

"I'm too busy working."

"Uh-huh." He stared at Nate. "You know, not every woman is like Diane."

"I'll look at the plans over the weekend."

"Keep an open mind." Chris wasn't sorry he'd brought up Nate's former wife's name. It was time for him to move on.

"I will." Nate frowned at the empty can in his hand. "Maybe it's time for a new start." He looked at his brother. "That goes for you too, you know."

"I know." Chris shifted his gaze to a coconut palm tree. He stared at it as if it were different from the others flanking it.

I wouldn't mind a new start with Miss Jeanine Stewart. Too bad somebody got to her first.

FOUR

"What do you mean, you can't make it, Lisa?" Jeanine rolled a pair of jeans and tucked them into the open dufflebag waiting on her bed. "We planned this weeks ago. I had to do some heavy trading to get off." She stared at the T-shirt in her hands, then put it beside the jeans. "I'm almost finished packing."

"I know. I can't tell you how sorry I am. Something came up. Maybe we can try for next week?"

"I'm sure something would come up then, too. I have three days off, and I'm not wasting them."

"But you can't go . . ."

"Bye, Lisa. See you when you have time for a friend."

Jeanine broke the connection before Lisa could finish. She stared at the phone for a long minute. Then she sighed and punched the redial button.

"Okay. What's the story?"

"Both Kimo and Lou called in sick. I have to drive the concrete mixer to the site myself. With all of the glitches, I'm sure the builder is having second . . ." Lisa hesitated. "And third thoughts about giving me the contract. Do you know how long it's been since I've driven one of those things? I hope I don't hit the wrong control and drop a load on the highway." Her heavy sigh came over the line. "I wouldn't bail out if there were any way to avoid it. They need this load to finish the lobby. I'm truly sorry." Again her sigh reached Jeanine. "Sometimes I wonder if I did the right thing in starting this business. Just because I worked for Dad in his business in Los Angeles doesn't mean I can run a successful business on my own." She paused again. "You don't want to hear my latest excuse. The bottom line is that I ruined your weekend."

"Don't start doubting yourself." Jeanine sat on the edge of her bed. "You've done great. I'll bet you couldn't find any business that doesn't have a few problems."

"But this is my biggest contract ever. This is my proving point. I'm afraid that the only thing I'm proving is that I'm trying to operate way beyond my ability."

"How many loads have you delivered to this job?"

"I don't know. A lot."

"And how many didn't make it to the site?"

"Those materials almost didn't."

"This is not a game of horseshoes. 'Almost' doesn't count. Did the delivery reach the site?"

"It was a little late, but yes."

"Was the project delayed because of it?"

"No."

"Have you ever driven a concrete mixer before?"

"Yes."

"Then stop trying to make me pity you. A woman's gotta do what a woman's gotta do."

"What are you going to do?"

"I'm going to Maui and hike the Lahaina Pali Trail and camp out just like we planned."

"You're not going alone?"

"I might hook up with a tour group. Or I might not. It's not like I haven't hiked it before."

"You know you shouldn't go alone. Especially you shouldn't camp alone. Are you sure Kay's plans haven't changed?"

"She's got a refresher course this weekend. They

wouldn't change that schedule unless there was an emergency."

"If you wait a few weeks . . ."

"I'm going this weekend as planned. It's not the wilderness you have to be afraid of, it's the people."

"That's true, and you'll be out there either alone or with strangers." If a dial tone had reached her, Jeanine would have thought Lisa had hung up. Finally a sigh drifted to her, followed by words. "Wait about twenty minutes and I'll see if they can wait until Monday for the load. I can fly back here Sunday night and . . ."

"No way. I'm not going to be the cause of a business problem. Much as I hate to say it, in this case, business has to come first."

"Thanks for understanding. I wish you'd wait. I—I'd like to hike, too."

"This isn't a special one-to-a-customer deal. We can go together after your building project is finished. As a celebration." Jeanine glanced at the sleeping bag beside the door. "I gotta go."

"Please think again about going alone, especially the camping part."

"I will."

"Promise?"

"Yeah."

"You have your fingers crossed, don't you?"

"Bye, Lisa. Talk to you Monday evening when I get back."

Jeanine stared at the sleeping bag, then finished packing. She looked at the bag again as she picked up her suitcase, shrugged, and left the bag in place. *No sense in being foolish. I can camp another time when both Lisa and Kalele can go.*

***

Two-and-a-half hours later Jeanine stood in line at Da Brudda's car rental office in Maui. Fifteen minutes after that she was driving a jeep out of the lot. She turned onto Highway 380, rolled down the windows. The mixture of scents that was only Hawaii drifted in. She turned on the radio. When the weather report came on, she switched stations. Today's weather would be the same as yesterday's, which would be the same as tomorrow's. She smiled. *Just another day in paradise.*

She reached Highway 30 and headed north, skirting the beaches. *I have to stop at a beach when I return tomorrow. Maybe I'll stop and get a plate lunch and eat at one of the tables.* She smiled again. *One of the best decisions the state made way back was to make all of the beaches public.*

She reached the hotel and condo section in Lahaina, but bypassed it and turned right onto Lolo Road. A small hotel a few miles inland along the curvy road was more to her liking.

"I'm Al. This your first time here?"

"No. I stayed here a couple of times before."

"I'm new here. I guess that's why I didn't recognize you. I'm just helping my uncle during my summer break. I hope you enjoy yourself."

"I know I will. Do they still have the show in the shopping center on Fridays?"

"Yeah. Nothing ever changes around here. Tonight the *keikis*, the kids, from the dance school perform. Folks always like to see them."

"I know I do."

"You gonna just hang loose for the weekend, or you got plans?"

"I'm going hiking tomorrow."

"Hiking? That's too much dirty work." He laughed. "Give me a board and a little surf, and I forget about everything."

"I know what you mean. I love surfing, too. I decided to do something different this time."

"As they say, 'whatever floats your boogie board.'" They both laughed as Jeanine picked up her bags and walked to her room.

Excitement bubbled in her as she unpacked her few things and put them away. It was still with her as she drove to the shopping center later that evening.

She watched the kids from the local dance school perform for an hour. *I gotta learn to do that,* she thought as the teenagers swayed and moved their hands to the lyrics, "Where I live, there are rainbows," one of her favorites. She laughed to herself. *Maybe if I'd started at the age of the little ones, by now I'd be half as good as these kids are.*

She stopped for dinner at the food court. A variety was offered. It only took her a second to decide against the Philly cheesesteak. She had learned a long time ago that unless the bread was flown in from Philadelphia, it wouldn't be the same. She shook her head. *And who ever heard of Swiss cheese on a cheesesteak?* She settled for stir-fry chicken and sat at one of the tables. She had Marilyn Tyner's latest book with her, but she didn't pull it out. Instead, she just sat and enjoyed the breeze blowing in from all sides, mixing with the island music from the sound system.

Half an hour later, she drove back to the hotel totally relaxed. The mood stayed with her when she reached her room.

It would be nice to have someone to share this with, she thought as she got ready for bed. *Somebody to talk about the show with.* Chris Harris's image drifted to her mind as if summoned. She shooed the image away. After she was under the top sheet, he came back. This time she let him stay.

Far off a rooster announced the morning dawn. *Somebody needs to buy him an alarm,* Jeanine thought as she glanced at the clock on the nightstand. The sun still had at least an hour before it had to get up. The rooster hollered again, as if he hadn't been heard the first time. *I wanted an early start, but this is ridiculous.* She sighed and sat on the edge of the bed and stretched awake. She pulled the hiking guide from the stand and opened it to her marked page. The pink-highlighted trail still looked good. A frown flitted across her face as her gaze stole to the suggestion in bold print advising hikers to go with a partner. *I'm not going far, this trip.* She nodded. *But I am going to get a good hike in.*

By the time she was ready to leave her room, the sun had painted a hint of color into the sky.

After a bigger breakfast than usual, she was in the jeep, her large backpack was stowed in the back, and she was driving down the road. After a stop for bottles of water, she continued to the parking lot at the foot of the trail.

Three other cars were there, but nobody was in sight. She slipped her backpack on, grabbed her binoculars, and headed inland.

An hour later, after climbing uphill the whole time, Jeanine reached an almost flat section of trail. The rich, damp smell of living plants surrounding her grew stronger. The sound of rushing water attracted her, and she followed it to a small clearing. A waterfall tumbled over a hill thick with ferns and other water-loving flora.

She wiped at the sweat on her forehead and looked over the bluff. The hill sloped steeply before stopping at the edge of a small pool. On the far side of the pool, water escaped into a fast-running stream. She shook her head. *It looks refreshing, but I'm not going down there. They'd have to send a rescue party to bring me back up.* Nothing but the sound of gurgling water, birds, a few frogs, and leaves rubbing together reached her. *If anybody ever found me.* She walked back to the trail. After stopping to drink some bottled water, she glanced at her watch and continued forward.

Twenty minutes later she came to a fork in the trail, examined both possible paths, and then took the left one. She wiped sweat from her eyes, drank more water, and followed the narrow path deeper into the forest.

Several times she had to make decisions about which trail to follow. *What good is a map if there are no landmarks?* She frowned up at the canopy of green overhead. An old joke came to her: "I'm not lost. I know exactly where I am. I'm right here." It wasn't as funny as it was when she'd heard it the first time.

She examined her surroundings carefully. After hesitating, she crossed her fingers and took what looked like a path to the left.

Twenty minutes and another bottle of water later, whatever trail there was had been swallowed by the greenery. She walked a few more feet and then stopped.

A small valley dipped below her. Tall plants growing in neat rows filled the area, right up to a small walled tent at the far side. A man standing in front was talking to somebody inside, but Jeanine couldn't hear what he said. She didn't need to. She understood the gun he was holding. She raised her binoculars and watched as he turned toward the plants. She held her breath as he seemed to focus on her before his eyes moved past her. *Good-looking guy.* She focused on the gun for a second. *As deadly as he is good-looking.*

Quietly, she backed up until she was farther under the trees. She ducked behind a thick trunk, hoping the man hadn't seen her. Then she backed up some more and listened.

Crops of marijuana weren't unusual in Hawaii. The weather made growing it ideal, and the government fought a constant battle against it. Kalele had told her about flying with DEA agents to make a bust on the Big Island. Still, Jeanine had never been this close to it before.

She held her breath and listened. Again she was aware of the absence of any human sounds. *Just me and them,* she thought as she peeped at the man once more. *If anything happens to me, nobody will ever find my body.* Despite the heat and humidity, she shivered. She kept watching, but eased her body back even more when his gaze panned her way a second time. Again she forgot to breathe. When he finally went inside, she remembered to give her lungs some air. Then, glad for the sound-deadening vegetation underfoot, she turned around and slipped away.

A few feet more and at a much quicker pace, she went back the way she hoped she had come.

When she reached a fork, she hesitated, then turned right. She jogged, only slowing each time she had to make a decision about which way to go. Once she followed a trail, only to turn around when it narrowed to nothing several yards further. When a turn took her to a wider trail, she followed it. Finally she heard a car door slam and voices. She smiled for the first time since her discovery. *Beautiful sounds.*

She rounded a final bend after a few yards and stood facing a parking lot. She had felt indifferent the first time she got into the rental jeep. Now she felt like kissing it.

She got behind the wheel and tried to insert the key into the lock, but her hand shook so much she couldn't manage it. She laid her head back and closed her eyes. She took several deep breaths. Then she tried again. This time she succeeded. Slowly she drove out of the lot.

When she reached Highway 30 again, she hesitated, then pulled into a gas station to ask for directions. Ten minutes later she drove into the police parking lot. She breathed deeply before getting out of the jeep. *This feels as bad as going to the principal's office in school. I didn't do anything, but I still feel nervous.* She shook her head and went inside.

"I started not to come," Jeanine told the man who introduced himself as Detective Hagasi. "I don't know how I can help." She shrugged. "I can't even tell you exactly where I was. I'm not even sure that what I saw was pot. I . . ."

"Just tell me what you can. The fact that you saw a gun means they weren't growing flowers to sell to tourists."

When Jeanine had finished talking, Detective Hagasi went to a large map on the wall.

"Let's see if we can trace your route."

"Okay." Jeanine shrugged and went over to the map.

By the time the detective had interrupted to question her at several points, they had a rough idea of the area where she had been.

"Now what?" she asked.

"Now we'll take it from here."

"But how will you look for it? What if I was wrong about one of the turns? I told you that I'm not sure."

Hagasi hesitated. "You don't have to be exact. We'll get a chopper to search from the air. We'll be able to spot anything growing that shouldn't be there."

"You have a chopper?"

He hesitated. "We use civilians." He held out his hand. "Thank you for coming in."

"Will you let me know if you find them?"

"You'll read about it in the paper. I expect we will. Again, thank you for coming in."

I gave him the report. The least he can do is let me know if I was right, Jeanine thought as she drove to the hotel. She assumed she had calmed down, but her mind returned to the scene in the clearing. She needed several deep breaths before she could get out of the car. Legs that seemed to have had their bones removed managed to take her to her room.

No exploring alone, Jeanine promised herself when she awoke Sunday morning.

After breakfast she decided to go to Haleakala National Park. She'd been there several times before, but each time she went, she learned something new.

Two hours later she had barely started the drive to the summit when a small group of bikers riding down—or, rather, coasting down—passed her.

As she drove through spritzing rain, clouds, and sunny spots, more bikers, followed by a van with a biking company logo on the side, whizzed past. *How do they keep from going over the side?* She glanced at the faces of the passing bikers. *They don't look like they're having fun. They can't see much of anything except the road.* She shrugged. *I guess they'll have something to tell the folks back home.*

She stopped at the visitor center but didn't go in right away. She grabbed her camera and went to where several people had gathered around a small blocked-off cinder bed. There, in the middle, was a beautiful silversword plant, open at its fullest. Jeanine had seen others at various stages, but this was the first time she had been blessed to see one in full bloom. She took pictures. It was beautiful. But it was doomed. The silversword waits nearly fifty years to flower, and then dies. She glanced around at several small plants scattered in the same cinder bed. They would take their turn. Jeanine sighed as she went into the visitor center.

Despite her plan not to explore, she went back to the jeep for her jacket. *I'll take the short trail. I'm sure others will be there, too.*

She decided on the shortest self-guided tour, taking pictures whenever she saw something of interest. Forty-five minutes later she was in the jeep and driving back. She bought lunch and went to Mala Beach park. She smiled as she watched the waves kiss the beach and then retreat. Her frightening experience of yesterday seemed to fade. She tossed bread scraps to the finches that had approached as if knowing that she would feed them. She watched the waves a while longer; then she left.

She stopped at Whalers Village in Lahaina and browsed. Then she returned to the hotel.

After dinner at a small restaurant nearby, she returned to her hotel room and picked up the phone.

"Did you find them?" she asked Detective Hagasi when he picked up the line.

"I told you the newspaper would report it if we did."

"What happened? Couldn't you find the site? I didn't think I was that far off from the location we figured out on the map."

"We found the site, but we were too late. The marijuana had been picked, and the men were gone."

"Do you think they'll be back?"

"It's doubtful. The tent was gone."

"Then I just wasted your time."

"Not really. You helped us pinpoint a recent site. Even if they don't use a specific site again, they often stay in the general area. Especially if they don't know that they've been discovered. You're sure he didn't see you?"

"I'm sure." She thought about the gun the man had held. She remembered how he had scanned his surroundings with it, as well as with his gaze. *If he had, I'd still be up there.*

"Again, thank you for coming in. Never be reluctant to report a suspected crime. Better a false report than letting a criminal get away. In this case your report was valid. We just missed them. Have a safe trip home."

After Jeanine hung up, she sat on the private lanai outside her room and watched night creep over. Later she went inside and packed.

By noon on Monday she was taking her seat on the Aloha Air flight back home. By three o'clock she was in her house, getting ready for Tuesday.

FIVE

"Girlfriends, I'm telling you, I was one scared sister." Jeanine leaned her head back against the wall in the women's steam room and sighed. She blotted her face even though she knew that the steam would bring out more sweat immediately.

"I told you not to go alone." Lisa shifted on the bench beside her. "I told you to wait until I could go with you."

"Nothing happened to me."

"Just because we don't pay for a mistake doesn't mean we didn't make it," Kalele added.

"Fortune-cookie wisdom?"

"No." Kalele shifted to a lower bench. "Something my mother still tells me when I do something stupid and nothing bad happens."

"So, what did Detective Hagasi look like?" Lisa asked as she adjusted the towel covering her hair.

"Like he's one week away from retirement."

They laughed as all three wiped their faces at the same time.

"I really needed this." Jeanine moved down to the place beside Kalele.

"Rough day?"

"Not really. I only had two flights. I was supposed to have a third, but a man stuck in the Dark Ages refused to go with a female pilot. Poor Bill had to do a turnaround."

She shook her head. "I tell you, just when you relax because the color barrier has faded a lot, a throwback shows up, and you're in a battle that you thought had already been won."

"I've had a few of those." Kalele nodded. "I call them 'stuck-in-the-barefoot-and-pregnant rut.' Was he alone?"

"No. He had a wife and a teenage daughter with him."

"I feel sorry for them. Especially the daughter."

"Better feel sorry for him." Jeanine laughed. "You didn't see the look on his daughter's face when he was making a scene. I won't be surprised if she ends up a pilot herself." She laughed again. "Or in a field even more male dominated."

"I know how you felt." Lisa nodded. "I had to battle to get my first construction contract. I've also had other battles since then." She poured a ladle of water over the hot rocks and coughed as a cloud of steam sprang up. "At the beginning I pretended that I was just doing the legwork for L. W. Enterprises. I let them think that the brains of the company were in a male head. After I got a signature there wasn't a thing they could do without breaching the contract." She shook her head. "You should have seen the looks on some of my subcontractors' faces when they asked to speak to the boss and found out that it was me." She smiled. "Things are opening up a bit more, now. I don't get called 'little lady' as often." Her smile widened. "I wonder. If I were eight feet tall and weighed five hundred pounds, would I still be 'little lady' to chauvinists?" They all laughed.

"How's the building coming along?" Jeanine asked.

"Right on schedule, thank God." She smiled. "My part is finished. Pat is still working furiously on the interior. She ordered the furnishings soon after we started building. As soon as the final touches are finished, she'll get the offices and apartments set up."

"You and Pat got it going on. You should call yourselves 'Sister Act.' " Jeanine shifted to the lowest bench.

"I can just picture how many 'good ole boys' would call for estimates if we do." Lisa sighed. "I'm not dwelling on negativity. The builder where I just finished isn't like that. In fact he contracted me to build his brother's house. He also referred me to another architect." Her smile widened. "Next week I meet with a company that's building a timeshare resort near the golf course near Hapuna. He said that I'll probably get the contract."

"All the way over there? That's a long haul."

"Yeah, but it's a big job. The profit will be worth it. Speaking of which, you guys want to share a fringe benefit?"

"What's that?"

"The builder is having an opening reception in three weeks. A lot of big-time folk will be there. Come with me and see what we built." She smiled. "At least what my tradesmen built and Pat's expertise finished."

"Exactly when is it?"

After Lisa told them, Jeanine and Kalele agreed to go.

"You know I'm always down for good food," Jeanine said.

"Yes, you are." Kalele laughed.

"It's a good thing you're so active."

"That's one reason why I do all this stuff. So I can eat more than just lettuce and an occasional carrot." She looked at them. "Speaking of eating, how about going to Bubba Gump's for dinner? I have a taste for shrimp." She stood. "The other reason I exercise is that I just feel better when I do." She tightened the towel around her body. "You guys ready to go? Much longer in here, and they'll have to mop me up and carry me out in a bucket." First one to Bubba's make sure we get a good table."

"There are no bad tables at Bubba's," Lisa pointed out.

"True," Jeanine and Kalele said at the same time. They laughed as each went to her own car.

Twenty minutes later they were seated in the restaurant facing another spectacular sunset. They were quiet until the only thing left was a streak of orange skimming the horizon.

"Isn't it amazing how each one is different?"

"Yeah. As the song says, 'Ain't God Something?' "

They nodded and watched the last bit of color disappear. Then they focused on the next day's schedules and whether they would meet to go jogging.

"You're going to love your new house. I promise." Chris stood beside Nate, watching as heavy machinery pushed debris into a pile and scooped up what was left of Nate's house. Nate watched silently as the final load was dumped into the truck bed. He turned to watch it drive away.

"That was my home. I had a lot of memories tied up in there."

"I know it's rough." Chris placed a hand on Nate's shoulder. "Look on this as a chance to start over. Once you see your new house, you'll be sorry you didn't do this a long time ago."

"I guess so." He frowned. "I don't know. Maybe I should have kept my furniture." Nate still stared at the road even though the truck was out of sight.

"Don't put new wine in old skins."

"Getting Biblical on me?"

"When you got that stuff secondhand, it was going to be temporary. That was three years ago. It's time to move on, Nate." He patted his shoulder. "Come on. I'll buy you a steak." He took Nate's arm and led him to their cars. "Afterward we can go to your apartment and check over the plans again to make sure you don't want to make any last-minute changes. In a couple of months you'll be unlocking the door to your new house."

Chris patted Nate on the back, then led him to the driveway. "See you in a few."

Ten minutes later they were seated at the Steak and Surf.

"You already planned your housewarming?" Chris grinned at Nate after their orders had been taken.

"Housewarming? You got to be kidding. Guys don't have housewarmings."

"You can start a new trend."

"Let some other guy be the pioneer. I'll buy my own toaster."

"Okay." Chris shrugged. "I'll back off." The waitress brought their orders. Chris stared at the food. A frown replaced his grin as if something were wrong with it. "Uh, have you seen Jeanine Stewart lately?" He picked up his fork.

"Casual doesn't work on you, Chris." Nate grinned. "I told you to let me get her number for you." Nate took a sip of beer, then cut off a piece of steak.

"Have you seen her?"

"You know I see the pilots every time they have a flight. She's a pilot. Ergo, yes, I have seen her."

"Ergo? Ergo?"

"That's my new word from two weeks ago. This is the first time I got a chance to use it." He grinned. "Like it?"

"I hope you'll move on to another word." Chris leaned on the table. "Did she say anything about her weekend?"

"She doesn't exactly share her life with me. She thinks I want her to crash, remember?"

"Didn't say a word, huh?"

"I'll bring her number with me when I come home from work tomorrow."

"I don't . . ."

"Spare me." Nate held up his hand. "The last time you acted like this was when you were a junior at Central High and you were smitten with . . ." He stopped at Chris's frown. "Another new word."

"Forget getting another word. Get a modern dictionary. You don't look like a 'smitten' kind of guy."

"As I was saying, you were hung up on that senior track star. It took you months of moping, walking in a daze and forgetting your school ID, before you said more than hello to her." He shook his head. "I never did get that. You had scouts watching you quarterback every game, trying to decide whether to offer you a scholarship. You faced those giants on defense, and some of them made The Bus look as if he was built like a high school punter. Still you managed to do your thing. And you were afraid to ask her out."

"I was young and foolish."

"What's age got to do with anything? You can be smitten . . ." He paused, waiting for Chris to say something. When he didn't, Nate continued. "You can be foolish at any age."

"Speaking from experience?"

"Mine and a lot of other people's."

"Maybe I'll stop by one day."

"Maybe I'll let you know when she's flying."

"Maybe we should go." Chris stood. "You finished?"

Nate looked down at his plate. "I don't think this bone is gonna grow more meat on it, so yeah, I'm ready." Nate stood.

"Good. I've got a long day ahead tomorrow. We're down to crunch time on the building." Chris pulled out his wallet and picked up the check. He glanced at Nate. "I got it. It's the least I can do for a homeless brother."

"Excuse me if I'm hurting too much to laugh."

"The hotel is temporarily temporary. In a few weeks you can move into one of the apartments in our building. I could have had them make a priority of finishing one, but the noise and dust would have made it impossible to live in."

Fifteen minutes later they were sitting at the small table in Nate's room, going over the plans.

Fifteen minutes after that, Chris was on his way back to his house. *It would be nice to have somebody to go home to.* He shook his head. *Uh-uh. It would be nice to have Jeanine Stewart waiting for me. I'd kiss her hello and wrap her in my arms. Then we would go upstairs. Maybe we'd make it to our bedroom.* A horn blew and a car pulled around him. *How long had the light been green?* He shifted into gear, but shifted back as the light answered his question. *Long enough for it to show red again.* He leaned back. *I've got to get her out of my head. She's been there almost constantly since the minute I first saw her.* He shook his head again. *The only way to do that is to talk to her.* When the light turned green again, he moved through the intersection. *Yeah, that's what I'll do. I'll talk to her. Real soon.*

Despite his promise to himself, the opening reception for the new building came, and Chris still hadn't called Jeanine. He called Nate several times but changed his mind and pretended that he was calling for something besides Jeanine's number. He had called himself a "wimp" so often that he had lost count. It just didn't work. Finally, two days before the opening, his mind and time were filled with last-minute details, and thoughts of Jeanine left him alone for a while.

"Wow. I am impressed." Jeanine glanced around the huge lobby dividing the apartment side from the office side of the new building.

Gigantic crystal chandeliers bounced light off the rich mahogany reception desk and the low tables scattered among plump chairs and sofas were set up in conversation groups. Jeanine glanced to the side and noticed glass-paneled doors tucked behind heavy tropical-print drapes. The doors were open to allow the cross-breeze to ventilate the room.

Linen-covered tables, laden with a variety of finger foods, were placed strategically so that guests didn't have far to walk to get refreshments. White-jacketed men and women circulated, carrying trays of hot hors d'oeuvres.

"I'm impressed, too, and I'm proud to say that I had something to do with this." Lisa smiled. "L & W's work really looks good, doesn't it?"

"Oh, yeah! Double wow!" Kalele added.

"My touches didn't have anything to do with it, huh?" Pat came toward them.

"Of course they did, my dearest sister. Without your decorating touch, this would be merely an unfinished, plain building." She winked. "Don't tell my workmen that I said that." She laughed.

"I forgot how good you are at that even without bread."

"Bread? What are you talking about?"

"Buttering people up," Pat answered. As they laughed, the man who'd arrived with Pat stepped beside her. "This is Carl." Pat smiled up at him. "He's planning to redo his house, and I wanted him to see some of my work."

After introductions, Pat and Carl moved off, and Jeanine, Lisa, and Kalele walked toward one of the tables.

"Wow!" Chris stopped in the doorway. He was not looking at the actual proof that his dream had come true. If he hadn't already examined every inch of the lobby from floor to ceiling, he wouldn't have been able to describe a thing around him. His attention was focused on the woman standing a few feet away. "Jeanine Stewart." His words were low, but he was talking to himself, so it didn't matter.

He stood as if he had stepped into a patch of quick-drying cement. *Jeanine Stewart in the flesh.* He exhaled slowly. *And what delectable flesh it is.*

The top of Jeanine's fitted red dress, streaked with hot pink, was suspended from thin straps tied on top of her shoulders. *What beautiful shoulders. How would they feel if she allowed me to wrap my hands around them? If I could ease her against me until I was almost as close as that lucky dress? If she allowed me to untie the straps, to slip the dress down her body until I could see her fullness uncovered?*

Chris swallowed hard. He felt a familiar pressure below his waist, but he couldn't look away from her. He did manage to force his gaze away from her top. It did little good.

That dress clings to her waist the way I would like to, he thought. The sarong-style skirt hugged her hips before dropping to her knees, where it stopped as if it knew it would be a shame to hide her fantastic legs. His tightness increased. Still, he continued to caress her with his gaze. He lingered on her firm, full legs, trying not to imagine being fortunate enough to be allowed to smooth his way up and down them, before he moved to her feet. The white straps pretending to be shoes added two inches, tops, to her height. *She'd come up to my shoulder if I held her close.* His pants had become uncomfortably tight and were on the edge of being obscene. He moved his gaze to her hair. It didn't help. *The way those curls are piled on top of her head, she would come just under my chin. I could find out if it's as soft as it looks. Then I'd release it.*

He swallowed hard and, for the first time, wished he had decided to install air-conditioning in the lobby. He frowned. Or maybe an ice pool. *I'd move closer to the breeze coming in the door if I thought it would help.* He shook his head. *Why didn't I hire a group to play dance music instead of background music? You have lost it,* he answered himself. *Can you imagine what effect she would have on you if you really got to hold her? Everybody within viewing distance would know how you felt. Just stay away from her.* He ignored his common sense's advice. *I can go speak to her.* He nodded, but still stayed in place. *I can say, 'Remember me?'* He frowned again and shook his head. *I'll make it up as I go along. There's got to be something better than that to say. Why can't I think of it?*

Finally, he tore his gaze from her and scanned the area around her. *Where's her friend? I know he didn't let her out alone, not wearing that dress. What's she doing here, anyway?* He noticed that two women were standing close to her and frowned as he looked hard at one of them. *What's Jeanine doing with Lisa Williams?* He took a deep breath and relaxed enough to allow a smile to appear. *That's it. I have to speak to my contractor, don't I? I have to compliment her on a job well done. It doesn't matter that I did that during our walk-through. She deserves more words of approval.* He walked over to them before he could talk himself out of it.

"Hi. Good job." He was speaking to Lisa, but his gaze was still stuck on Jeanine.

"Thank you," Lisa said. "And thanks again for the referrals. We'll have more work than we can handle."

"No problem. When I find good professionals I like to help them out when I can." He managed to glance at her, but his gaze flew back to Jeanine as if she were a magnet for him.

"Chris, this is my friend, Kay . . . I mean Kalele." Lisa smiled. "And this is Jeanine Stewart. They're both pilots."

"I've already met Mr. Harris." Jeanine hesitated before touching his outstretched hand.

"Really? You never said so when I talked about the building project."

"You never mentioned his name."

"Oh." Lisa frowned. "Didn't I?"

"How was your trip with your friend?" *May as well get it out into the open. The more I know about him, the better chance I'll have to get him out of the way.*

"Oh, she went . . ." Jeanine didn't give Lisa a chance to finish her sentence.

"Fine. How is Sarah?" Jeanine's expression was as cool as his was warm.

"Sarah? You know Sarah?" *What did I do?*

"Did I hear my name?" A slender woman, just a few inches shorter than Chris, smiled and wrapped her arm through his.

Figures he'd go for the tall, skinny type. Jeanine forced a smile. *It's none of my business.*

"You two know each other?"

"I don't think so." Sarah frowned. "I have a terrible memory. I'm sorry if I don't . . ."

"No, you don't know me. I—I just heard Nate mention your name."

"You know Nate?"

"I heard my name." Nate, an overflowing plate in his hand, joined them. "I have to make sure nobody is telling lies about me."

"With all of the truths out there, nobody has to lie." Sarah turned her smile on him.

"See that? Sis is trying to start something. I'm doing my best to be nice, too."

"Yes, you are. For a change." Sarah leaned over and kissed his cheek. "I know how hard that is for you."

Sis? Sarah is Nate's sister? She's Chris's wife? No wonder Nate asked about her.

"Oh. What?" Jeanine asked as Lisa nudged her away from her thoughts.

"Are you going to keep your name a secret from Sarah?"

"Oh, no." She held out her hand and managed to avoid seeing how far she would need to go to get away from the group. "I'm Jeanine Stewart."

"How do you know my brother?"

"I'm a pilot for the same helicopter company."

"Great. One day you'll have to tell me what bad thing you did to make that happen and how you like seeing my brother so often."

"Sure." *Please don't let her invite me to dinner with them. She seems so nice.* Jeanine sighed. *Too nice. I can't think of a reason not to like her.*

"Did Nate invite you here?"

"Why do you ask it like that? You think somebody like this wouldn't bother with me?" Nate glared at Sarah.

"No. Don't get prickly. I just . . ."

"I invited her. Hi, I'm Lisa Williams." Lisa held out her hand. "I'm the building contractor."

"That is so fascinating. I'll bet you run into all kinds of problems with men stuck in the Dark Ages."

"You just don't know."

Jeanine thought of a way out. *I don't need an excuse. I'll just say 'excuse me,' smile, and walk away. I can do it.* She frowned. *The smile part will be hard, though.* She took a deep breath. *I can do it. I'll just . . .*

"So you've been working with my brother? I hope he wasn't one of the ones who gave you a hard time."

"Brother? Chris is your brother? I thought Nate was your brother? I thought. . ." Jeanine forgot that she was going to leave the group.

"This isn't a one-to-a-customer deal," Chris said. For the first time that evening, he relaxed. "Nate," his smile widened, "Sarah, *and* I are siblings."

"Siblings? You're siblings?"

"Same mama and daddy." His smile centered on Jeanine and settled there. "Sometimes we wonder about Nate, but there's never been any doubt about our sister, Sarah." He squeezed her shoulders as if trying to prove that he was her brother.

"If you'll excuse us, I'd like to show Jeanine around." He put his hand under Jeanine's elbow and gently led her away.

"Don't mind us, Bro," Nate called after them. "We can fend for ourselves as long as the food holds out." His laughter tugged at them, but neither of them turned around. Chris continued leading her to the side garden.

"You thought what?"

"Huh?"

"Back there you started to say what you thought. What was it?"

Jeanine hesitated. Then she shrugged. "Doesn't matter." She stepped out of the building. A brick path through the thick grass carpet led her to a bench beside a koi pond.

"It does to me. I think it's important." It was Chris's turn to hesitate. "Who did you go to Maui with?"

"What business is it of yours?" She stared at the huge multicolored fish that seemed to be trying to climb out and make her feed them. She turned the handle of the fish-food dispenser so her hands would have something to do. Then she let the pieces filter through her fingers, but she didn't notice how the fish swarmed as close as they could get to her. She was concentrating on Chris, wondering what he would say next, hoping she would like his answer, wondering why it was so important to her.

"None. Not yet." He gently turned her to face him. "I would like it to be. I want to make sure I'm not wasting both of our time." She looked up at him, and his expression intensified. "If you . . ." He frowned. "If you have somebody in your life, I'll try to back off, but I felt something in the hangar the day I met you, and I thought you did, too. If I'm wrong, just tell me and I will back off." His voice lowered. "It will be hard, but I'll try."

He held his breath for what seemed like hours before she answered.

"You didn't imagine it." She blinked and looked away. "Then I heard Nate ask you about Sarah, and I thought she was . . ." She frowned. "Your wife or, at the least, your Somebody Special."

"She is special. She's my sister."

Jeanine shrugged. "I thought you were a player."

"I never did play that kind of game, not even when I was younger." He held her hand.

"That's good to know."

"Yeah."

They rose from the bench and stood close enough for Chris to feel her warmth. He looked at her long enough to notice the faint sprinkling of freckles over her nose, long enough for him to imagine holding her closer and kissing those freckles. Long enough for him to feel his body heat rise as he imagined . . .

"Crab cake, Mr. Harris? Miss?" The waitress standing beside them asked.

How long has she been here? "No, thank you." Chris smiled at her. He watched her go back inside. *I should thank her for keeping me from embarrassing myself in front of my guests.* He drew in what he hoped would be a cooling-off breath, then turned his attention back to Jeanine. "I promised you a tour. I like to keep my word. Let's walk this way."

"Okay."

He placed his hand under her elbow again and headed for the far side of the pond. *Am I touching her to guide her? Uh-uh,* he answered himself right away. *I'm touching her because I had to touch her*. He smiled. *I hope the breathlessness in her voice is because of me.*

They reached the palm trees standing watch on the edge of the lawn as if to guard the beach just beyond.

"Just in time for sunset." The breathlessness was still there. "Beautiful." Jeanine smiled. "This is one thing I love about Hawaii. The beautiful sunsets."

"That's not the only thing of beauty here right now." Chris put his arm around her waist. When she didn't pull away he eased her against his side. Much as he was aching to do so, he didn't kiss her. There would be time for that later. She had been filling his thoughts for so long that it felt as if he had known her for months, but he wasn't sure she felt the same way. *I don't want to scare her off.*

For now, he'd be satisfied to just hold her and watch nature trying to match her beauty.

SIX

"Come on, Jeanine. Tell us." Lisa did a final stretch.

"Yeah. She who withholds truth from friends will be denied truth herself." Kalele smiled as she straightened up.

"You made that up."

"You got that right. One day . . . ," she clasped her hands together and looked to the sky. "Please make it soon." She looked back at the other two. "We'll have news to share with you, and we won't do it."

"Okay. Okay." Jeanine took a deep breath and released it slowly. "Let's get started so you both can get rid of your aggression. Really, there's not much to tell." She jogged toward the bridge with her friends beside her.

The memory of the little time she had spent with Chris came back to her as vividly as if it were happening now. *I wouldn't mind if it were,* she thought. The beads of sweat that glistened on her face had little to do with her jogging and a lot to do with the memory of the intensity in Chris's gaze.

What would it have been like to have him hold me closer? To be in his arms? To have his hands touching more than my back? How would his hands feel stroking my breasts? Sending heat spiraling through my body? Her breasts hardened as if her daydream were a reality.

How would it feel having my body aching, wanting more? And him giving it? She tried to gain control of her thoughts, but couldn't. *When will we take the next step?*

"Hey. Earth to Jeanine. Where are you?"

Jeanine blinked, and her fantasies came back to solid ground, *We haven't even kissed and already I'm in bed with him.*

"I was just thinking."

"I'll bet you were," Lisa laughed. "You're sweating a whole lot more than we are." She followed the path with the others and headed toward the first bridge.

"We don't need more than one guess, but I still want to hear every detail from you," Kalele said.

"Nothing happened." Jeanine glanced at the ducks quacking at them. "He showed me around the complex and then took me home."

"And?"

"And nothing."

"Your nose is gonna grow." Kalele glanced at her. "Wisdom from Pinocchio, before you ask." She laughed.

"What did you do? Shake hands good-night?" Lisa asked.

"No," Jeanine smiled. "He kissed me on the cheek."

"The cheek? The cheek? What's wrong with him?"

"Nothing. He said he didn't want to rush things."

"You agreed?"

"Yeah. We've got time. I'm not going anywhere and neither is he." She slowed her pace. "If he is, I'd rather he goes before we get in any deeper."

"I guess you're right," Lisa said as they jogged closer together to let another runner pass. "Some people use jumping into bed as an introduction."

"Yeah. Then they exchange names," Lisa added.

"Anything worthwhile is worth waiting for." *Now all I have to do is make sure I remember that.*

"And it looks like he is sure worth waiting for." Lisa laughed. "He is one fine example of male perfection."

"My thoughts the first time I saw him." Jeanine told them of her first meeting with Chris. Then the conversation turned to Lisa's project. After that each one drifted into her own zone.

It's been a long time since any woman has had that effect on me. Chris leaned back in his chair. *I might have to borrow Nate's word: "smitten."* He grinned. *It was all I could do not to press her against me and claim her as mine right there in the garden. Then I would have congratulated myself for not kissing her in the lobby.* He shook his head. *What would she have done if I did?* He shook his head again. *She's too important for me to risk scaring her off.* He frowned. *Getting overly cautious in your old age, aren't you? Just trying not to blow it. I've got to stop this one-way conversation with myself before they put me away.*

The intercom buzzed him out of the thoughts wrestling with each other. *I'll have time. She's not going anywhere. She's no more interested in a short fling than I am. I want to make sure that I do this right.* He picked up the phone and made himself focus on business. Later he'd make a personal call. He allowed a slight smile at the thought of hearing her voice. Then he spoke into the phone.

Jeanine let herself into her house. *A slow, luxurious bath, I think. Maybe a couple of vanilla-scented candles.* She sighed. *They're not birthday candles, but I can still wish that Chris were here.* She grinned. *Is that tub really big enough for two?* Her grin widened. *I wouldn't mind finding out. And they want us to think that only teenage boys have raging hormones.*

She had just filled the tub when the phone rang. She hesitated, then took the cordless phone into the bathroom with her. After she stepped into the hot water, she pushed the talk button.

"You took so long to answer that I thought you weren't home," Chris's deep voice reached her. Jeanine leaned back against the inflated pillow fastened to the back of the tub.

"I haven't been home long."

"I hope I'm not disturbing you."

You have no idea. Jeanine shifted in the tub. "It's okay."

"I'd like to see you again."

"I'd like that, too."

"I don't know your flight schedule."

"It varies. What do you have in mind?"

"It's too early to tell you what I have in mind." He paused, but not long enough for her to respond. "Besides, I'd rather show you."

"Oh." Jeanine knew he wasn't talking about the time of day. She sat up straighter. *This water is too hot.* She shook her head. *It's not the water.* "I'm not going there."

"Good idea. Who knows where it would lead." He chuckled. "I know it's short notice, but do you have plans for dinner? I mean tonight? Will you go with me? I would have called sooner, but . . ."

"Yes. I mean no. I mean . . ."

"I had a client cancel on me. I didn't know I'd be free this evening. I promise that next time I'll . . ."

"No, I don't have any plans, and yes, I'd be glad to go to dinner with you."

"I don't usually wait until the last minute. I . . ."

"Chris?"

"Yes?"

"I said I'll go to dinner with you." She smiled. "Do you always have trouble with this?"

"With asking a beautiful woman out to dinner?"

"Thank you, but I meant with taking 'yes' for an answer."

"Not usually." His voice relaxed. "I really want to see you."

"I want to see you, too. What time?"

"How about now?"

"You have to give me time to put some clothes on."

"You're not dressed?"

"I don't take a bath with my clothes on."

The only sounds to reach Jeanine were those coming from outside the house. The phone added nothing. She shifted, and the water made a sloshing sound as if trying to fill in the quiet.

"I'm going to hang up, now. I'll see you in a while. Probably a long while. I have to take a cold shower. If I could figure how to have ice cubes come out of the showerhead, I'd do that."

Jeanine laughed. "See you in about an hour and a half?"

"I guess. Yeah. If the shower hasn't helped by then, it never will."

Jeanine hung up and leaned back. *I should have told him that if he succeeds with that ice-cube idea and decides to market it, I'll be his first customer.*

She got out of the tub and dried off. *Adding cool water to the bath wouldn't have helped.* She smiled. *Nothing would. Nothing except Chris.* She shook her head. *What am I getting myself into?*

After pulling out and then discarding everything in her closet, she stood back and stared into the space as if expecting something to say, "Wear me." She shook her head. *A closet full of clothes and nothing to wear. What a cliché.* She went back over her clothes again, hanging up the ones she decided against. When she had finished, a two-piece royal-blue-and-white outfit was left. She slipped it on. The scoop-necked top, held by spaghetti-thin straps, hugged her while the skirt draped over her hips before falling in soft folds to mid-calf.

My hair? What do I do with my hair? She frowned. When in doubt, pin it up. She fastened a blue clip to her loose curls in a pile on top of her head. She had just finished her make-up when the doorbell rang.

She rushed to the door, but stopped a few feet from it. She took a slow breath and let it out just as slowly. Then she opened the door and smiled.

"Hi." *I hope I don't sound too anxious.*

Chris stood in the doorway, staring. *She looks better than good.* He grinned. *Get it together, fool.*

"Hi, beautiful."

"Hi. Come on in." She stepped aside. Chris paused in front of her as a whiff of her perfume reached him. He dared to let a finger trail down her cheek, but resisted the urge to let his mouth follow. "I'd ask if you're ready, but I can see that you are."

"Why, thank you, kind sir." Her smile widened. "Yes, I'm ready." She stepped onto the porch.

Chris watched as she locked the door. Then he placed his hand on her waist as if he had to persuade her—as if she didn't seem as eager to go with him as he was to have her company.

"I thought we'd go to Terri's Down Home Cookin'. Okay?"

"Fine with me."

"I would say it's the best soul-food place on the island, but . . ."

"Since it's the *only* soul-food place, there would be no contest even if her food were a bad example," Jeanine said, finishing his sentence. Their laughter mingled as if it was meant to be.

During the ride to the restaurant they discussed their activities of the past week.

They continued the conversation after they went inside.

"Why architecture?" Jeanine asked after they were seated. "How did you decide what you wanted to do with your life?"

"My parents said they gave me a set of those little connecting building pieces for Christmas one year when I was really young, and I never gravitated to anything else. As I grew older, the blocks got smaller and the sets bigger. I used to build dollhouses and even furniture for Sarah's dolls. The way Mom tells it, I always had one of her dolls in some new building that I had just finished. The year we went to Orlando, they took me to a store that sold more kits than I imagined existed. They even had huge buildings and creatures on display, all built from the sets. I forgot about all the theme parks in the area. Mom said Dad was sorry that he had spent a small fortune on tickets. He said he could have bought one of each set in the store for what he paid for tickets to the theme parks." Chris laughed. "Somewhere along the line I started drawing plans before I built something." He shrugged. "There was never any question about what I wanted to do." He looked at her. "How about you? Why did you choose to become a helicopter pilot?"

After the waitress set their meals in front of them, Jeanine answered.

"When I was growing up in Philadelphia, we used to go to the Willow Grove naval base's air show each year. Everybody else loved the planes. I was fascinated by the choppers. They're so versatile. They can set down almost anywhere. They can be used for many purposes."

"Aren't they dangerous?"

"No more than any other vehicle."

"Cars stay on the ground. If they crash, they're still on the ground and people have a better chance of surviving." He sampled the barbequed ribs on his plate.

"Are you one of those people who believe that people shouldn't fly? That what the Wright brothers did was not a good thing?"

Chris shrugged. "These ribs are good."

"Yes, they are." Jeanine stared at him after tasting hers. "I'll take your non-answer as a 'yes.'" She set her fork down. "Let's follow that idea. If people were meant to build, their hands would have built-in tools. Right?"

"Okay." He held up a hand. "I don't want to fight with you." *I'd much rather make love.* Chris frowned. *Back off before you scare her away.*

"Is something wrong with the food?"

"No, it's delicious." He looked at her and hoped his desire wasn't showing. "What about that problem you were fussing with Nate about?"

"He checked the engine. The chopper has been fine since then."

"But what if it happens again? What if the next time you can't control it? What if . . ."

"What if another car plows into us on the way home? What if the brakes fail as we're going around a sharp curve on the mountain? What if a section of the ceiling over our heads falls on us right now?" She took a sip of iced tea.

"Okay, okay." Chris pinned her with a stare. "I just don't want anything to happen to you."

"That makes two of us." She smiled.

The conversation turned to safer topics. Chris told

Jeanine of his plans for Nate's house and the new project that he was about to begin. Their conversation stayed on safer topics for the rest of the meal.

During the drive home the quiet filling the car was comfortable. When they reached Jeanine's house, the tension Jeanine felt matched that in Chris.

"I had a great time," she said as she turned to face him. "I . . ."

Chris covered her mouth with his, blocking any words from getting out. He pulled back, looked into her eyes, and then claimed her mouth again. Jeanine felt herself lean into him. Her hands found his chest. His tongue danced with hers, and her hands felt for a resting place around his neck. She tried to move closer. Finally Chris eased his mouth from hers. He cradled her in his arms.

"That first kiss is always awkward," Chris's words rasped. "I thought I'd get it over with."

"Good idea," Jeanine managed to squeeze out. She brushed her hands back and forth across his chest. *I don't have to wonder if he is as affected as I am. His body is telling me that he is.* She stepped back.

"I'd better go inside."

"Yeah, you'd better."

Neither moved.

"I have to go."

"Yes, you do." He held her arms softly but didn't pull her close again. "I can't tell you how much I want you, but it's too soon."

"Yeah. Too soon." She tried to nod, but only managed a half-hearted effort, and that was weak. "Way too soon."

"I'd better go." He rubbed his hands up and down her arms. "Now."

"Right now." She pressed against his chest instead of moving away.

"Now." Chris skimmed his mouth across hers.

"We can't do this." Jeanine pulled her mouth away. "I'm sorry. I shouldn't have . . ."

"Yeah. We can't." He groaned, but he released her and backed away. "Good night, sweet thing." He smiled, shook his head, then backed away. "I finally understand that line about parting being sweet sorrow. Dream of me." Then he turned and walked down the steps. After he got into his car, he waved before he drove away.

Jeanine stood fixed in place long after his car had left her driveway.

Dream of him? How did he expect me to sleep, much less dream? She grinned and leaned against the door. *Is there some direction booklet that tells you how long you have to wait before it's not too soon?* She went inside. *When it happens we'll probably set off an eruption that will make Pele jealous.*

She went into her bedroom, but just sat on the bed. *What if Chris were here with me right now? What if he unfastened my dress like this?* She slid the back zipper down. *What if he touched me? What if he explored my body with his hands, his mouth, until he discovered hot spots that I'm not even aware of?* She shook her head and felt her breasts harden. *He's not even here, yet my body is ready for him.* She groaned. *What am I going to do?*

She finished undressing, but didn't pull on her night shirt. Instead, she stretched out on top of the covers and wished for just a bit of a Philadelphia winter—just enough to cool her hot body.

SEVEN

Jeanine awoke before her alarm went off. She had tossed all night, but she felt refreshed. She smiled. *I'm on a love high.* Her smile widened as she went into the bathroom. *Is this what love feels like? Have I really, finally found love?* She turned on the water in the shower but didn't step in. She felt on the edge of something. *I've only known him for short while. Can love happen this fast?* A crease formed between her eyebrows. *I've heard of love at first sight, but I wasn't sure that such a thing was possible.*

She knew the water temperature was perfect; still, she didn't move. *Love.* She nodded. *I'm in love with Chris Harris.* Her smile returned wider than before. *If he can make me feel this way with little more than a kiss, what will actually making love with him do to me?* She stepped into the shower. *I can't wait to find out.*

Her smile stayed as she got dressed. Even putting on two distinctly different shoes didn't erase the feeling. She thought of an old song about the second time around. *Love is beautiful the first time, too.* She carefully picked the mate for one of the shoes and slipped her foot into it, discarding the mismatched one.

The answering machine was blinking when she went into the hallway. She frowned. *Was a message here last night, and I missed it?* She smiled. *It's understandable.*

I did have something else to occupy my mind. She pushed the play button.

"Good morning, beautiful. I guess you've already left. I just called to thank you for last night." His low rumble skipped along her spine. *If he could bottle that, he'd only build because he wanted to.* She tried to frown, but couldn't. *I don't have time for a cold shower,* she told herself. *You'll have to handle this without help from water.* She leaned against the wall and listened to the rest of the message. "And to ask you to dinner tonight." He chuckled. "And to hear your sweet voice." His sigh was heavy enough to reach Jeanine through the phone. "Pick you up at seven? Call me if it's a no-go. Of course, you can call me, anyway." Again he left a space. "I hope you didn't sleep any better than I did."

Chris's voice ended, but Jeanine stared at the phone as if waiting for more. Or as if waiting for him to find a way to come through the line and hold her. Then she took her keys from the table and left the house.

Just as well, she thought. *If I had talked to him I might not have made it into work at all.*

Two flights and many hours later, Jeanine was on her way to her car, finished for the day. She smiled. Finally she could free her mind to think about Chris. *I'll see him in a few hours.* He stayed in her thoughts all the way home, but the dinner that they would share was not her main focus.

After she got home she went for a short run alone since Lisa and Kalele couldn't make it. Thinking of Chris helped her stay in the zone. When she finished she wasn't as relaxed as usual. She was going to see Chris.

She forced herself to choose a dress without emptying

the closet. She had just left the bedroom when the doorbell rang.

"Hi, sweetness." Chris greeted her when she opened the door. He eased her against him and claimed her lips. Slowly, but too soon he pulled back. "Better than any dessert we can order." Desire simmered in his gaze. "I missed you."

"It's only been a few hours," she teased.

"What's time got to do with it?" He brushed his lips across hers again.

"Not a thing." *The entire outside is full of air, and still I can't find enough to breathe.* She met his stare with hers. "I know. I missed you, too."

"I guess we'd better go before we miss dinner, although missing dinner isn't always a bad thing. It depends on the reason, doesn't it?" Chris stepped back and let his gaze slowly move down her and then back to her face. "Beautiful." He grinned. "And I like the dress, too."

"Just something I had hanging around the house." She laughed and took his arm. He laughed with her as they walked to the car.

"How was your day?" Jeanine asked after they gave the waiter their orders.

"Long. Until about half an hour ago."

"I mean your work."

"It *was* work to keep my mind on the plans I was drawing up and not on seeing you. I hope my plans included bathrooms in the units. If not, lots of folks will be in awkward situations."

"Oh, Chris, Chris, Chris." Jeanine shook her head. "What am I going to do with you?"

"Are you open for suggestions?"

"Not yet. Anything worth having is worth waiting for."

"Uh-huh." He nodded. "Fruit takes a while to ripen."

"What?" She frowned at him as the waiter set their plates in front of them."

"I couldn't think of anything else to rationalize waiting."

"That was lame."

"I know." His smile disappeared. "I also know that we're moving fast. I don't want anything to mess up what we have growing between us."

"Neither do I." She touched his hand. "Neither do I," she repeated. She leaned back. "Tell me about the plans you're working on. Big project or little?"

As they ate, Chris told of the design for a new resort. "They want a mix of condos for both full-time owners as well as time-share owners. The plans call for an initial building to accommodate fifty units with shops on the ground floor to supply basic needs so people won't have to go out every time they need a loaf of bread or a quart of milk. If that's successful, they plan to put up additional buildings. They have plenty of space."

"Don't you wonder when we'll reach the time-share saturation point?"

"Speaking as an architect/building designer, I don't question it. I just give thanks for the business." He squeezed her hand. "Now your turn. Tell me about your day."

As they finished eating, Jeanine talked about the two flights. "None of my passengers had ever been in a helicopter before. Two couples were celebrating anniversaries. One was the twenty-fifth, and the other was the thirtieth." She smiled. "Both couples held hands during the flight. You could tell that they're still in love." She sighed. "That's what I want."

"You'll have that." He touched her hand.

"I hope so." She sighed again. "The second flight was a different story. The family of parents and two children was okay. The other two passengers were a married couple, but the way they argued, I don't see how they can stay together much longer. I doubt that they saw anything. They got on board arguing, kept it up during the whole flight, and were still at it as they walked away from the bird." She frowned. "That, I don't want."

"You're not that type." Chris set his napkin on the table. "Ready, or do you want dessert?"

"I'm ready."

They left the restaurant with Chris's arm around her shoulder. They rode to her house with him answering questions about the progress on Nate's house.

"Home again, home again." He turned off the engine.

"Jiggity jog." Jeanine finished the nursery rhyme and looked at him.

Neither spoke as they walked to the house. They reached the porch and, as if on cue, turned toward each other. Still silent, Jeanine walked into his arms and rested her head against his chest. Chris's arms folded around her. She pressed a kiss to his chest. His arms tightened.

"That's a waste of a perfectly good kiss," he said as he eased her chin up. "I have a better idea." He claimed her mouth to show her. *I'm standing on my own lanai, but I'm lost,* she thought. Then she opened her mouth to him and whatever thought might have been waiting to come out got lost, too.

His hands stroked up and down her back. Hers mimicked his movements. Their tongues touched, tasted, and explored each other. Chris widened his stance and Jeanine moved into the cradle his thighs formed. His hand found the side of her breast, and the kiss deepened. His other hand trailed fire to the fullness, finding the hard tip waiting. He traced a circle around it, almost touching, but barely missing.

Jeanine moaned and Chris swallowed her moan. His

mouth left hers and kissed its way along her neck. She pressed her breast into his hand as her own hands found a way under the back of his shirt. She stroked his hard muscles and felt them ripple under her fingers. His fingers finally found the swollen tip waiting. He brushed across once, then stopped.

Jeanine gasped and moaned again.

"It's okay," he whispered against her cheek. She felt the night air caress her back as his fingers slipped the dress zipper down. He eased the dress from her shoulders. If her hips hadn't stopped it, it would have slid to the lanai floor. And she wouldn't have minded one bit. What he was doing to her kept her from caring about anything else.

His hands skimmed her back and she moaned at the feel of him replacing the breeze. She shifted closer against his hardness. He groaned and found the clasp of her bra. She lowered her arms and let it slide down, too.

He took advantage of the new part of her available to him. He rubbed across her back, and she rocked against him. He shifted his chest from hers and found the dark, hard tips waiting for him.

"Beautiful," he whispered before his mouth claimed one. His tongue circled the peak before drawing it into his mouth.

Jeanine gasped and tightened her hold around his neck.

"I wouldn't want the other perfect tip to feel neglected," Chris said before he claimed it.

Jeanine drew his head closer and pushed herself into him. Then she frowned and pulled back. "I—I can't." Her words were weak, as if all of her strength was somewhere else. Or as if she hadn't wanted to say the words. She reached for him, but pulled her hand back before she touched him. "I'm sorry. I'm so sorry. I didn't . . ." She shook her head and stared at her feet.

"It's okay. I don't want us to do something that you'll

be sorry about tomorrow. There's no hurry. We'll wait until you're sure." He smiled and moved a finger gently down her cheek before his hands found her waist. "I'm not going anywhere." He grasped her dress. Slowly he lifted it into place. When it reached her breast, Jeanine gasped. He had made them more sensitive than they had ever felt before. *What's wrong with me? It felt so right. Why did I stop?*

Chris took a step away from her and made himself lean against the railing.

"How many dates constitute enough?" His grin caressed her.

"What?"

"How many do we need to get to know each other well enough?"

"Oh." She looked into his eyes. "I think—I think we're almost there. I don't want us to blow what we have going. I'm sorry. I . . ."

"It's okay. It's killing me, but I want you enough to wait until you're ready." He pushed off from the railing. "I'd better go before my ability to be noble disappears." He touched his lips to hers. "See you tomorrow?"

"Yes. Same time?"

"Yes. We're throwing a lot of 'yesses' around, aren't we?"

"Yes." Her smile was shy. "I—I know it's not the one you wanted to hear."

"Not wanted. Want. But I'll wait until the time when we both want the same thing."

"Thank you for being understanding." She shrugged. "You probably think I'm acting like a Victorian stuck in the present day."

"I think you're acting like a woman who wants to be sure before she takes this to the next level. We'll only get a first time with each other once. It has to be right."

He nodded. "I'd better leave before I try to persuade you to do something you might regret." His expression intensified. "I don't want to do that. See you tomorrow."

Jeanine watched him walk away. She was still standing in the same spot as he drove away.

Did I do the right thing? She shook her head. *If he only knew how close I was to the "yes" that he wanted to hear.* She sighed. *If he had pushed, would I have been able to stop?* She touched her lips, and the memory of the kiss they had shared flew back as if waiting for a new memory to add to it. No kiss had rocked her like that before. She closed her eyes. *Did I do the right thing in not having him continue? Not letting him finish what we started? I've only known him for a short while, but it seems like months.* She frowned. *It felt like it, too.*

She picked up her bra and clutched it to her. The night stillness settled around her. Somewhere, a long way off, somebody's rooster crowed. She blinked hard. *That rooster doesn't know when the time is right, either.*

She sighed again and, on legs still weak from what had just happened between her and Chris, with her breasts still sensitive and aching as if they ached badly enough, he would come back, she managed to go inside.

She undressed slowly. *What if Chris were doing this for me? What if he were unzipping my dress again? What if his hands were skimming it off my body? What if his touch were letting him learn about what he had uncovered? What if his mouth were teaching me what I like? What if he were here with me now?* She slid her panties away from her moistness and worked at getting her body back to normal. *What if he were here to discover how ready I am for him right now?*

She took a shower, and the agony of knowing that she could be sharing it with Chris stayed with her.

A little later she slid into bed. She closed her eyes, but

she knew it would be a long while before she found sleep. Instead of sheep, she tried to count the reasons why they should wait. There were a lot fewer of them than there were sheep.

EIGHT

Jeanine went to work the next day. Whenever her mind wanted to take her back to the night before, she forced it to stay on her flying. She knew, although it felt more right than anything else ever had, it would be better if they waited. Finally her last flight was over and she was on her way home. She smiled as the warmth of the night before warmed her now. *We can still fool around, though.* She grinned and shook her head. *Playing with fire never appealed to me before.* She frowned. *I never had anybody like Chris to play with before.* She sighed. *Nobody could consider what we shared "playing."*

Once home, she changed into her running clothes. She was looking forward to seeing Kalele and Lisa. Their work had messed up their running schedule. *How much do I tell them about Chris? Not too much. I don't want to jinx things.*

She was on her way out the door when the phone rang. *Lisa or Chris?* She shrugged. *Caller ID would let me know, but where's the fun in that?*

"Hi."

"Hi, Jeanine," Lisa's voice was thin. No happiness colored the words.

"Why can't you come with us this time?"

"I'm sorry. I really am. It's this new project. We're just starting up, and we've hit more than a few snags." She waited. When Jeanine didn't say anything, her words rushed on. "You know this is our biggest project to date. If we can't handle it, we'll never get a chance at a project this size again." Again she waited. Again Jeanine kept silent. "Look, when things quiet down, after we settle into a routine, I'll be back. As it is, I don't expect to even get to the gym for a long time." She tried a chuckle, but it died before she finished. "I'll have to dust off my old treadmill and snatch some time when I can. Jeanine, I'm sorry. I'm really sorry."

"Yeah, I know," Jeanine sighed. "I was the one who said work comes first." Her voice softened. "You just make sure you work out at home. When your project cuts you some slack, I don't want to have to slow down my pace while you get back up to speed."

"Thanks for understanding."

"I don't have a choice. I don't make enough money to feed both of us, so you have to keep your company in business. Call me. You can't work round the clock."

"I will. I'll call you. I promise."

Jeanine hung up and stared at the phone. *She'll be all right.* Then she left to meet Kalele at the park.

"How's it?" the other woman asked when Jeanine reached her.

"Fine," Jeanine answered. "Been waiting long?"

"Just got here."

"Let's get started."

"Lisa's not coming?"

"Nope. It's just the two of us."

"Work, huh?" She stretched with Jeanine.

"Got it in one. She said the new project is kicking her butt."

"She says that at the start of every new building project."

"She swears she'll work out at home."

"For her sake, I hope she does."

They started walking, but soon broke into a jog. Today Jeanine's zone included Chris. She smiled as she ran. She was going to see him tonight. Her smile widened. *I know "seeing" will include some touching, too.*

"Hey. Who you running from?"

"Sorry." Jeanine slowed to their normal pace, but kept smiling. *It's more like running* to, *not from.*

An hour later they were walking to cool off.

"I have something to tell you." Kalele stopped walking and faced Jeanine. "I'm afraid it's gonna be just you for a while."

"You quitting on me, too?"

"Not because I want to. And not because of work, either. Duty calls, literally. I've been called up to active duty."

"Oh. I forgot you were in the reserves." Jeanine stood still and looked at her.

"The president didn't forget. Besides, one weekend a month and two weeks every summer won't let me forget."

"When do you go?"

"Next week."

"Next week? No more notice than that?"

"That's the way it goes sometimes, especially these days."

"Do you know for how long?" They began their cool-down stretch.

"No." Kalele shook her head. "You can't go by what they say when they do give you a time frame. This time they were more vague than usual. They didn't even give us a general idea." She rolled her shoulders and finished her stretch.

"Do you even know where you're going?"

"As of now, somewhere in the Middle East." She inhaled slowly as she stretched up. "Of course, that might change."

"Oh." Jeanine blinked hard. "You tell the president that he'd better send you back in the same condition you're in now."

"I'll be all right. I'll be doing the same thing I'm doing now except for less money."

"They need to fix that."

"Yeah." Kalele smiled. "But why should they? We have to go, regardless." She watched as Jeanine completed a final stretch. "You have a few minutes before you go?"

"Sure." Jeanine sat on a bench near the parking lot, and Kalele sat beside her. "What's up? You don't have a cat for me to watch while you're away, do you?"

"Nothing like that." She smiled. "I found out something you might want to take advantage of. In three weeks there's a training session for civilian pilots who want to fly special assignments for the police like I do sometimes. You sounded interested when I told you about it awhile ago. With me going away, they'll probably need another pilot. I have the information in my car." She shrugged. "I brought it just in case."

"Okay." *I'm not as enthusiastic as I was before.* Jeanine frowned. *I can't let everything go because of what Chris and I are working on.* She felt her temperature go up a degree just thinking about exactly what that was. She suppressed a smile. Then she frowned. *I will not be one of those women who cling to a man like that.*

"What's the matter? Change your mind?"

"No. I'm still interested." She stood. "Ready?"

"Sure."

They walked to Kalele's car.

"You'll still have to stick to our routine until you leave,

though. I don't want to do this alone until I have to, so no excuses. In fact, if you don't report until late on the day you leave, I might make you work out before you get on that plane."

"I know that won't happen. Departure time is always when the sun is still in bed, so that's out. Until then, it's you and me. Let's not talk about it anymore. Okay?"

"Okay."

She handed Jeanine the brochure. "Call me if you have any questions. Of course, if they can wait, I'll see you at the gym tomorrow. Right?"

"Absolutely. It's my favorite place."

"And if I believe that, you'll sell me Diamond Head at a good price, and because this is my lucky day, I get to keep all of the diamonds embedded in the mine, right?"

They laughed and went their separate ways.

On the drive home, Jeanine glanced a few times at the brochure on the seat beside her. Each time she frowned. *I think I know how Chris will react, but I hope I'm wrong.*

"Hi, beautiful," Chris placed a lingering kiss on Jeanine's cheek when he got to her house that night.

"Hello, handsome." She grinned. Then she placed a hand on either side of his face and pulled his mouth down to hers. What started as a G-rated kiss soared to X-rated in a few seconds. Still, a good ten seconds more passed before she eased back from him. "Ready?"

"I'm more than ready, but you're probably talking about leaving."

"You know I am." *But I'm as ready as you are for the other, too.*

They ate at a small restaurant that Chris had discovered near the site of the new building he was planning. They probably would have found the food delicious, but neither could tell what they ate. They were too busy concentrating on each other. Finally Jeanine stopped pretending to eat and placed her napkin beside her plate.

"I'm finished."

"Me, too." Chris smiled. "I just didn't want to rush you."

His arm was around her waist as they walked to the car.

"I was very tempted to buy a sports car with a stick shift," Chris said as he got behind the wheel for the drive back. "I'm glad I didn't. If I had, I couldn't do this." He held her hand after he turned on the motor and put the car in gear. "Of course, if I had been anticipating meeting you, I would have skipped the bucket seats, too." He brushed his lips across hers. "But then again, maybe that wouldn't be such a good thing. I could never concentrate on my driving with you pressed against me." He glanced at her and pulled onto the road. "In fact, I'd better drag my mind away from that thought before I have an unexpected encounter with a tree, or worse, with another car." He smiled at her and drove down the road. Their hands were still clasped together when they reached her house.

"Want to come in?" *We lucked out the last time we did our thing at the front door. If one of my neighbors had come past . . .* She shook her head. *The story they could tell.*

"Change your mind? I saw you shake your head."

"No, I was just thinking of something else." She smiled up at him.

"If the offer is still open, you know I do. I have to talk to you about something." His easy smile was gone.

"Okay." Her smile left, too. *He's breaking up with me before we even get started,* she thought as she opened the door. "Coffee?"

"No, thanks." He followed Jeanine into the living room and sat on the couch.

"What is it?" She sat at the other end, poised at the edge. *Here it comes.*

"I have to go away for a while." He frowned.

"Away?" *Is this how he breaks up?*

"Yes."

"For how long?" *Why did you ask that? Do you want your feelings trampled on? Do you want him to see how you react when he says "forever"?*

"For two weeks. I have to go to L.A. for a conference and then to D.C. for a meeting. I leave in a week."

"Oh. Is that all?"

"Two weeks isn't long enough for me to be away from you? You want me to stay away longer?"

"No, no." Her words rushed out as she shook her head quickly. "Of course I don't." She shrugged.

"Well, what was the 'Is that all' about?"

"I thought you were going to tell me something else."

"Like what?"

"It's not important."

"It must be if it made you say something like that."

"I thought you were going to tell me that you found somebody else." She didn't even glance at him.

"You thought what? Somebody else? After what we've had so far, what made you think that?"

She stared at her lap and was surprised to see her hands clutched together.

"I don't know." She looked at him. Then she shrugged and looked away again. "I guess what we have seems so good that I'm afraid it's going to end before I'm ready."

"I don't intend to end it, so you might be stuck with me long after you start to avoid me."

"That won't ever happen. I . . ."

"Hey. What are you doing way over there?" Chris

pulled her near. "Maybe you're the one tired of what we have growing between us."

"That will never happen as far as I'm concerned, either." She tilted her face up to his.

His mouth found hers, and he pressed his lips against hers, pulled away, then found them again. She opened her mouth to him and he entered. His tongue touched hers, danced a bit, then withdrew. He found her lips again and tasted them.

Jeanine moved closer still. Mouths together, Chris eased her onto his lap. His mouth sampled her cheek as his hand found her breast. He stroked around the tip, and it hardened in anticipation. He made it wait too long, then he brushed a finger across it gently, then replaced his finger with his mouth. Jeanine's hand tightened on his chest before she found the way inside his shirt. Once there, her fingers stroked back and forth across his nipples. His groan matched her moan. Then slowly he removed his mouth. The air on the dampness he left behind did nothing to cool her. Slowly they moved a few inches apart.

"Dessert never tasted so good." The heat in Chris's gaze matched one in hers. "I'd like a second helping, please." He reached for her.

"I—I hate to do this, but we—we have to talk." She took a deep breath, but it didn't help. His gaze kept throwing fire at her. She forced herself to move a few more inches away from him, when what she really wanted was to feel his mouth on her again.

"Now?" He frowned. "You want to talk now?"

"I—I'm sorry. But I think we should before we . . ." She tried a deep breath again. This time it helped a little, but only a little. "Before we go on." She managed to stand. She glanced at her blouse, and heat flooded her face as she thought of why it was unbuttoned. She pulled the edges together and covered the damp spot on her bra.

Despite shaky hands, she managed to get one button back where it belonged. *When did he open it? I didn't.* She frowned. *Did I?*

"What is it that won't wait?" Chris stood. The proof of his arousal was obvious.

Jeanine clasped her hands together to keep from reaching to him. "I'm sorry."

"For what just happened?"

"No." She shook her head. "I'm sorry that I waited until now to say 'let's talk.' I—I didn't expect us to reach this point so quickly." She looked at the floor. "I'm sorry."

"You already said that."

"Yes." She dared a glance at his face. Frustration met her, but not anger. *Maybe he won't react the way I think he will.* She took another step away from him so it would be harder for her to close the space.

"I have some news, too. I'm going to enter a training program."

"And that's why you stopped us?" He ran a hand over his hair. "Because this training program starts right this minute?"

She glanced at him. His face looked a little more relaxed. *Is that the hint of a smile at the corner of his mouth?* She felt some of her tension leave. *Maybe there's hope.* "No, in two weeks."

"And I leave in one. Your training starts a week before I get back." He let a smile show itself. "When I return, we can work around our schedules. The worse time will be when I'm on the mainland. We won't be able to steal time together." His expression intensified. "I don't know how I'll be able to stand not seeing you for those two weeks." He moved close to her and clasped his hands behind her back. Then he rocked her slightly from side to side. "You have become such a part of me." He placed a quick kiss on her mouth. Then he looked into her eyes and released her. "When I get back, we can make up for the time we were apart."

"My training lasts for three weeks."

"You'll have another two weeks of training after I get back."

"Yes."

"Well," he smiled again. "We might not get to see each other as often as we'd like to, but neither of us will be busy all day and all night. They'll have to release you sometime. We might even be able to steal lunch together a few times those weeks." He touched her cheek. "And we might even manage to eat some lunch during our meetings." He reached for her, but she took a step back and shook her head.

"The training program is on Oahu."

"Oahu?" Now it was his turn to widen the space between them. "Three weeks on Oahu? Exactly what kind of program is this? Are you learning to fly a new type of helicopter? Nate didn't mention anything about that, but he doesn't tell me everything." His smile was weaker.

"I'll be training to participate in police operations." She stared at him as if trying to see into his thoughts before he showed her a reaction. *There. I got it out.*

"What?" He took another step away from her. "You're joining the police force?"

If Jeanine hadn't seen his smile before, she would never have known that he had given it to her.

"No." She shook her head and ignored the uneasy feeling growing inside her. "The police department has only two helicopters, and both of them are stationed on Oahu. Sometimes they have to use civilians for operations, especially on the other islands."

"Why do you want to do this?"

"I've been fascinated by the idea ever since I met Kalele."

"And she does this?"

"Yes," she nodded.

"That's where you got this idea."

"I guess. Partly." She shrugged. "Yes."

"I'm going to ask you a question a version of which your mother probably asked you at least once when you were growing up: If Kalele jumped off a bridge, would you follow her?" He looked at her.

"If it was for a good reason." She met his gaze.

"I'm just trying to understand why you want to do this." He frowned and shook his head slowly, as if trying to undo what he had heard.

"I have skills that can be helpful to the police." Her stare intensified. "I think I should use them."

"I don't like the idea."

"Who said you have to?" She crossed her arms across her chest. "Why do you have to like it?"

"What?"

"Why do you have to like it? This is what *I* decided to do." Her glare was as strong as his was. "I still decide for me."

"It's dangerous. You could get hurt."

"As they say, you can get hurt crossing the street. That doesn't make people live their whole lives on the same side of the street."

"I care about you." He reached toward her. "I just don't want you to get hurt."

"I care about you, too, and I don't want you to get hurt, either. Tell me, do you intend to continue hanging around construction sites? Just a few days ago a man fell off a building he was working on. And don't tell me about hard hats," she said when he opened his mouth. "That man's hard hat didn't help him."

"That's not the same thing."

"No, it's not." She shook her head. "What you do is

not as safe as what I do. Construction site accidents happen more often than helicopter accidents."

"I don't want to argue with you." His frown didn't go anywhere. "Will you at least think about it some more?"

"I've already thought about it. A lot. I made up my mind a long time ago that, as soon as I had an opportunity, I'd take the training. I want this, and I'm going for it."

They both wrestled for control as if trying to make the other one holler "uncle." Finally Chris shook his head and slowly turned away.

"I guess I'd better go."

"I guess so." Her voice barely reached him. He opened the door and turned back toward her.

"I'll call you."

"Okay."

She closed the door behind him and frowned. *What just happened?*

Chris got only four blocks away. After going through two stop signs, he pulled over, turned off the engine, and leaned back. *What happened back there?* He frowned as he stared out the windshield as if the answer were outside. *One minute we're ready to fall off the edge of something beautiful together, and the next we're at each other in a whole different way.* He shook his head as if that would make the last ten minutes erase like an unwanted tape. *Ten minutes, if that long. That's all it took to take things back way before square one and to build a wall to prevent anything from ever developing between us.*

He turned the engine on and pulled back onto the road. *Why does she have to be so set on putting herself in danger? Why is she so stubborn?*

NINE

Jeanine awoke the next morning with none of the happiness that had kept her company when she knew she would see Chris later in the day. She wasn't sure she would ever find that euphoria again. *What will get me through today when I can't anticipate seeing Chris tonight as I have every evening for . . .* She frowned as she got dressed. *We haven't been involved for long.* She sighed. *But it seems like months. It seemed as if we were meant to be together. And now . . .*

She concentrated on finishing with her usual morning routine. She tried hard not to think of how close she and Chris came to making love last night. *If we had, how could it have hurt any more than it does right now? I hadn't planned for us to get to that point so soon, but it seemed right.* She shook her head. *Maybe it's good that it didn't happen. Maybe I don't know him well enough to take that step. Evidently I don't know him well at all.*

She sighed again and left the house. *I should be relieved that this came up now rather than later,* she thought as she walked to her car.

She got in, but just sat. *I should be, but I'm not. The heart doesn't always follow the head.*

She got through the day struggling to keep her mind on flying and all of the duties that went with it rather than trying to figure out how to resolve the impasse that stood like a stone wall between her and Chris. She was pleasant and said the right things to her passengers and hoped that they couldn't tell that her heart wasn't in it.

At three she was finished with her last flight. *Any other time I would be glad to get off early. Today I wish I had three more flights.*

"Bye," she said to Nate.

"See you tomorrow?"

He looks as if he wants to say something else. Jeanine waited. She didn't have any reason to rush home. When he didn't say anything more, she answered him.

"Yeah. I'm scheduled for two flights." She looked at him for a few seconds longer. Then she shrugged and walked away.

Did he look at me funny just now? Did Chris tell him what happened? Did he tell him about the blowup? She frowned as she got into her car. *Probably not. Chris won't get any support for his attitude there. The way Nate loves those birds, he'd take to the air, too, if he could. Faulty depth perception is just an annoyance for most people. For those who wanted to be pilots, like Nate, it was an insurmountable obstacle.*

She pulled out of the parking lot. *Anyway, it doesn't matter who knows. It won't change things. Chris is a controlling, stubborn mule, and I'm better off with him out of my life.*

Her ride home wasn't long enough to convince her of that. She doubted if any ride would be.

She tried to avoid looking at the answering machine when she got inside. Then she tried not to be disappointed when the light wasn't blinking, possibly signaling that Chris was ready to apologize. She stared at it a few seconds longer as if she had the power to make it change and give her the message that she wanted to hear. Then she forced herself to get dressed to meet Kalele, thankful that she didn't have to go running alone today.

The two women completed their warm-up ritual, then took off. Kalele led the way. Jeanine forced herself to stay back with her friend instead of trying to outrun her memories of Chris. Then she struggled to make herself satisfied with keeping to the pace.

They finished their run, but Jeanine never did find the zone. Her mind had decided to dwell on Chris. It was as bullheaded as he was. Jeanine followed Kalele to a bench, thankful that they were ending their run this way instead of her having to leave immediately. Now she had a little longer before her thoughts of Chris crowded in on her again.

They talked about the training program, about Kalele's leaving, and a little about Lisa and how they hoped her job was going as planned and that she'd be able to run again with Jeanine really soon. Jeanine felt a twinge of guilt because her hope was mixed with a bit of selfishness.

"How come you aren't rushing off?" Kalele asked after they had run out of things to say as Jeanine still sat beside her. "You and Chris have an argument or something?" Kalele smiled.

"Yeah."

"What?" Kalele turned to face her. "You did?"

"Yeah." Jeanine glanced at her then looked at the ground.

"Wow. Was it serious?"

"Oh yeah."

"You guys really seemed to have found something special. Want to talk about it?"

"No." Jeanine still stared at the ground as she slid her

foot back and forth, making a rut in the sand. "Not right now. It hurts too much." She shook her head. "Last night, I found out that he's a chauvinist." She crossed her arms. "I'm glad I found out so soon in our relationship." *But it wasn't soon enough to keep me from being hurt.*

"It's about the program, right?"

"He doesn't like the idea. He says it's too dangerous."

"There is some danger involved."

"That's not the point. I don't care if it involves bungee jumping into a steaming crater; it's my decision to make." She glared at a palm tree a few feet away as if it were to blame. "I don't tell him what to do." She nodded. "Yeah. I'm glad I found that out about him now instead of later." *Later might have devastated me so much that I couldn't work.* "Better now than later," she said again as if trying to convince herself that it was true.

"I'm still sorry. I thought you two had something going."

"Yeah, so did I."

"If you want to talk some more about it, you know I'm here."

"I know." Jeanine stood. "I know. Thank you." She sighed. "I'd better be going."

She took her time getting to the car and then drove the long way home. She stopped at the supermarket even though she didn't need anything. After all, she had no reason to rush home.

Again the answering machine caught her attention when she got home because again it was stuck on steady red and zero.

Later, after she picked over the chef's salad she had bought at the supermarket, she lifted the phone. She stared at it as if looking for directions, then put it back.

It's his *fault.* He's *the one who's wrong. If he cares as much for me as I thought he did, he'd call me.*

She went to sit on the lanai to get away from the dead phone. *If he really cared, he wouldn't bother with the phone. He'd come over here, get down on his knees, apologize, and beg me for forgiveness.*

She watched the beginning of the sunset. For once, watching the sun drift out of sight in glorious shades of orange, reds, and yellows didn't make her smile. Tonight it was just another way to pass time. She sat staring into the darkness as if waiting for the sun to do an encore. Then, when it was late enough so she wouldn't have to wait too long to go to bed, she left the darkness and went inside.

She followed her nightly routine, the one she had followed for forever until Chris came along to change it.

She crawled into bed without trying to understand why a new routine was harder to let go of than an old one.

The next two days dragged by the same way that day one had without Chris. Not every pain eased with the passing of time.

Jeanine began to cross off the days until it was time to leave for the training program. She didn't want to think about the countdown to the training being also a countdown away from her time with Chris.

I don't know how I got hung up on such a stubborn woman. Chris quit pretending to read the sheet of paper on the desk in front of him. *After three readings, one more try wouldn't help.* He glared at the paper as if it were written in some language he had never heard of. Then he rocked back in his chair and, even though he needed to make some decisions before leaving the office, he ignored the entire desk.

I could call her. He swiveled his chair to face the window. *And say what? I was wrong? I don't believe what you're planning is dangerous?* His scowl could give lessons to thunderclouds. *I'm not lying about this. What she plans to do* is *dangerous.* Another question surfaced. *But is it a danger that I could live with?*

The intercom intruded. For once he was glad. Maybe it was an offer to let him rebuild every building on the island. Maybe a project that big would keep his mind off what he had almost had.

"What is it?"

"Nate wants to talk with you."

"Okay." *Not a big project, but maybe enough to take my mind off the beautiful armful who has been disturbing me since I saw her last.* He shook his head. *Too long ago.* "What's up?"

"Is it too late to make a minor change?"

"Nate, you have made at least three so-called minor changes in the past week."

"I decided that I want the kitchen back where it was in the original plans."

"What does it matter? The amount of cooking that you do, you only need a microwave, and that would rust from disuse." He shook his head. "However, I'll see what I can do. Is that it?"

"When's the last time you saw her?"

"That doesn't have anything to do with your house."

"She's been looking about as bad as you do, and believe me, brother, you been looking bad."

"I'll get back to you on your changes."

"You need to fix things."

"Go find an engine to meddle with."

"I didn't get the whole supply of family mule headedness, did I? Seems like you took a big chunk before I got here."

"I'll call you about the changes."

Chris replaced the phone gently when what he wanted to do was throw it down. *I could call her.* He shook his head. *What would I say? I changed my mind? What you intend to do isn't so dangerous after all?* He walked over to the window. *If I could pull that off, what happens when she leaves for the training? I just kiss her good-bye and let her go? And what about when she actually has to fly a mission into a dangerous situation? How could I handle that?* He shook his head.

I can't lie. I still know it's dangerous. I can't spend the rest of my life wondering if she'll come back each time she's on a mission. It's bad enough that she flies that pregnant bug every day. Why the need for more danger? Does she have a death wish? He shook his head again. *She's got me talking to myself. Who said anything about the rest of my life, anyway? I've only known her for a few weeks.*

He gave up on the papers and closed the file. *But they were the best few weeks of my life.*

He closed his eyes and the memory of the feel of Jeanine against him intensified. Jeanine's softness pressed against his hardness. Her soft, warm breasts, heavy in his hands, sweet in his mouth. Her mouth, giving, promising. *Cut it out. You can't have her. There is no way around this wall between you. Get over her.*

Face back in neutral, he grabbed a few folders, jammed them into his briefcase, and slammed out of his office. He was glad everybody had already left. If not, in the morning, he would have had to apologize to every one of them for his tirade.

She's got me so twisted up, he thought as he drove home. *Why couldn't she work in an office? If she were satisfied to just fly routine flights, I could probably handle that. Why this need to save the world? Why couldn't she let somebody else do that?*

***

The phone rang, and Jeanine grabbed it before the third ring. "What's up?" Jeanine asked after Lisa's voice greeted her. *I'm glad to hear from Lisa, but why couldn't her call come after the one I've been waiting for?*

"My stress level is what's up. Murphy is embedded deeply in this project and won't find somebody else to go mess with."

"Talk to me." Jeanine settled into the corner of the couch. It had been too long since she had talked to her friend.

"The first snag was when the wrong size beams were sent. Not once, but twice. Somebody at the company where I get my materials can't read a simple order form."

Lisa continued to tell Jeanine her problems, and Jeanine managed to follow the conversation. This was what her friend needed from her. Fifteen minutes later, Lisa stopped talking.

"Other than that, everything's all right?" Jeanine asked.

Lisa's laughter came over the line.

"Girlfriend, I needed this. You just don't know. Oh, sorry. After the last fifteen minutes, I guess you do know." She sighed. "You don't know how much talking to you helped."

"You have been walking off some of that daily stress on the treadmill. Right?"

"Most of the time. How about you? I talked to Kay, and she told me about her orders. You going to keep it up after she goes, right?"

"Right. Until I leave. I'm entering the training program to work with the police the way she does. It's a three-week program on Oahu."

"You can tear yourself away from Mr. Bronze Hunk for that long?"

"He won't know when I'm gone."

"Oh, no? Girlfriend, now it's your turn to talk to me."

Half an hour after she had picked up the phone, Jeanine hung up. She leaned her head back on the couch and closed her eyes. *Now what do I do with the rest of the evening? If I manage to find the answer to that, what do I do with the rest of my life?*

TEN

"You did what?" Chris's glare made Jim, his assistant, back up a step.

"We need an aerial view of the site."

"We never needed one before." *How did I miss something as important as this?* He released a harsh breath. *I know how.* He pulled his attention away from the reason he had missed it and focussed on Jim's response.

"We never had a project this size for a site configured like this before. There are some tricky aspects to it."

"Okay. For what day did you make reservations, and what company did you use?" *Please let it be any one of the other five companies.*

"Tomorrow." Jim took a step forward.

"Tomorrow?"

"This could hold us up. I figured the sooner the better. They book up fast. We want a private flight, so a pilot and a chopper have to be available, and there has to be no booking conflict." Jim's words rushed on. "It's a good thing I booked when I did. They aren't available for the next week and a half. That would run us into your conference dates. It would be costly to make changes in the plans based on aerial photos. We don't want that, do we?"

"You know we don't." *How did I miss it?* He forced his mind back to the situation. *I'm glad* somebody *has his mind on business.* "What company did you use?" But he already knew. Fate was messing with him.

"I thought we'd throw a little business to Nate's company." His stare collided with Chris's. "Look, if you don't want to go, I can go and fill you in from the photos I'll take."

"I'd better go myself. I drew up the initial plans."

"Look, Chris. I thought it was okay for me to do this."

"It is. You were right." He shook his head. "I'd better get back to this paperwork and make sure I have what I need together so one flight will be enough." *It's too much to hope that another pilot is assigned to the flight,* he thought as he watched Jim leave. His jaw tightened. *If she can take it, I can too.*

For the rest of the day Chris processed the paperwork piled on his desk as if he were hoping for the Clean Desk of the Century Award and the judging were at the end of the day. Most of that time he managed to keep Jeanine out of his thoughts. But that wasn't the case when he got home late that night. She seemed to have crouched in some dark corner of his mind and waited to spring on him when he didn't expect it.

Standing at his front door, he held his keys, but didn't open the door. *What is she doing here?* he thought as she planted herself in front of his mind. *I never brought her here. I never had a chance to before things fell apart. Why is she here?*

He closed his eyes and leaned against the railing. Memories of the time they had spent on her lanai seeped through him as powerfully as flowing lava. He could almost feel her pressed against him, almost feel her smooth skin under his hands, almost hear her moan as he stroked her hard nipple, almost taste her mouth as he swallowed her moan. Almost savor the rough texture of the hard point as his tongue tasted that, too.

He grunted and opened the door. If almost doesn't count

in something as simple as a game of horseshoes, no wonder it didn't help ease his tension with his memories of Jeanine.

He changed and went into the gym next to his kitchen. *Maybe I can run off this frustration until it's down to a manageable level,* he thought as he started the treadmill.

An hour later, glistening with sweat, he turned off the machine. *If it hasn't worked by now, it's not going to.*

He went into the shed, grabbed the pruning shears, and started chopping. *Mr. Igashi will kill me when he sees this.* He thought of the meticulous care the gardener took with the plants. Once he had watched him examine a bush. He had walked around it several times, then cut about two inches. Each time he followed the same ritual before pruning a branch. When he finished, the bush looked almost the same, but better.

Chris looked at the ground in front of the section where he had just worked. *I wonder how long it will take the bushes to recover from my hacking.* He shook his head and walked back inside. *I hope Mr. Igashi doesn't have a weak heart.*

Just before Chris shut the door, he glanced back and frowned. *I also hope he's as gentle as he seems to be. Otherwise he's going to make me apologize to the garden before he kills me.* He put the shears away. He thought of the other mess he'd made, the more important one.

His body was tired, but his mind was acting as if it had been resting and waiting for him to stop what he was doing so it could open memories.

He showered and tried not to imagine sharing the stall with Jeanine. He didn't want to think about gliding soapy hands over her body and her doing the same to him. He certainly didn't want to imagine entering her right there in the stall and then, after their lovemaking, repeating the soaping process all over again.

Tomorrow, he thought as he got ready for bed. *Maybe it won't be her. Maybe it won't be as bad as I think.*

Chris knew by the way Nate looked at him when he entered the hangar the next morning that his maybes were wasted.

"You need to mind your own business."

"I'm not going to lie about influencing the assignment. Somebody needed to do something. She's just as bullheaded as you are. Ten years from now you two would still be plodding along, avoiding each other."

"What?"

"I'm reading up on psychology. Interesting stuff."

"You better go find some lab rats to practice on."

"Chris, you gotta find a way around this."

"Sure, doctor." He stared at Nate. "Does she know?"

"She doesn't have a clue."

"I wouldn't want to be you tomorrow."

"She might thank me and bring me a heaping platter of home-cooked soul food."

"She'll probably make you switch to reading ancient poetry, and I'd make her taste any food she brings first." He stalled for a few seconds. "Do I go inside or what?"

"Check in at the desk that you passed. You have an orientation and a film first."

Chris hadn't been able to trade his glare for a smile, but at least his face wouldn't make the representative think that his anger was for her. He followed her inside to the viewing area.

"Please wait here."

Chris wished he could borrow a smile from her. She seemed to have a big supply. He sat on the built-in bench facing a TV. Music drifted into the room, and the clear, smooth voice of Iz singing "Over the Rainbow" reached him, trying to soothe him. It didn't manage completely, but Chris was in a better frame of mind than when he awoke that morning. *Too bad there's no real way over the rainbow. I could use the fulfillment of a few wishes.*

After the orientation and a short film, he and the representative went over the specifics of what Jim had requested.

"If you need to get more shots of a particular area, just tell the pilot. Our video camera mounted beneath the cockpit will photograph the entire flight. Of course, you won't be under any obligation to purchase the video, but if you want to, just come to the desk when you return. Any questions?" When Chris shook his head, she led him out of the terminal and to the gate.

There she is, he thought as his gaze found Jeanine standing beside the gate and looking at the open folder she was holding. He saw her look up; he watched as her stance tightened at the sight of him.

"Chris."

"Hi, Jeanine."

"You two already know each other. Good." She nodded. "We can skip the introductions. You have your flight plan?"

"Yes." Jeanine held up a folder, then tucked it against her chest as if she needed a barrier between her and Chris. "If you're ready, we can leave." She looked past him as if talking to somebody behind him.

She acts as if I don't know what's behind that folder. As if I haven't felt what she has covered. As if I haven't tasted her. As if I don't know how smooth, how soft, yet how firm her breasts are. As if I don't remember that they are sweeter than any other chocolate that I have ever tasted. As if . . .

He forced his mind to focus on the reason for the flight. To think of how many feet of rebar he would use in the construction of the current building project, of how many gallons of paint it would take to cover the walls and ceilings even though painting wasn't part of his job. He tried to concentrate on anything else to get his mind off Jeanine so his body could appear acceptable to anyone who saw him, provided they didn't look too closely.

He followed her to the chopper, not sure whether he wanted more space between them so he could see her walk, or whether he was glad he only had to look at her back. In the end, he was grateful that the chopper was nearby. He didn't say a thing as Jeanine made sure he was situated properly. He was still silent as she got in. *What is there to say that would make a difference?* he wondered.

"Wait a minute, Jeanine," he shouted over the noise of the engine as she reached for the controls. "This wasn't my idea. None of it. I didn't plan . . ." He let his hope rise as her hand paused before it reached the stick. His hope disappeared when she wrapped her hand around the stick in a grip definite enough to let him know that he wasn't doing any good. The tightness in her jaw was further proof that the only plus from this trip would be the pictures that he took.

"It doesn't matter." Her tone was loud enough for her to be heard above the noise and was as determined as her posture. "If it wasn't you, it would be somebody else in that passenger seat. A flight is a flight. They all help pay the bills. I'm glad for the change in flight patterns." She hadn't looked at him since speaking his name at the gate. Then it had been only a glance, but he had seen the hurt shining in her eyes.

"Jeanine . . ."

"If you put on the headphones, you can let me know when you have all the pictures you need. I'm sure they told you that the chopper has a camera mounted underneath and that you can get a copy of that video as well. If you're ready, we can get under way." She stared directly at him, and Chris wished for the passing glance of before. The hurt had been replaced by shards of ice.

"I'm ready." His gaze met hers and hers slid away. He knew the desire burning in his eyes showed her exactly what he was ready for and that his answer had nothing to do with a helicopter flight and everything to do with her. He also knew that it made no difference to her.

The next words Jeanine spoke to him were the same ones she used for every passenger. Her voice was neither heated nor frigid. Worse, it was neutral.

She went over instructions about the equipment, the headphones, and she verified the flight pattern. She instructed him on what to do in an emergency, too, but she didn't tell him how to get them over this impasse. She acted as though they had never had a relationship for an impasse to impede. *Impersonal. And it's killing me.*

Finally they were lifting off.

Fifteen minutes into the flight, which felt like hours, Chris disrupted the muted whir of the rotor blades. He was grateful to the inventor who had built a microphone into the headphones.

"I'm sorry." *That's a start,* he thought.

"For what?"

"For . . ." He frowned. *What am I sorry for?* "For what happened between us." He shook his head. "I mean for the rift between us." *Even if he never got a second chance to get close to her, he'd never be sorry for the short time they had had.*

"You can't help the way you feel."

"That's what's killing me; the way I feel."

"I—I mean the way you feel about what I intend to do." Her sigh reached him through the headphones. "This discussion is a waste of time." Her voice sounded as sorry as he felt. "I refuse to change my mind, and you can't."

"Jeanine . . ."

"Make sure your camera is ready. We're approaching the site that you requested. I plan to circle it from every angle and from both directions. If you want me to repeat a particular pass, let me know."

Chris struggled to concentrate on the reason for the flight as he ran off a roll of still shots. Then he switched to the video camera. Even though the chopper was filming, he still wanted his own shots. He knew what the plans called for, and he wanted to make sure that he had the information he needed.

"Do you need me to fly over an area again?"

"No. I'm finished." *Please don't use the word "need." Not unless it's the need that we both want to satisfy.* He hoped that he wasn't really finished—that *they* weren't finished. That this wasn't the last time he'd see her and be this close to her.

"I'll head back, then. We should . . ." The whirring stopped as if somebody had cut off the sound. "No. Not again."

As Chris watched, Jeanine worked various controls.

"What is it?"

"May Day. May Day." She followed with the flight identification code. "We've lost power." She gave the coordinates of their position over the radio even while fighting for control as the chopper tried to drop. "Attempting autorotation," she said in a voice that gave no clue that there was a problem.

She pulled back on what Chris hoped was a miracle control. He relaxed his grip on the seat a bit—too little to measure—when he felt the chopper stop its fall. Her feet worked the pedals, and her hands were busy as she repeated her message.

He tightened his fingers even more than before when

they didn't go back to the original elevation. Jeanine's next words were no surprise.

"We're going down."

ELEVEN

"Down? You mean we're going to land?" Chris knew that wasn't what she meant. Still, he hoped.

"We've lost power. The engine is off."

"Off? Can't you turn it back on?"

"That's a negative." She shook her head as if the verbal answer wasn't enough to convince him of how much trouble they were in.

Chris watched as she held one hand steady on one of the controls while the other toggled switches and pushed buttons and her feet worked the pedals. Her hand flew back and forth between the controls as she repeated, "May Day, May Day," in a voice that sounded as if she were carrying on a normal conversation. Chris didn't want to consider that maybe the communication connection was just as dead as the engine.

I knew that something shaped like this shouldn't be able to leave the ground. He frowned. *A pregnant bumblebee without wings,* he thought. *That's what they look like.* He tightened his harness belt as well as his grip on the front of his seat.

"What are you going to do? What *can* you do? Do we just . . ." He swallowed hard. "Do we just fall?"

"Not quite." She shifted the position of a control slightly. Without the noise of the engine, the sound of the turning of the rotor blades was alone in the air.

"I thought the engine was off. What's keeping the blades turning? What's keeping us up?" *Why question a miracle?* ran through his mind.

"We're gliding."

"Gliding? How can something so heavy and shaped like this glide?"

"Chris, I'll explain everything once we're on the ground."

He watched as Jeanine's gaze alternated between the instruments and the outside. Her hands finally quit moving, grasped the stick, and held on. *I hope we're both alive for that conversation.*

He swallowed any other words that he had, but he couldn't stop a gasp from escaping when he looked out the front window. Power lines loomed ahead as if waiting to catch them. He released the breath that he hadn't realized he was holding when the chopper shifted enough to the side to barely miss the wires. *Another two inches and . . .*

"Brace yourself. We're over the Kohala area." Jeanine nodded to the right. "No houses, so we won't put anybody on the ground in danger."

Brace myself? His frown grew deeper. *If I hang on any tighter the edge of this seat will be in my hands and a lot of good it will do me then.* Chris tried not to look in the direction that Jeanine meant, but with the mountain close beside them—almost close enough for him to scrape his hand or snatch leaves from the trees if the window were open—he couldn't ignore it. *A mountain is within touching distance, power lines tried to fry us, and she's worried about houses?*

"I'd like to clear those trees, but . . ." Her voice drifted away before the end of the sentence.

Now she's worried about trees? What about the mountain?

They seemed to be following Route 270 along the side of the mountain. Jeanine managed to keep air between the chopper and rocks. Chris could feel the bottom of the chopper scrape the tops of the trees as it continued to fall. *Better the trees than the mountain, but no jungle is strong enough to support something of this weight,* was his last thought.

"Nate?"

Nate pulled his attention away from the diagnostic machine on the bench on the stand in front of him and looked at the young woman approaching from the terminal.

"Hey, Carla. You must have done something outstanding for Hal to free you from the desk." He smiled at her. "Come to see how the dirty half lives?" He held up his hands to display grease from the machine he was working on.

"Hal needs to see you." If she had a smile, she kept it to herself.

"Can it wait? I just hooked this sucker up."

"He needs to see you right away." She was speaking to him, but her gaze touched everything except him. Nate frowned as he turned off the machine. That wasn't like her.

He started talking as soon as he reached the office door. "Look, Hal, I know I said I'd have that engine finished by yesterday, but I ran into a snag. I have the final diagnostic running right now."

"This isn't about that engine."

"Then what?"

"Our chopper went down."

"What?" He stared as if Hal had spoken in a language that he didn't understand.

"Jeanine called in a 'May Day.' We heard it, but the FAA notified us, too."

"What went wrong? Where? Are they all right? My

brother was . . ." He stopped, then spoke again. "*Is* on board."

"Sit down and I'll tell you what we got from Jeanine, but it isn't much." He looked at Nate. "She said the engine had failed and that they were going down." His gaze slid away from the pain in Nate's eyes. "The FAA officials are on their way over here. Hopefully, they'll have more information for us by the time they get here."

"When did this happen?"

"About fifteen minutes ago."

"And you're just telling me?"

"I was waiting to see if there was an update." Again he looked at Nate. "It wouldn't have made any difference whether I told you right away or not."

"Fifteen minutes is a long time. Where were they?"

"Her last message said they were over Kohala."

"Toward the mountain or the ocean?" Nate's eyes were open, but he was picturing the tall, long-silent volcano that dominated that entire area.

"She would have been with the wind." He shook his head. "She gave her coordinates, but she was still moving."

"She kept telling me about that engine." Nate frowned out the office window. *How can the sun have the nerve to be shining?* "She chewed me out a couple of times about it. I teased her, but I swear I took her seriously." Nate shook his head. "I checked that engine out every time she had a problem with it in addition to the regular checkups. I put that thing through every test there is." He frowned. "What did I miss? It's my fault. I must have missed something." He shook his head again. "Maybe I don't know as much about these birds as I thought I did."

"Don't blame yourself. We don't know what happened."

"Yeah, we do. We know that one of our birds went down because of engine failure." He looked at Hal.

"And we know that I'm responsible for maintaining the engines of these birds."

"I have faith in your ability. If you didn't find something, nobody else would have."

"Yeah? Then why are we having this conversation?"

"Look, Nate. Jeanine is one of the best. She knows how to handle an emergency like this."

"Yeah." Nate stared at the floor. "But if I had done my job, she wouldn't have had to."

The two sat in silence, hoping that radio contact from Jeanine would break in, hoping that she and Chris were safe on the ground. Neither Nate nor Hal mentioned the chopper accident of three weeks earlier. It was a different company, but a chopper is a chopper. He thought about the families with new gaps in them.

Half an hour later three men in suits were led to the office by Carla. Nate knew before they opened their mouths that they were from the FAA.

"I'm Tom Imano from the FAA." Imano glanced at the men with him. "These are Agents Sullivan and Monroe."

"Agents? What kind of agents? Are you FAA, too?" Hal faced them. "I've never known them to send three investigators. What's going on?"

"We need to see your records for the chopper that went down." Agent Monroe stepped forward.

"Look. Nate is my best mechanic. He's not at fault here."

It was as if Hal hadn't opened his mouth. Imano looked at Nate. "The records, Mr. Harris."

"Nate?" Hal looked at his mechanic.

"I got nothing to hide, although folks usually say

'please' when they want something." He let his stare wrestle with Monroe's before he spoke. "This way."

Nate led them back to the shop. He'd never before noticed the silence when all of the equipment was turned off. He'd never paid a bit of attention to how quiet it was when a bird wasn't waiting a few yards away with its engine running or when a machine wasn't putting a piece of equipment through a test.

He opened the top drawer of the filing cabinet and pulled out a bulging but neat folder.

"Is this just for the chopper that went down?" Monroe asked as he took the folder from Nate.

"That's what you asked for, isn't it?"

"We're going to want to see the records of the other choppers, too, but first we need you to tell us the history of the one in question."

"It's all there." Nate nodded at the papers he had given them.

"We'd still like you to tell us in your own words what work you've done on it, starting with the first and working forward. Even routine service checks. Records aren't always as complete as they should be." He glared at Nate. Nate met his stare. Neither man looked away.

"My records are complete. You need an audio version, give me back the papers and sit down. Or stand if you want to."

He nodded toward the only clear bench in the shop. Then he pulled the chair from his desk, lifted the folder from the agent's hand and sat.

"Is this the first trouble you've had with this helicopter?"

As he pulled a sheet of paper from the folder, Nate repeated the complaints from Jeanine, starting with the first one. He read the specific dates, the nature of each complaint, and what action he'd taken.

Going through the papers, he was interrupted many times by Monroe. Finally he reached the last sheet of paper.

"This is the paperwork from the pre-flight checkup today." He looked at each of the three men, then went back to Monroe. "What's going on here?" The men just stared at him. "I need to know if I missed something. I need to make sure that, if I made a mistake, I won't make it again."

"You got your training in the Air Force?"

"You evidently already know that or you wouldn't ask. Don't play games with me. In addition to Jeanine, I got a brother in that chopper. You know something. I want in on it."

Instead of answering, Monroe turned to Imano. "Thank you for your time, Agent Imano. We can take it from here. We'll let you know if we turn up anything of use to you."

Imano looked from one to the other and then back at Monroe. "I'd better get back to my office."

After Imano left, Monroe turned back to Nate. "Purple Heart. Many other medals. Honorable discharge. Your commanding officers speak highly of you."

"So, you can read and memorize and you know how to use a phone. What's that got to do with the price of pineapples?"

"Tell us exactly what Miss Stewart told you each time she complained about the chopper. Use your notes if you have to."

"My memory isn't bad, either." He gave the details of each conversation with Jeanine after she had experienced trouble with the chopper.

"Any problems with your other birds?"

"No."

"What was different about this one?"

Nate frowned. Then he pulled out the records of all of the choppers and spread them side by side on the bench.

The agents watched silently as he worked from the most recent to the oldest, cross-checking the records.

"Here." He held up a sheet of paper. "I replaced a part in the engine of Jeanine's bird two weeks before her first complaint." He frowned. "I've replaced the same part in the others."

"From the same shipment?"

"No. We don't keep parts like that in stock. It's not that often that I have to replace it. I got that part from a new supplier." Nate leaned back. "The part was bad. I didn't make a maintenance mistake."

"You didn't make a mistake."

"You gotta tell me more than that." Nate folded his arms across his chest. "What agency are you from, anyway?"

"We've had problems with parts."

"You're not FAA."

"The name of our agency isn't important."

"The Blue Eagle? You had this problem with the Blue Eagle. I read about that. Those crashes were caused by bad parts?"

"The investigation is ongoing."

"Why didn't you notify us about the parts so we could pull them? You guys act like you're only a half-inch below God. You couldn't have prevented this? How long have you known? Have you at least shut the company down so nobody else has this problem?"

"We haven't come to any conclusions yet."

"I'll bet you made damn sure that none of those parts are in Air Force One."

This time Monroe looked away. Then he stood. Nate stood to face him. It was all he could do to keep his hands at his sides. And he managed that only because nothing he could do would undo the accident. Finally the agent spoke.

"I'd check any other replacement parts you have on hand before installing them if I were you."

"That won't help my brother and Jeanine, will it?"

Nate wasn't surprised when he didn't receive an answer.

Monroe and Sullivan left, and Nate stared at their backs until they turned the corner. Then he went to the file cabinet and began pulling out repair records. If he was lucky, no crucial parts had been replaced recently and few, if any came from the company in question. He'd definitely have to pull them. Even if they came from the regular supplier, he'd still check. He hoped Hal wouldn't have to cancel any flights, but if he did, that would be better than taking a chance on having another chopper fail. Nobody should have to go through what he was going through right now.

He opened the maintenance folder for each of the choppers and began a line-by-line check. He had to work hard to keep from thinking about the one faulty part that he had installed. *I try to save Hal a few bucks and look what happened.* He made that thought go away so he could concentrate on what he had to do.

TWELVE

Jeanine grabbed her head with one hand and, eyes closed, groped around, trying to find something to use for leverage—something to push against so she could get free. "Let go of me. Let me go." She struggled, and the pain in her head squeezed tighter. *What's holding me? It hurts too much to be a nightmare.*

She opened her eyes a slit, and the muted light entering her eyes fed the pain. She closed them again. *Think, Jeanine. Think. Where are you?* She rubbed her hand across her head, took a deep breath, and then slowly opened her eyes again. The pain got no worse.

The world around her was tilted as if somebody had decided that it was the equator's turn to be on top and the heck with its effect on people. The instrument panel in front of her was sideways, like the rest of the world. *Chopper. I'm in my chopper.* Pressure on her left shoulder increased each time she moved. *Shoulder harness.* Her hand fumbled with the strap holding her in place. Finally it released and dropped her against the dark side window. She closed her eyes and lay in a heap until everything stopped spinning around her.

Chris! Her eyes flew open. Despite the pain in her head that increased when she moved, she turned to look into the back seat. If not for his shoulder harness, Chris would have been crumpled against his side window. Instead, he dangled, swaying gently as if in an infant's swing.

"Chris." Jeanine touched his shoulder. She didn't dare disturb his position any more than that. She frowned. *Shoulder harnesses were supposed to keep you safe, but I don't want to take a chance. What if he has a neck or back injury?* She swallowed hard. *Harnesses were supposed to protect you, and helicopters were supposed to stay in the air until you decided where to land them.* She scrambled toward him and crouched there, but she allowed her voice to be the only thing that touched him. "Chris. Wake up. Open your eyes. Chris."

At the sound of his name, he shifted. Jeanine felt some of her tension leave when, arms and legs thrashing, he struggled against his harness. *At the least, he has a little movement.* "Open your eyes," she demanded again. She touched his shoulder when he turned his head and looked at her. "Good. Can you move your legs?"

"Yeah." He bent his knees and extended his legs and struggled to free himself. "A whole lot better if I weren't tied up."

"Wait a minute. Brace yourself." *Dumb. Against what? Air?* Quickly she opened the clasp, and he dropped to the window and grunted.

"We have to get out of here." Jeanine used the window as the floor and tried to push against the other side window, which was now on top.

"Where are we??" Chris crawled to the front until he was standing beside her. He rubbed his head.

"I'm not sure, but we have to get out of here." Water splashed against the windshield, on the side. "The handle is stuck, and I'm too short to put enough pressure on it."

"I know we're in the ocean, but how deep?" Chris asked even though the water sloshing over his feet and rocking the chopper told him that it was deep enough.

"Let me try." He shoved against the door above them and tried to force the lock. "We'll have to jimmy it open. Do you have a tool kit?"

Jeanine was already pulling a canvas bag from under the pilot's seat before Chris finished asking for it. She handed it to him and tried not to notice that it was dripping wet. She also tried to ignore the fact that waves were shifting the chopper.

"Any idea how far from shore we are?"

"I'm not sure. We were still gliding after I checked our last coordinates."

Chris stared at her for a few seconds. *I wish I could promise her that everything will be all right and that I could erase her worried expression. I wish that* she *could promise me the same.* He exhaled harshly. *We're both alive. That counts for a whole lot.*

He unzipped the tool bag and peered inside. He pulled out an instrument resembling a gun with a very short muzzle that ended in a wide point. What looked like a nail was built into one side. In spite of the situation, he smiled slightly. He carried one of these in his car. He'd never used it, but he'd read the directions carefully. He and Jeanine didn't need to cut the seat belts, but they definitely needed the nail and the pointed end.

"Cover your face."

He drew back and then hit the windshield with full force. The nail made a tiny hole and the glass crackled into tiny pieces, but the pieces still clung together and to the frame. He hit it again, this time with the wide point. Glass rained down like small diamonds. A wave gave them a split-second warning before it spat water through the window, which now served as a door.

"Let's get out of here." Chris grabbed Jeanine's arm.

"Wait a minute," Jeanine said as another splash of water hit them.

"Come on." He tugged harder as another, stronger wave joined them in the chopper.

"Okay." Jeanine grabbed the folder from the pocket between the front seats and tucked it inside a plastic-coated canvas bag. "Hand me your cameras." She zipped the bag closed and tucked it inside her jacket. "Let's go."

Chris boosted her up to the section of the chopper that was still showing sky. He quickly followed her and dropped outside, landing beside her.

Water lapped at their pants legs, dampening their shins. As they left the chopper it shifted a bit more and settled deeper into sand. A wave pushed against it, and it shifted still more toward open sea.

They waded the few feet to shore and turned back to face the ocean. They watched as the chopper shifted as if trying to right itself. The wave pulled back, and the chopper stayed on its side while being dragged a short distance by the current.

Chris and Jeanine moved up onto the beach as far from the ocean as possible. They stopped only when Kohala Mountain blocked them. Then they turned back to the ocean and watched waves take turns trying to wash away the sliver of sand they were standing on. More waves pulled at the chopper as if in a tug-of-war—one they were winning.

"Now what?" Chris glanced around. "Are you familiar with this coastline? Which way?"

"I know enough about it to know that we're going to get a lot wetter. This strip of beach disappears for about a hundred yards, shows up again, then disappears again. It skips along like that for miles, even more so when the tide is coming in. There are occasional trails leading to the top. I'm hoping that we can find one before we have to go far."

She glanced out at the horizon, still blue, but showing hints of fire orange and gray. "It will be dark before long. We need to get moving. The beach has already disappeared in that direction." She gestured to the right, then headed left. Chris let her pass, then followed her.

"Does anyone know where we are?"

"Somebody should have gotten our May Day, but our coordinates were changing as I was broadcasting." She turned sideways to get around a rock jutting in the way. "They'll have the general area." She looked at the sun slowly floating into the ocean. "It will be dark soon, and they have to get civilian pilots to search. They'll wait until morning."

"So we're on our own tonight." It wasn't a question, and Jeanine didn't answer.

They walked on. In spots, their shoulders brushed against the cliff. Even so, they were slogging in water. Then the beach disappeared completely.

"Hand me the pouch." Chris waited until Jeanine took it from under her jacket. He placed it inside his own, then rolled up his jacket and shirt until they were under his arms with the pouch tucked inside to keep dry. Then they moved forward again.

After a few seconds, Jeanine plunged into water so deep that only her head and shoulders were above it.

"Wait." She said and stopped at an unusually wide section of sand. "Maybe we can climb up higher from here. There's nothing but water ahead." She stood back as far as possible and looked at a cliff.

"It looks like a cave up there." Chris pointed halfway up. "Now to get up there." He ran his hand along the base of the cliff as high as he could reach. "There's a hollow up here." He turned to her. "Come here. I'll give you a boost. Feel if there's a handhold within reach."

He grasped her waist and lifted her.

"I got it. Come on up. There's room for both of us this far."

Chris followed. As Jeanine inched to the side, then

up, then to the side again, Chris trailed her as if they were engaged in a game of Follow the Leader. They continued their movement up, sideways, and then up again. A time or two they had to move in the opposite direction to find a handhold, but each sequence got them closer to the cave. They reached it just as the ocean swallowed the last sliver of sun.

"This is it, huh." Chris walked from the opening into the shallow cave. He only got a few yards before he reached the far wall. Jeanine was at his side.

"All the comforts of home." Jeanine shook her head. "I certainly don't mean to sound ungrateful." She looked around. "This is the size of a generous closet, but I'm thankful that we found it. I wasn't looking forward to spending the night in the water." She looked out at the ocean, but couldn't see a thing. "Especially since the moon took the night off." She zipped her jacket up the last inch. "I think that tropical Hawaii is going to prove how cool it can get at night." She walked along the back of the cave, sat as far from the opening as she could get, and leaned against the wall. She brushed her hand across the floor. "Sand? Up this high?"

"Time can change anything but the past, and sometimes people's minds play tricks on them about that." Chris frowned. "The wind has probably worked on these rocks since they rose from the ocean."

"Yes, and a hurricane from time to time most likely added to the sand that was already here." She shook her head slightly. "That gives me another reason to be glad that no hurricanes were in the forecast for anytime soon."

"Yeah. I'm also glad that the cave is empty instead of one of those used as a burial place by the original Hawaiians." Chris settled closer against her. "Come here." He pulled her against him. Regardless of the circumstances, it was almost worth it to hold her again. He wrapped his hand around her shoulder and held her close.

"This must be what James Weldon Johnson meant when he talked about darkness 'blacker than a hundred midnights down in a cypress swamp.' "

"He sure got it right, didn't he? We'd better stay back here until daylight. I've got something else to be thankful for. My head doesn't hurt as much as it did at first. How is yours? Did you have a hard pounding when you first came to?" The catch in Jeanine's voice wasn't caused by the hard climb. The recent memory of the pain in her head had nothing to do with it, either. *I forgot how it feels to be in his arms. How could I forget something that feels as good as this does?*

"Probably worse than yours. Mine felt like somebody inside my head was practicing on a kettle drum." Chris's voice sounded as if it had scraped against the cliff.

"No way could it be worse than mine." Jeanine fought the urge to feel his chest against her breast.

"We'll call it a tie. Okay?" Chris's hand moved back and forth along the side of her arm.

"We—we should take off our wet shoes." *I should move away,* she thought. *I should follow my own suggestion.*

"Um-hmm." His hand found her upper arm and stayed.

Jeanine took a deep breath and put a few inches between them. Careful to avoid touching him, she took off her shoes and socks. Chris did the same.

"The ground is warm." She pressed her hand down. "The sun heated it for us." She rolled up her pant legs until the damp sections were no longer against her legs, but she knew the wetness would soak through. *One minute at a time,* she thought. She hesitated, then unzipped her wet jacket and took it off. The shivers that started were only partly from the cool air and the wet clothes.

"You have to take off your shirt, too." Chris spoke

with logic, but Jeanine just sat there. "Here." He unbuttoned his jacket and handed it to her. She waited a few seconds, then pulled her shirt off over her head.

She reached for his jacket and quickly put it on before she dared to glance at him.

"Thank you." She zipped it, resisting the urge to snuggle into the warmth that he'd left. She inhaled, and a slight whiff of his aftershave teased her from the collar.

"There's not a puddle to lay my coat on to protect your dainty feet, so this is the best I can do."

"Dainty feet?" Jeanine laughed in spite of the situation. "My shoe size is at the far reaches of the women's section in any shoe department." Her laughter died when Chris moved against her again. He kept his hands to himself, but his side burned along hers. She frowned. "I'm sorry for this."

"Did you do something wrong?"

"I don't think so." She shook her head. "No, I didn't. I don't know why, but the engine failed."

"Just like you've been telling Nate for a good while."

"Yes."

"So he *did* miss something."

"I don't think so. He's the best at what he does, but don't tell him I said that." She took a deep breath as Chris moved and his arm rubbed against hers. She shook her head. "It was more than something being missed during a checkup." She exhaled. "I think it was a lot more. I've never heard of anything like this happening before."

"Then it's not your fault." The faint sound of the waves lapping at the shore below kept rhythm as if a conductor were directing them. Neither Chris nor Jeanine seemed aware of the sound.

"I'm sorry, too."

"What are you sorry about?"

"Trying to run your life. Trying to tell you what you can't do. I don't have that right."

"I won't ever give anybody that right."

"I can understand that. I wouldn't, either." He wrapped her hand in his and held tight. "It's just that I don't want anything to happen to you. Tonight made me realize that anything can happen at any time. We could have been killed. Just a few weeks ago a chopper went down and members of several families died."

"I know. I also know that today, somewhere, many more people were killed in car accidents. And others in robberies, and still others for various reasons. Whoever said that tomorrow isn't promised was speaking the truth. We can't focus on what might happen. That could drive us crazy." She took a deep breath. "As for your worrying about me, remember that I don't want anything to happen to me, either."

"I know. It's just that I care about you. I care more than I thought I would ever care about anybody again." He rubbed his thumb slowly back and forth across the back of her hand. "Please say that you forgive me."

"I do. I—I think we should move on." *I also think that if he keeps this up, either my hand will burst into flames or my whole body will need cooling off.*

A slight gust found its way into the cave. A tremor flittered through Jeanine. "It's going to be a long, cold night."

"I have an idea that could help warm us and make the night pass faster." Chris moved his hand around her shoulder and began stroking there.

"What—what is that?" *I feel as if I just ran a marathon at my top speed. Twice.*

"We could share body heat." He brushed his lips across the side of her face. "There are several ways we could do that." He turned her slightly toward him. She completed the turn.

"Like what?" She barely got the words out when he covered her mouth with his. She pressed closer and grasped his arms. He drew back.

"This is one way."

"I—I think it's working." She traced a line down his jaw.

"Of course, it might aggravate our headaches." Chris rubbed his hand up and down her back. "But I'm willing to take that chance."

"What headache?"

She slid her hands around his neck and rubbed her body against his chest. He groaned and his hands found a way under the jacket. Hers discovered a way under his shirt. Her fingers rubbed up and down the hard muscles of his back.

"I know you just put this on, but you have to take it off, please." Chris slid the zipper of the jacket down and pushed it off her arms. "Okay?"

"But now I'm cold," she lied. *I feel as if I'm sitting under the full sun.*

"Not for long." His hands inched across the swell of one breast, hesitated long enough to circle the hard tip, then inched to the other one and repeated the movement. "Your bra is wet," he whispered against the side of her face while his hand covered her breast and stroked over it as if trying to rub it dry.

"Maybe—maybe I should take it off, too." She pressed her lips to his chest.

"Good idea." His mouth found a spot on her neck and tasted.

"You have to . . ." The rest of Jeanine's sentence got lost as Chris nipped lightly at the place where her shoulder and neck met. She felt her pulse jump there as if trying to meet him. "You have to take off your shirt, too. I don't want to be the only one . . ."

"Baby, you won't be the only one in any of this."

He quickly unbuttoned his shirt and shrugged it off. Then his hands moved to her back. In a few seconds her breasts were free of the clinging, restraining lace.

Before she had time to react to the feel of the air on her bare skin, Chris's hands were covering her breasts. She and Chris were in total darkness, yet her eyes automatically closed as if she needed to heighten the sensations even more—although they were already pushing the edge between pleasure and total release.

His hands moved slowly, as if trying to memorize every smooth inch of her. His finger slowly circled one tip in an ever-shortening spiral. He skimmed the tip and moved to her other side. Jeanine pushed against his hand even as her own stroked the front of his pants.

"Not—not . . ." she moaned as he brushed a finger across one hard tip, pulled gently, and then moved to the other breast. "Not fair. The waist of your pants didn't get wet in the ocean." She brushed across the zipper that was keeping her from touching him. "Mine did." She gasped as Chris slowly drew her breast into his mouth and rasped his tongue across it before he suckled. She moaned again and, although she was already on the ground, grabbed him as if to keep from falling.

He gave one more nip, then released her. "I want to be fair." Desire filled his voice. "I guess I should take them off," he whispered. But instead he moved his hands to her hips, then brushed his way across her front, tracing small circles over the mound between her legs before moving back up and easing a finger under the lacy elastic at the waist of her panties. "What a shame. These are wet, too." He inched them partway over the fullness of her hips and stopped.

"I guess I should take them off." Her words whispered as if all of her strength was in use elsewhere.

"We can help each other." Chris grasped the lace that was keeping him from touching her and moved it down her legs.

Jeanine's hands managed to slide his zipper down. She brushed once across his hardness before moving her hands back to his waist. There she tugged and pushed until her hands finally touched only skin.

"Come here." Chris stood and pulled her up beside him. He shoved his pants off and spread them out on the floor of the cave. Then he reached for her and eased her panties the rest of the way from her body. His hands moved back to her waist and his mouth sampled one breast before he released her and stroked a hand along the side of her fullness. "Beautiful."

"How do you know? You can't see me." Heat was radiating from every spot he had touched.

"I can feel. And I know beautiful when I taste it." He captured her mouth again, and they became lost in a kiss. Their hands wrapped around the sides of each other's hips as the kiss deepened.

Chris stroked his hands along her backside and pulled her against him. Jeanine cupped his behind and rubbed herself against the proof of his maleness, his desire for her. She managed a slight smile when his body tightened even more against hers. Their tongues met and danced as if practicing for the performance of their entire bodies.

"Come with me." Chris helped her to the floor and onto the spread-out pants. Once there, he captured her mouth again and pulled her against him. Then he eased away from her.

"No. Don't go."

"I'm not going anywhere, baby." He fumbled with the pocket of his pants and pulled out his wallet, dropped it, but managed to find it again. Jeanine smiled at the sound of a foil packet being ripped open.

"Let me help."

"If you do, we won't need it."

Quickly he was back against her, sharing a kiss. He nestled between her legs, and she shifted them to accommodate him. She pulled him down to her and tightened her hold on him as he entered her. She gasped and he stilled.

"Okay?"

"More than okay."

Chris began to move slowly, but increased as Jeanine learned his rhythm and joined him in the ancient dance of lovers since time began.

Coupled together, they moved faster, as if trying to catch up to something—something more wonderful than either had experienced before.

Jeanine felt that she was climbing a hill, a mountain, running up the steepest slope of the tallest volcano in the world and at recording-breaking speed. She was almost at the summit. Almost there. And Chris was with her.

As if obeying some internal order, they moaned each other's name just before dropping from the volcano's summit.

After they returned to Earth, Chris, still holding Jeanine in his arms, found the jacket and spread it over them.

Twice during the night their lovemaking dislodged it, and he had to pull it over them again. Neither complained.

THIRTEEN

Gray sunlight, filtering through thick rain clouds, poked at the two wrapped in each other's arms. Jeanine pushed her back against the warmth cradling her. The arms tightened around her. She remembered, smiled, and opened her eyes just enough to allow a sliver of light to enter.

"Good morning, beautiful." Chris pressed his lips to her cheek. "The light may be dim, but it's bright enough to see that my assessment of you last night was correct." He pressed a kiss against her neck. "How are you feeling?"

"What you're doing to me is fantastic, and it's warming me in a way, but truthfully, I'm cold." She shivered slightly.

"Truthfully, me, too." He sat up and took her with him. "I hate to say it, but we'd better put on some clothes."

"I agree." Jeanine handed him his jacket. "I'll put on your shirt."

"You sure? The jacket has long sleeves."

"The shirt will come down farther on my arms. It will have long sleeves on me." She pulled it on and stood. The shirt stopped just above her knees. "Even though they're still wet, I think we'll be warmer if we put our pants on." She leaned against the back wall and forced her feet through the damp pant legs.

Chris put his on at the same time. Then he walked

over to her and pulled her to the floor and held her close again. He pressed a kiss on the top of her head.

"They won't search for us in this, will they?" Chris asked, looking out at the rain trying to raise the level of the ocean.

"I doubt it." She shifted closer to him. "But it doesn't look as if it's going to rain all day," she said. "Doesn't it look lighter out on the horizon?"

"A little." He covered her hands with his. "Last night was unbelievably fantastic. It was so off the charts that I was afraid I'd awaken and learn that it was just a dream."

"If it was, I had the same dream." She snuggled against him. They sat for a while, listening to the rain play a pattern outside the cave. Now and then the wind would blow a spray inside, but it always dropped before reaching them.

"I have an idea." Chris took the things out of the pouch and carefully laid them against the back wall. Then he stood. "I can't go hunting for breakfast, but I can try to get us some water."

He took his jacket off and draped it around her shoulders. She watched as he walked toward the cave's opening. The sight of his broad back, even in the dim light, made her smile.

I'm stuck in a cave on a cliff during a storm with no food and no water, and all I can think about is how good it felt sleeping in his arms last night. And the incredible lovemaking before that. I have no idea when we'll get out of here, but all I want right this minute is to rub my hands along his body. Slowly at first. Very slowly so I don't miss a single spot. Then, after I've had enough of that, I want him to sink into me, fill me, make me complete. I want him to take me on the same journey he took me on last night. She grinned at the feel of the moisture forming as her body prepared for another trip. *Several times.* She took a deep breath. *Dirty young woman.* Her smile grew. *And it feels so good. Not as good as the actual experience, though. Patience,* she told herself. *Soon,* she promised. She watched as Chris leaned out of the mouth of the cave and held the pouch open.

"Be careful. Don't fall."

"No way. Not after I finally found you. I have too much to look forward to." He glanced back at her, threw her a smile. "No, not too much. I should say that I have so much more to look forward to."

From where she was sitting, she could see his eyes fill with desire. His glance lasted only a few seconds, but that was long enough to stoke the fires that her thoughts had kindled. She didn't even try to calm her feelings.

She kept her gaze on him as he focused his attention on the pouch. She didn't hold her breath, but she did feel tension grab every muscle of her body and take control as he seemed to stand close enough to the edge to fall. Some of the tightness slipped from her when, after what seemed like hours, he came back and handed her the pouch.

"You first."

"No. You caught it."

"Call it chivalry, machismo, whatever. You first. Unfortunately," he nodded toward the outside, "as you can see, there's plenty more where that came from."

"Okay. Thank you." She took the pouch and smiled up at him before she drank.

"Keep looking at me like that, beautiful, and when I catch some water for myself, it will boil away in the pouch. In fact, wet or not, the pouch might burst into flames."

"Sorry." Her smile widened. "Nobody plays cards with me twice. They complain that I telegraph my hand." She drained the pouch and handed it back to him. Then she drew her knees to her chest and tucked the hem of the shirt around her ankles.

"Hold that thought. When I finish here, we can discuss the message you're sending to me. We'll also see if we can think of an appropriate answer. One mutually satisfying."

He captured enough rain for a couple of long swallows, then went back to sit beside her. They cuddled for warmth as well as just to be close. Their eyes held on the sky as if they could will it to hurry and empty of rain.

Gradually, the clouds began to drift off. About an hour later, the distant sound of chopper blades split the air.

"Will they see our helicopter?"

"Yes, but I don't know how soon. I don't know how far out the waves dragged it."

"Then they won't know that we're not still inside it."

"No." She thought of what might have been. Then she thought of what she had been given instead of death. The sound grew louder. "Come on."

Together they ran to the opening. Chris took off his jacket and waved it in the soft breeze that had replaced the strong wind of the storm. They yelled even though they knew there was no way they could be heard over the engine noise.

They watched as the chopper circled a spot in the water close to where they'd gone down, but a long way along the shoreline from their cave. It hovered as if pointing out the spot to somebody else.

"They've found it."

They continued watching while the search chopper widened its circles, slowly following the shoreline but in the opposite direction.

"No! Over here!" They yelled harder. Chris waved the

jacket more furiously, but the helicopter continued its pattern away from them, still following the shore.

The sound of the engine faded; yet Jeanine and Chris remained at the opening with their arms wrapped around each other. The jacket, clutched in Chris's hand, was lifted every now and then by a soft gust. They added nothing to accompany the muted sounds of the waves below and the far-off engine.

Chris pressed his lips to her forehead, and she pressed a kiss to his chest. Then they stood as still as if they had become part of the cave floor.

Gradually, so gradually that they weren't sure whether their imaginations were at work or if it was really happening, the sound of the helicopter grew and expanded until it was a sweet, deafening roar. They watched as it moved in a pattern no straighter than the flight of a bee and much, much slower. Finally, it flew directly toward them. It hovered for a few seconds far enough away for the blades to clear the cliff but close enough for Jeanine and Chris to see the pilot looking at them.

The wind from the chopper blades pasted their clothes against their bodies and dropped the air temperature ten degrees, but they smiled as the pilot gave them a thumbs up, then flew directly overhead.

Within minutes a wire basket slowly lowered to the cave's opening and swayed there. The wind moved it like a playground swing at full speed, making it impossible for Chris to grab it. The chopper shifted to one side, and Chris's fingertips grazed against the basket, but the wind snatched it away. Then it disappeared, but they could still hear the chopper.

"They won't leave," Jeanine yelled as she placed her hands against his chest. She continued to stare out of the opening.

"What will they do now?" Chris's words managed to rise above the roar. He enfolded her in his arms again.

"I'm not sure. Probably wait for the wind to die down or try a different angle."

"I vote for the second option." He squeezed her gently. "Whichever they decide, they found us. We can wait."

The sound of the engine quit, and Jeanine and Chris had to get used to its absence.

"What happened? Do they have engine problems, too?"

"I doubt it. They probably shut down so the blades can't create an additional wind problem."

A long fifteen minutes later, the basket seat appeared in the center of the opening. This time the wind helped swing it toward them instead of away. Chris grabbed it and helped Jeanine inside. A few minutes later it was Chris's turn to ride. Soon he was sitting beside her, wrapped in a blanket that was a twin to the one draped around her.

The copilot pushed cups into their hands, and they swallowed hot coffee gratefully. To Jeanine, who usually drank tea, it was the most delicious drink she had ever had.

Soon, they were wheeled into a hospital on gurneys, too tired to protest.

After being treated for dehydration and mild concussions, Jeanine and Chris were resting in different wings of the hospital. She had been dozing off and on when a nurse's aide came in.

"I'm sure you'd prefer to wear these when you go home. The clothes you had on will be stiff with salt when they dry." She held a small stack of folded clothes.

"Where did those come from?" Jeanine shifted, but she was too tired to sit up.

"A Miss Lisa Williams brought them. You were sleep-

THE "THANK YOU" GIFT INCLUDES:

- 4 books absolutely FREE (plus $1.99 for shipping and handling).
- A FREE newsletter, *Arabesque Romance News*, filled with author interviews, book previews, special offers, and more!
- No risks or obligations. You're free to cancel whenever you wish with no questions asked.

INTRODUCTORY OFFER CERTIFICATE

Yes! Please send me 4 FREE Arabesque novels (plus $1.99 for shipping & handling). I understand I am under no obligation to purchase any books, as explained on the back of this card. Send my free tote bag after my first regular paid shipment.

NAME ______________________________

ADDRESS ______________________ APT. ______

CITY ______________ STATE ______ ZIP ______

TELEPHONE (   ) ______________________

E-MAIL ______________________________

SIGNATURE ___________________________

Offer limited to one per household and not valid to current subscribers. All orders subject to approval. Terms, offer, & price subject to change. Tote bags available while supplies last.

Thank You!

AN015A

THE ARABESQUE ROMANCE CLUB: HERE'S HOW IT WORKS

Accepting the four introductory books for FREE (plus $1.99 to offset the cost of shipping & handling) places you under no obligation to buy anything. You may keep the books and return the shipping statement marked "cancelled". If you do not cancel, about a month later we will send 4 additional Arabesque novels, and you will be billed the preferred subscriber's price of just $4.50 per title. That's $18.00* for all 4 books for a savings of almost 30% off the cover price (Plus $1.99 for shipping and handling). You may cancel at any time, but if you choose to continue, every month we'll send you 4 more books, which you may either purchase at the preferred discount price. . . or return to us and cancel your subscription.

* PRICES SUBJECT TO CHANGE

PLACE
STAMP
HERE

THE ARABESQUE ROMANCE BOOK CLUB
P.O. BOX 5214
CLIFTON NJ 07015-5214

ing, and she didn't want to disturb you. She said to tell you that she'll talk to you in the morning." She set the clothes on the chair. "Mr. Harris's brother brought clothes for him, too." She smiled. "They came together and they asked so many questions. They even peeked in on you and watched for a long time, making sure you were really you and that you were all right." A frown pushed her smile off her face. "Maybe I shouldn't have disturbed you, either. I probably should have checked with the nurse first, but she was away from the desk when they came. I know that you must be exhausted, but I didn't want you to worry about what you were going to wear home."

"I hadn't thought that far ahead." Jeanine yawned.

"Oh. Then I'm really, really sorry." She glanced at the clothes, then backed away. "I'll let you sleep." She reached the door, but turned. "Can I get you anything before I go?"

"No, thank you." Jeanine covered another yawn.

"Okay, then. Have a good night's sleep."

Before her footsteps had disappeared, Jeanine was asleep again.

After breakfast, Jeanine and Chris were released. Both of them were protesting riding in wheelchairs when the orderlies pushing them stopped side by side outside the hospital.

The small crowd gathered out front—photographers with television-station logos on their cameras, people with note pads, and others with microphones—showed how important their crash had been.

The crowd barely gave the two of them enough time to stand before shouting questions; they surged forward. Chris put an arm around Jeanine's waist and held her close. *Is the sunlight hurting her eyes as much as it is mine?* He frowned at the crowd. *This noise isn't helping.* He tried to block the ache in his head that was feeding on the noise so he could listen to their questions. Unfortunately, each one was different, and he couldn't make sense out of any of them.

A man came forward from the group; two other men followed him. The first man glared at the crowd, then turned his back on them and handed Jeanine a business card.

"We'll handle this. No interviews. We're conducting an ongoing investigation." He stared at the crowd for a few seconds more, then turned back to Jeanine. "We need to talk with you. Both of you. I'm Tom Imano, FAA." He nodded toward the men beside him. These are Agents Monroe and Sullivan."

"We need for you to come with us," Monroe said. He didn't give her a card. He hadn't even said "hello."

"Chris. Jeanine." Nate pushed through the crowd and ran to them. "Are you two okay?"

Monroe moved in front of Nate. "We need to talk to them. They'll see you later." He turned to Chris. "Follow me."

"Oh yeah?" Nate said, stepping around Monroe. The agents hesitated, then, without waiting for an answer, turned and strode toward a black parked car. None of them looked to see if Jeanine and Chris were following.

"You coming with me?" Nate asked.

"I think we'd better go with them," Chris smiled. "We want to find out what went wrong, too."

"We need to take him home and let Mama teach him some manners." Nate glared at the car. "Give me a call if you need a ride or something afterward. Something like help getting rid of the wanna-be intimidator."

"It's okay. I'll call you if I need you." Chris's voice softened. "Stay cool, Little Brother. We're okay."

The crowd, no longer held back by the agents, surged

toward them. Some of the reporters up front managed to walk backward. Microphones were thrust into their faces as if they were trying to make up for the time the agents had made them lose. Jeanine and Chris ignored them as best they could.

Chris reached for Jeanine's hand and they walked toward the car, followed by a crowd that would make the largest entourage look skimpy. The back door of the car was open well before they reached it, but they didn't hurry.

"Please get in." Monroe sounded as if saying "please" hurt his whole body.

"What is this about?" Chris asked after they were seated. It was Jeanine who answered as the car pulled away from the curb.

"This is routine whenever any aircraft goes down." Jeanine hesitated. "If there are any survivors."

Chris tightened his hold on her hand and wrapped his other arm around her shoulders.

They rode that way, trying not to think of what could have happened to them, until the car stopped in front of a four-story building. Jeanine looked at it. It was an office building, but there was no sign on it. *If a building came in a plain brown wrapper, this is what it would look like,* she thought.

Monroe opened the door and waited for them to get out. *Do they charge him for every word he uses, or is being rude part of his job description?* She frowned. *What is his job, anyway? Exactly what kind of agent is he? He never said.*

"Agent Monroe will take it from here," Imano said. He drove away before Jeanine could say anything to him. She turned to face the man holding open the door to the building.

"This way."

"No."

"What?" For the first time his face showed an expression.

"Not until I know why we are here."

"We're investigating your crash. Please come with me."

"The FAA does that. Why did Mr. Imano leave?"

"It's complicated."

"We both have college degrees. Try your explanation on us."

He stared at her. When she didn't back down, he answered.

"We think it's more than a routine crash, but you know as well as I do that there is no such thing as a routine crash. I really don't want to go into it out here. Please come inside."

Jeanine stared back long enough for three cars to drive pass.

"Lead the way."

FOURTEEN

Half an hour later, Jeanine leaned back in a chair and crossed her legs. She didn't like the man behind the bulky desk. He had stormed into her life only a very short while before, but so far he was a little below slug status on her Dislike List. Still, she was relieved at what he had said. She glanced at Chris and then back at the man.

"So I didn't do anything wrong?"

"No."

Agent Monroe wore the same expression that he had when he was first introduced to them. Jeanine wondered if they deducted from his salary each time he used a different one. She pushed.

"There was nothing I could have done to prevent the accident from happening."

"No." He stood. "Thank you for coming in."

"Why?" She uncrossed her legs, but she didn't stand.

"Why what?"

"There's always a reason for every accident, whether on land or in the air. Are you telling us that Nate did something wrong?"

"No."

"If it wasn't my fault and it wasn't Nate's fault, then it had to be the chopper." She frowned. "But I know Nate checked that bird more than he checked any of the others, and he checked them as often as warranted.

What was it? A part?" She nodded. "A part must have been defective. But how could that happen? Don't companies have to meet some standards? Doesn't the government have to give approval before anyone does business? Don't they have to have licenses?"

"Yes."

"Then what went wrong?"

"Your mechanic . . ."

"Nate. His name is Nate Harris." Chris leaned back to make it harder for him to reach Monroe in case the thread holding him in check snapped.

"We spoke to Mr. Harris as soon as we were notified that your chopper went down. He ordered parts from a supplier that wasn't his usual source."

"Was the company an illegal operation?"

"No."

"Parts don't have to be ordered from the same place every time, do they? People in all sorts of businesses order from different companies all the time. That's called free enterprise. It's okay to shop for the best deal. Civilians do it all the time. I'm sure businesses do the same thing, too. Even the government buys parts from companies based on competitive bids. Isn't that true?"

"Yes."

"There's something that you're not telling us."

"It's complicated."

"Our college degrees haven't been revoked." Chris leaned back farther.

"There's no reason to give you any more information." He held out his hand. Jeanine didn't move.

"That chopper has . . . Make that *had* been giving me trouble for a long time. Is this the first you found out about it?" She shook her head. "It couldn't be. You came with the FAA rep to question us, and I know that maintenance records go to the FAA every month." She glared at him. "You knew about this." Her words were deliberately slow, as if that was necessary for Monroe to understand her. She stood and leaned on his desk. "How long have you known about the part? Or are there more than one? How many other choppers crashed because of bad parts? I've heard of three crashes recently. Was it because of the same part? How many others have there been that we don't know about? Why didn't you notify everybody who flies helicopters?"

"There's an ongoing investigation. We . . ."

"Why?"

"Why what?"

"What's the magic number? How many crashes have to occur before you decide to order a recall or at least notify the public?"

"I understand that you're upset."

"Upset doesn't begin to describe how I'm feeling."

"What's going on here?" Chris moved up to stand a little in front of Jeanine.

"I'm not at liberty to say." Monroe walked from behind his desk. "Thank you."

"You know what you can do with your 'thank-you.'" Chris glared at him.

"The Blue Eagle. This is what happened in the Blue Eagle crashes," Jeanine said. "That's your interest. And you never notified anybody outside the military that there was a problem."

"I'm not at liberty to divulge . . ."

"You saw how the reporters were on us." Jeanine folded her arms. "Maybe you'll tell them more than you're telling us."

"You can't go to the media."

"Want to watch us?" She stared at him. "You know how, in the movies, when some big in-charge type is trying to shut somebody up and the person is running? I always wondered why the people with the information didn't contact every newspaper, every television reporter, every investigative reporter in the world, and give them every bit of information that they had." She glared at him. "Once something is out, silencing the source won't be necessary." She sat back down. "Unless you plan to shoot us here and now, explain the callousness on the government's part."

"This is classified. We have to look at the bigger picture." Monroe hesitated. "I can tell you this much: the defective parts weren't meant to be used by civilian choppers. One of the supplier's employees decided that his salary wasn't enough. He probably figured that, in a warehouse full of parts, nobody would notice if one got lost occasionally. We know of only seven that made it into civilian choppers."

"And he gave you this information." Chris stayed where he was. He was still struggling to convince himself that the world wouldn't necessarily be a better place without this agent.

"We got what information we could." Monroe thought of how they found what was left of the greedy employee in the empty warehouse only the day before. Even the dust had been removed. He frowned. They had been so close.

Jeanine sat motionless for a few minutes. Chris was still. Monroe didn't move, either. Then Jeanine nodded quickly and gripped Chris's hand.

"Civilian choppers? You said civilian choppers. The parts they sold us were meant to fill a government contract? Their bid was accepted by you guys."

"Yes."

"I'm not going to ask if you checked the company. I'm afraid of what the answer would be. Did you get the guy?"

"We're on it."

"The choppers that went down in the Middle East . . ."

"You should leave now."

She nodded. "Yes." Her voice was weak. So much of her strength was focused on trying to understand the magnitude of what they had just been told. And what they hadn't been told.

"We really are still digging into this." Much of the hostility that had been evident in Monroe had been replaced by concern. Maybe he was partly human after all. "What do you intend to tell the reporters?"

"Exactly what happened. That the engine quit on me."

"Good-bye."

Jeanine stood, but she didn't move away.

"Are we going to have to look under the hoods of our cars or check our apartments, or constantly look around us from now on?"

"You watch too many movies. We don't operate that way."

"Sure you don't." She threw him a hard look. "I've always believed that where there's smoke, there are flames nearby."

"You don't know enough to be a threat to our investigation. For your own good, however, you still shouldn't mention this." Her glare intensified. "The company doesn't know how much we know. If they find out that you know what little you *do* know, they'll assume that you know more. The danger wouldn't be from us." Jeanine exhaled slowly, but she didn't speak. Chris placed his hand under her elbow and eased her closer. Monroe continued, "I have a car waiting to take you home."

"We need to go to the airport and get our own cars." Chris fixed him with a stare. "Is that a problem?"

"No." Monroe picked up the phone and gave the change of orders.

"Are you sure we'll reach there okay?" Jeanine asked. "Or rather, since it is one of your cars, are you sure we'll arrive home okay?"

"You need to switch to G-rated movies. Or PG at the most."

Jeanine gave him one last look. Then she turned and left with Chris.

When they reached the outside, she glanced at a guy on the sidewalk talking to what looked like two tourists. She watched as he held out one of the brochures to them from a bunch clutched in his other hand. She smiled and felt some of her tension fade as she heard him say, "But it's a free luau. The best on the island. Probably the best in all of Hawaii. The presentation will only take about an hour."

"Some things are still normal," she said to Chris as she got into the back of the waiting car. "I'm thankful for that."

"As long as we build timeshare units, somebody has to sell them," Chris said as he climbed in beside her.

"Normal is a good thing. A very good thing."

They rode to the airport without speaking, but both were more relaxed than when they had left the office. Although Jeanine tried not to rush out when the car stopped, she had the door open before the wheels stopped rolling.

"Thanks." She looked at the driver. His answer was a nod. She stood close to Chris and watched as the car pulled away. They stood in place, watching the vehicle as it followed the curving sidewalk to the gate, rounded the corner, and disappeared.

"Do you think that's the end of it?" Chris turned her toward him.

"I'm afraid not." She glanced around and frowned. "Oh, no." She stared at the spot where she had left her car. She stared at an empty lot. "I just know that, on top of everything else that happened to us, somebody did not steal my car."

"Hey, you two! I'm so glad to see you." Nate rushed up. He grabbed them and wrapped his arms around both of them at the same time. He squeezed, sniffed, then released them. Then he pulled them close again in what was almost a death squeeze. "Are you okay? The Gestapo didn't try to harm you, did they? Why didn't you call me? I'd have come to get you. How are you feeling?" He shook his head. "Dumb question. Don't answer that." He let a sliver of sunshine come between them and him. "Talk. Say something. Say anything just so's I know you're all right."

"Do you know what happened to my car?"

"Yeah." He nodded. "That's easy. We took it to your house yesterday." He shrugged. "Figured you might not feel like driving as soon as you got out of the hospital." He turned to Chris. "I can drive you home if you need me to, and I can catch a ride in with somebody tomorrow."

"We're okay." Chris squeezed Jeanine's shoulders and she nodded.

"You sure? The boss said it wouldn't be a problem."

"We're sure." Jeanine smiled slightly. "No smart remarks?"

"This is too serious for that." He frowned. "I—I thought we'd lost you. I was afraid . . ."

"That somebody would blame you."

"No." The word exploded from him. He shook his head. "That's not true. I thought I'd never see . . . " He wiped at the side of his face, then inhaled. "I swear. I know I joked and picked at you about it, but I swear I checked that bird out thoroughly each time it gave you any problem."

"I know. We talked with Agent Monroe. He said he talked to you and he explained as much as he had to." She smiled at him. "I'm kidding you." Jeanine touched his arm. "I know you checked. I know you were concerned." Her smile widened. "But if you're not careful, somebody might think you are soft-hearted, and that would blow your reputation so far away that you'd never get it back."

"Okay. Maybe I care." He mumbled. "A little." He managed a shrug.

"We'd better leave it at that." She shook her head. "I'd better go talk to Hal. I'll be right back, Chris." She started to walk away.

"Tell the truth and shame the Devil, Big Brother," she heard Nate say in his old voice. "Accident aside, I did the right thing when I got you assigned to Jeanine's chopper."

She laughed as she walked to the reception area. Nate was bringing some of her normal life back.

FIFTEEN

"You folks sure you don't want free tickets to a luau?" The slight young man threw the tourists a quick smile, then glanced back to the street. "It's the best on the island. Some say it's the best on all of the islands." He looked at them again. "Okay," he said as they shook their heads and walked away. "Have a nice vacation."

The tourists continued down the street, but the man wasn't watching them. His smile had left him as soon as they had. Luaus and fun took up no space in his thoughts. Now the building across the street held his attention more than the tourists had. Still watching it, he moved to the corner of the building behind him. Then he tucked the brochures into an envelope, pulled out his cell phone, and pressed a button.

"They left five minutes ago. No one has come out since. I'm leaving now."

He walked to the corner and caught the bus. He sat so that he faced the building, then stared at it until it was gone from view.

"I say we should do nothing," the man pacing across the cabin floor said. "There is no problem."

"We do not know what she told them. I saw her leave.

She is still, with them. If they were finished with her, she would have left."

"You are right about one thing, Hassan. We don't know what she told them. But we do know that we cannot change what she has already said. It would not help to take action now. It would only serve to draw more attention to us." He stopped in front of the young man and glanced at the three other men sitting on the battered sofa before continuing. "The action against the greedy capitalist may or may not have been necessary. We will never know. We do not need to give them anything further to examine."

"I was not in favor of hiring an outsider, Abdul. It was you who made that decision."

"And it was *you* who decided to take drastic action against him without orders."

"It was necessary. He knew things that he did not know he knew. They would have gotten information from him that would have been harmful to the cause, just as they might get such information from her."

"I did not order your action. You overstepped your bounds. If you are not careful, you will no longer be here when we are ready for the next step."

"Are you threatening me?"

"Threats are useless. I am telling you that I am in charge. I will be in charge until I get orders saying that I am not. As for the woman, you are right about one thing. We do not know what she told them," he repeated. "We can be sure, however, that whatever she learned she has already told." He continued to stare at the man. "Besides, she had nothing to tell except that her helicopter went down."

"I still say we should take care of her. Maybe there is something she will remember at another time that will hurt our cause. Then it will be too late to take care of her. I say we do it now."

"You are not in charge. This country calls itself a democracy, but a vote does not decide with us. We wait for further instructions." He glared as the younger man sat down in a chair with its stuffing coming out. Once in place he jiggled his leg as if he would rather still be pacing.

"I told them that you are not ready for this. I told them that you do not have the patience for such an operation, that you would better serve at home."

"You did not get a vote in this, either, Abdul." Hassan glared back.

"We will await orders. Until then we do nothing. Talking about it is not productive. We have better things to do."

He sat at the scarred desk and opened a laptop computer and made sure that he had an Internet connection. Then the only sound inside the cabin was the soft contact of his fingers with the keyboard.

"How are you feeling?" Chris asked once they were in her house. He pulled Jeanine into his arms and brushed his mouth across hers.

"Great, considering. Thank God that the memories are not as intense as they were at first." She rested her head on his chest, then pulled back. "I have to call Lisa. I know she's still worried."

"Yeah, and I need to call Nate to make sure he's cooled down. I want to make sure that he's not set on hunting down Agent Monroe and taking him apart like some malfunctioning engine. Poor Agent Sullivan might be included just for hanging out with such a turkey." At the words "malfunctioning engine," Jeanine drew in a quick breath. "Sorry, sweet." Chris kissed her cheek. My mouth ran on without waiting for my brain to kick in."

"No problem. I have to keep my mind on the fact that we survived. Besides, if he does get to Monroe, maybe

Nate can install the heart that they left out of the good agent." They laughed.

"Do you think that's a requirement for his job?" Chris asked. "You know, 'Wanted: able-bodied almost-human. Those with hearts or emotions need not apply.' "

"I'll bet he'd be at the top of that list." She picked up the phone. "As soon as I calm Lisa down, I'm cooking. I don't know about you, but the breakfast we had in the hospital was not what I would have ordered."

"You got that right." He pulled out his cell phone and walked away from her to make his call.

"Hey, Lisa. Glad I could get you." Jeanine leaned against the wall. "I'm fine." She shook her head. "No, I don't need you to come over. I'm already at home. Thanks for leaving the clothes for me." She nodded. "I agree. Friends have to make time for each other, but I still understand about your work. How's it going?"

She listened as Lisa told her about the status of the project. When she had finished, Jeanine said, "Give me a call when you're ready to go. It will be nice to have another musketeer with me to face those territorial geese." She nodded. "Yeah. I miss Kalele, too. Each time I check my e-mail I expect to see a message from her." She swallowed hard. "You're right. If . . ." She took a deep breath. "If she wasn't okay her family would have heard." She nodded. "Yeah, I know we're not the only ones who wish that the mess over there was over. Call me when you get a break from playing with those huge building blocks." She laughed and hung up.

Soon Chris put away his phone. Jeanine smiled at him. "Was Nate still angry?"

"I'm glad he didn't have to perform brain surgery or some other delicate operation today. As it is, I'm sure that whatever work he manages to do today, he'll check on tomorrow. I told him to go for a swim and cool off." Chris laughed. "I also told him that when he finished, the ocean temperature would be a minimum of ten degrees hotter." He nodded. "I got him to laugh. That means his anger is starting to subside."

"Just so he doesn't kill Agent Monroe. Not that he doesn't deserve it, but we need Nate." She shook her head. "But I don't want to spend any more time on that. Are you hungry? I can make an omelette."

"Yes, I am hungry." He pressed a kiss to her mouth. "And I want some food, too." He caressed her back before his hands came to rest on her hips.

"In order for me to cook, you have to let me go." Jeanine's hands ran over his back.

"Baby, you are cooking already." He rested his hands on her hips. "That's a hard choice." He drew her against him. "A very hard choice."

Jeanine rubbed against him twice. She smiled as he felt more like a stone against her softness.

"Maybe we can eat later." Her hands found a way under his shirt. "The refrigerator door is shut and the eggs can't escape. We can . . ." Chris's mouth covered hers. His hand found a path under her shirt, eased along until it found the swell of her breast.

"Yes, we can." He bent his head and covered the tip with his mouth. He released her and smiled when she moaned her protest. "Are you up for an experiment?"

"Since you're up," she circled the proof of his arousal. "I guess I am."

"We can compare making love in your bed to making love in a cave." He moved one hand between them and found the center of her arousal.

"I think . . ." Jeanine gripped his arm. "I think it's too much trouble to think." Slowly, she moved a few inches away and took his hand. "This way to my la-bor'a-tory." Her hand skimmed his chest. "If you're still interested."

"If I were any more interested, I'd explode."

"Follow me."

"Definitely."

The hall leading to the bedroom wasn't long, but they stopped three times to share a kiss.

"Why did you put the bedroom so far from the front door?" Chris asked and unbuttoned her shirt.

"It never seemed too far before." Jeanine undid the buttons on his shirt and pushed it down his arms.

"Probably has something to do with Einstein's theory of relativity." He unhooked her slacks and eased them over her hips.

"Distance . . ." Jeanine slowly unhooked his pants. "Is directly related to . . ." She brushed her hands along his hips before she slid his pants off.

"The level of desire," he finished. "Um hmm." Chris stared at her. "This is what I couldn't see last night." He grazed a finger over her breast and felt it harden under his touch. "I like lace." His words were husky. "Maybe I'll admire it later. I have something else in mind right now." He reached behind her and unclasped the hook. The lace fell away revealing her fullness to him. "Beautiful." He bent his head and captured one chocolate drop. "And sweet." He flicked his tongue over the tip and Jeanine grabbed his shoulders and moaned. She pushed against him.

Chris pushed her panties down her legs and lifted her onto the bed. Quickly he removed his pants, taking his shorts with them. Then he gazed at her.

"Don't," he pleaded when she tried to cover herself. "Let me look at you." He continued to stare as he fumbled to get his wallet from his pants.

"It would be easier if you looked at what you're doing."

"Looking away from you would be much harder." He shook his head. "I shouldn't use that word right now."

He pulled foil packets from the wallet and placed all but one on the nightstand.

"Do you anticipate a busy night?" Jeanine asked as she looked at the other packets. She felt, and sounded, as if she had just run a double marathon.

"I certainly hope so."

Chris went to her and ended the conversation with a kiss. He let his hands explore first one breast then the other. Then he traced circles over her middle, slowly moving to the soft mound protected by the thatch of hair. He stroked smaller circles, smiling at the moans escaping from Jeanine each time he came close.

"Are you ready for me?" His hand stilled on her mound.

"Any more ready," she managed to say, "and I'd be a puddle of liquid and nerve endings. Do you need help?" She asked as he opened the packet.

"As with last night, if you help with this, we won't need it." Quickly he rolled the condom into place, then returned to her. He positioned himself between her legs, but he didn't enter. "Your time to help is now," he murmured into her ear. He nipped her ear lobe, then eased into her and stilled. He waited as she accommodated him, then closed around him.

Together, in the daylight, they rode to the place that they had found last night. They made love with the sheer joy of having been through a disaster, having looked death in the face, and come out alive. They had used three condoms before, still locked together, they drifted into a satisfied sleep.

Later, with daylight managing to share the end of itself with them, the two stirred.

"I need sustenance. I need food. I am hungry." Jeanine

tried to shift her position. Chris moved enough to allow her to. Still they remained laced in each others arms.

"I hate to say it, but I agree." He stroked her thigh, which was on top of his leg. "I really hate to say anything that will mean the end of this."

"It's temporary."

"Promise?" He stroked again.

"Yes." Her hand brushed across his backside.

"Then I guess somebody has to make the first move."

A few minutes later they were still almost sharing the same space.

"Okay. On three we go." Jeanine stopped moving her hand, but she didn't remove it from Chris's leg.

"Wait. Do we go on three, or after three?" His hand reached the top of her thigh and waited.

Jeanine groaned and rolled from under him. "Don't look at me like that."

"Like what?"

"As if I'm a piece of chocolate cake and you're craving dessert."

"Chocolate is my favorite flavor."

"Stop it."

"That's not what you said a while ago. And a while before that. And . . ."

"I'll use the shower down the hall. You use this one."

"We're not going to share?"

"Not this time." She forced her legs to carry her to the closet when she really wanted to get back into bed. She draped a red silk robe over her arm. "Here. This is for you." She laid a white terry robe on the chair. "See you in a bit." She blew him a kiss and winked.

Chris watched the movement of her firm backside until she was out of the room. Then he rolled over onto his back and put his hands behind his head.

Yet another reason to call Hawaii "paradise." He

grinned. *This pushes all of the other reasons way down the list.*

Half an hour later he walked into the kitchen and wrapped his arms around Jeanine as she was standing at the stove.

"Hello, beautiful." He pressed a kiss to the side of her neck. "Red is a good color, but not as nice as chocolate." He slipped a hand inside her robe. He stroked her stomach before moving his hand up to capture a plump breast.

"Stop that," Jeanine said, but she made no move to separate from him.

"This? You want me to stop this?" Chris rubbed gently across the tip, felt it harden, then tugged it slightly.

"Chris." Somebody removed all the air from the room.

"Yes, my sweet." He rubbed again, then pulled his hand from beneath her robe. Reaching around her, he slowly gathered the edges of red silk together as if hiding her from sight would erase what she looked like from his mind. "I'm stopping, just as you wanted." He kissed her cheek before going to the table.

"I did not say that was what I wanted," she said as he turned back toward her. "I guess I'll have to put you to work to keep you out of trouble."

"If that's trouble, no wonder people find it so easy to get into."

Jeanine shook her head. "I'd ask what I'm going to do with you, but I know what your answer would be." She pointed to the overhead cabinet beside the sink. "Glasses are there. You can pour us some pineapple juice. Then you can set the table. By then I'll have our omelettes on the plates."

"Yes, ma'am."

A few minutes later they were sitting across from each other. *I could get used to this,* she thought as she passed him the mango jelly. *Real easy.* She took a sip of juice. *This is way too fast.* "We need to talk," she said.

"That sounds serious."

"It is."

"Are you sorry?"

"We should have talked before . . ." She frowned.

"Before we made love?"

"Yes."

"I seem to remember part of this conversation before." He shrugged. "Okay." He placed his napkin beside his plate and leaned on the table. "What put that frown on your face? You're not sorry that we made love? Are you?" He held his breath and waited for the "no" that would allow him to breathe again.

"I'm still going to enter the training program. I haven't changed my mind."

"And?"

"And I know how you feel about the program." She stared at him. "I'm still going to do it."

"Okay."

"Okay?" She leaned back in her chair.

"It's your decision." He touched her hand. "I meant it when I said that I have no right to tell you what you can and cannot do." He released a hard breath. "I care about you. I care deeply. More than I have cared about anybody before. I think that what we have can grow if we give it a chance. I also think you care about me, too." He smiled and his look lost some of its intensity. "Or are you just after my body?"

She laughed. "There is that." She nodded. "I care so much that it scares me. I've never been here before."

"Me, neither. We'll find our way together." He squeezed her hand. "Come on." He walked around to her. "Let's catch the sunset. We were a little too busy last night to appreciate it."

He smiled. "I would say that the sunset will be the perfect ending to a perfect day, but I hope not."

They sat on the glider on the lanai with their arms around each other and watched God change day into night. Then Chris turned to her.

"The people who rescued us—they went through the training that you'll go through? That's the kind of thing you'll be doing?"

"Yes."

"It seems safe."

"It usually is, but there is some danger." She watched him. "There have been cases when the rescue chopper crashed or when one of the crew members was killed attempting a rescue." He stared back, and his hand tightened on her shoulder. "I'm giving you the reality."

"I have to confess," he said, "I am never comfortable in the air. I only fly because it's the quickest way to travel. You know, 'If God had wanted people to fly, etc.' "

"Oh yeah. That's the one that's answered with: 'And if he meant for people to ride, he would have equipped them with wheels on their feet.' "

"Okay. You got me." He brushed a hand down her cheek. "Speaking of which, is it bedtime yet?"

"Speaking of which?"

"I couldn't think of a way to get from that subject to this one." He kissed her.

"I noticed that you didn't ask if it was time to go to sleep." She put a hand inside his robe and stroked his thick chest hair. "I wonder why?"

He stood and pulled her with him.

"No, you don't. You know that sleeping is not my primary objective." He untied her robe and pressed his mouth to the hollow beneath her chin. He flicked his tongue into the space, then tasted his way to the swell of her breast. He paused, then drew the hard puckered tip into his mouth. He smiled and lifted his head as she gasped. "Just as delicious as before. Shall we see if everything else is as delicious as before?"

Jeanine wrapped her hand around his arousal and brushed a finger along the underside. Chris groaned.

"I think that's a good idea." She moved her hand to his and led him to the bedroom. "I meant to tell you how nice you look in my robe." She pushed it open. "But I think that what's inside is much nicer."

"No problem." The robe was on the floor before he finished answering. "Your turn." The heat in his look flared when her robe joined his and her lushness was there for him to take.

Seconds later, they came together. This time there was no need to hurry. They were safe, and they had all the time in the world.

SIXTEEN

Three days later, the glorious, perfect evening outside the floor-to-ceiling windows in Chris's house was wasted on the two sitting at the small table overlooking the view. The breeze, entering the open window and trying to tease them with nature's abundant perfume, was wasting its time. Chris and Jeanine might as well have been in a basement room with no view or scent of the outside world.

"I wish I didn't have to leave you tomorrow." He rubbed a finger over the back of her hand.

"I wish you didn't have to go, either." She turned her palm up and enjoyed his touch there as he traced the lines.

"I wish the conferences weren't important to the future of my company." He squeezed her hand. "If those wishes fail, I wish you could go with me."

"If I went with you, you wouldn't attend enough sessions to make the trip worthwhile."

He sighed. "Maybe this separation is a good thing." He shook his head. "We couldn't keep going on as we have been."

"I won't play dumb and ask why not, because I know that, without a break, we'd both drop dead from exhaustion in about two more days." She grinned. "Marathon lovemaking makes that a distinct possibility." She caressed the side of his face, and he turned his head to place a kiss on her palm.

"Yeah, but what a way to go."

"Yeah." Her grin widened.

"Exercise is good for you."

"And we discovered the best exercise in existence."

"Absolutely."

Seriousness filled her face. "I'll leave for my training a week before you get back. Then I'll be gone for two more weeks after you return."

"I could come visit you."

She shook her head. "It's an intense program. No time for visits. Besides, there is no way I could concentrate on anything but you if you were around." She sighed. "Our timing is definitely off."

"Um hmm." He brushed his thumb along the fullness of her lower lip. "We both have to go. Fortunately, I know how we can work on both things before then." Heat filled his eyes. "I don't think of it as work, though."

"Both things?" She had trouble stringing the two-word sentence together.

"Yeah. We can get some exercise and work on our timing."

"I thought our timing was perfect."

"There's always the possibility that we can hit a new high."

"I guess we'd better get started trying, huh?"

"Oh, yeah. The sooner the better."

They stood at the same time. Arms around each other, they walked to Chris's bedroom.

They spent the night trying to accomplish the impossible: to stock up on enough loving to satisfy each of them for the next four weeks.

"I guess I have everything I need." Chris glanced around his bedroom in the barely there morning light.

"Everything except you." He kissed her and held her close as if he hadn't slept with her in his arms.

"They say that when you forget something, that gives you a reason to come back."

"I could never forget you." He claimed her mouth in a quick but searing kiss. "And you're the best reason in the world for me to come back." He touched his forehead to hers. "We have to stop this."

"Yes. We'd better go before the plane leaves you." Jeanine squeezed him close. Then she slowly moved away but still held his hand.

They let go long enough to put Chris's things into the car and for them to get in, but they held hands during the ride to the airport as if that would prevent business from separating them.

As they drove, the dawn gradually gained strength as if it knew that everybody would expect radiant sunshine and it had better get busy. Jeanine and Chris wished they had the power to hold it back.

"The sooner you leave, the sooner you'll come back." Jeanine ran a finger down his jaw and across his chin.

"That doesn't keep me from missing you already." He pulled her into his arms.

After several good-bye kisses, Jeanine watched Chris until he went inside the terminal. She watched as he waited in line and checked his luggage. He waved a slow good-bye and then went to the gate. She stood a while longer as if hoping he would change his mind and come back to her. Then she slowly got into her car and drove to her home, which would be lonelier now that Chris was gone.

"You sure you're ready for this?" Hal asked when Jeanine walked into his office later that morning. "You can take some more time off if you want. I can even get

Kimo to cover for you today if you change your mind. I already talked to him about that possibility."

"I'm fine. 'Good to go,' as they say." She smiled. "Really. I can get back on this horse and ride him into the ground, so to speak." She shook her head. "Wow. That was a bad expression to use in this case, wasn't it?" Her smile widened.

"I'm glad you used it and not me." Hal smiled back at her. "If you're really sure . . ."

"As sure as I've ever been about flying." She raised an eyebrow. "Unless you're looking to bench me, coach."

"Why would I bench my best player?" He leaned toward her. "Don't tell the others that I said that. It would hurt their feelings something terrible."

"Lips sealed and all that."

"Okay. Here's the passenger list." He handed her a folder. "You have a family of five: the parents, a sixteen-year-old boy, his thirteen-year-old sister, and their ten-year-old brother. It's the first chopper ride for all of them. The youngest has to do a report about his vacation, so he'll probably have a lot of questions."

"Ten-year-olds always have a lot of questions, report or not." She smiled. "A routine flight will be nice."

She was still smiling when she got out to the field.

"Hey, Nate."

"Your bird is ready. I checked it one more time a half-hour ago. It . . ." He shook his head slightly. "It won't give you any trouble." He moved closer to her and frowned. "I know that Monroe guy told you what they think happened." He inhaled sharply. "They should have told us before. Those guys don't care about people. What kind of government have we turned into when they do something like that?"

"I wonder the same thing." She tapped his arm with her folder. "We got to put it behind us."

"Yeah. I guess you're right." He shook his head quickly as if to get rid of what had happened. "Anyway, I pulled all the parts that I had gotten from that company and replaced them. I did that for all of the choppers. Thank God there weren't a lot." He frowned. "It's taking all I got not to go to that company and make somebody pay." His frown hardened. "If I don't see some results in the news soon about that investigation, I still might pay them a visit. They risked people's lives for money. Some of the recent crashes might have been because of them. We don't know how long they've been selling that junk." His face hardened. "I don't care what Monroe said, I called Lou at Green Paradise and suggested he test his birds. He'll pass the word. I'm not going to read about something bad happening that I could have warned somebody about." His scowl deepened. "I might go to that company warehouse, anyway, and work my way up to the person responsible."

"Chill, Nate. Armor, whether shining or dull, doesn't fit you. Everything is okay here, and you've passed the word on. You've done what you can do." She smiled at him. "Maybe, if you check through your catalogs, you can find a company that sells patience. If you do, order a big supply. Then double the dosage until it's gone."

"Not even close to funny."

She shrugged. "I tried."

"About the chopper. I tested everything three times. This is the first time we're flying since . . . since . . ."

"Since I went down."

"Yeah. Since that." He stared at her. "I'm sorry that . . ."

"That somebody sold us bad parts? That the government didn't warn you about them? I am, too." She touched his arm. "Don't go all soft on me. I won't know how to act with you if you do." She winked at him and went to the gate to wait for her passengers.

Two hours later, with the chopper noise in the background, Jeanine stood at the gate shaking hands with each of the passengers as they left. She answered any last questions about the flight. The ten-year-old had more questions than any of the others, but Jeanine's patience was just as evident at the end of the flight as it had been at the beginning. His final questions were about how he could get to be a helicopter pilot. *He reminds me of me at that age,* she thought as she answered him. He started to ask something else when his father put a hand on his shoulder.

"That's enough, Jesse."

"But I want to know . . ."

"Can he use e-mail to ask any other questions?"

"Sure." Jeanine smiled. "The address is in the brochure."

"Thanks for being patient. Jesse can get a bit intense when he's interested in something."

"It's all right. I understand." She looked at all of them. "We thank all of you for flying with us. If you ever come back to the islands, remember us." Her smile widened. "The tape of our flight will be available in a few minutes. You can wait for it in the gift shop. You might find something else in there that you want to buy."

"Yeah. I want some posters and a model kit and . . ."

As they walked away, Jesse continued to list what he planned to buy with his allowance. She chuckled. It sounded as if he intended to buy one of each item in the shop. Unless he had a whole lot of money, he'd blow it all before he left the airport.

"How did it go?" Nate came over to Jeanine and tried to look as if the answer didn't matter to him.

"Routine." She smiled at him. "It was a wonderful routine flight." She held the flight folder to her chest. "I'd hug you, but I don't want to start a new tradition." She laughed. "See you tomorrow." She hummed as she walked to the locker room. *I did it. I really did it.* She did a little celebration dance. *Except for the ripples of concern when I started up the engine, I was okay.* She laughed. *There's something to be said about facing your fears and staring them down.*

She changed into her running clothes in the locker room and drove directly to the park. Her life was back to normal. At least the recent normal.

She tried not to think of Lisa and Kalele as she ran her usual route. It was hard, but she managed a weak smile when the geese on the lake honked at her. She liked to think that they were just saying "hello."

She had to work hard to find the zone and even harder to stay in it. Her memories kept dragging her away. Finally she was finished running and stretching.

The quiet that greeted her when she opened her front door was way too loud. *How could I miss him so much?* She shook her head. *I haven't known him very long, but the intensity of what we have makes up for the short time.* She frowned. *This is just the first day. How can I stand four weeks apart from him?*

She didn't try to think of an answer. She knew there wasn't one. Instead, she decided to access her voice mail for messages. *That should be good for a few minutes*, she thought.

"Hi, baby, jet lag is kicking me, but I arrived here okay. Only thing—I'm missing something—you," Chris's voice rumbled, and sharp longing stabbed her before settling in as a gigantic ache. "I have this big, big bed and nobody to share it with. How am I going to get to sleep tonight without you against me? How will I be able to find sleep without you to help me exercise away the tension of the day?" His sigh reached her, and hers echoed it. "Even the weather misses you. It's raining. Everything is gray." He sighed again. "I can't believe that this is only day one. Who do we petition to get a few days knocked off each week so that four weeks become two? Or one? Or only a few days total? Not a permanent change, mind you. Just until we're together again." He exhaled loudly. "This is killing me. I miss you so much." He paused. "I got to go. I've got a workshop in ten minutes. They didn't waste any time. Be talking to you later. Stay sweet, but not so sweet that you attract any other bees."

Jeanine waited, but the next sound she heard was a dial tone. Still she sat for a while holding the phone close, as if she could pretend that it was Chris.

Later, she checked her e-mail. Despite her loneliness, she smiled when she saw a message from Kalele.

"I'm settled in. I thought Hawaii was hot, but that's like an Alaskan winter compared with this. I'm doing pretty much the same things that I was doing at home, but it's so different. I know a lot of the others over here wish that they were doing the same as at home. I don't know when I'll be able to write again or even access my e-mail. We're really busy. Has Lisa been able to run with you? I know that you still worry those geese even though I'm not there to make sure that you run. You have to stay in shape so we three musketeers can get back into our thing when I get home."

Jeanine read the message several times. Then she answered it. She hesitated while she was writing; then she told Kalele about Chris. Her news about him was too good to keep to herself.

When she finished at the computer, she sat on the lanai and watched the sunset. The streaks seemed brighter, richer than other sunsets, as if the sky were trying to cheer her up. It failed.

Even the sunset wasn't the same without Chris, she thought as she went inside the house after the last light of day faded and the moon took over.

As she climbed into bed, she knew exactly how Chris felt about sleeping in a big bed alone.

Jeanine filled the long days while she was waiting till it was time to go for her training with so many activities that she should have been exhausted when she got into bed every night. She took as many flights as allowed. She ran every day. Twice that week Lisa was able to get away and run with her. On those days Jeanine was grateful for two reasons: she got to see her friend and, at least for an hour and a half, her mind wasn't stuck on Chris.

As soon as she got back into her car, however, he sprang into her mind so strongly that it was as if her memories of him had been gathering strength while they waited for another chance.

During that week she went to every performance of every dance school in the area. She went to the movies and stared at the screen as if she was paying attention; as if she was making sense of what was in front of her eyes; as if she wasn't wishing that Chris was with her. As if she wasn't longing to be in his arms, making up for the days they had been apart.

Chris called from Los Angeles every night, and Jeanine had mixed feelings when he did. She was happy to hear his voice, but talking to him about how they would make up for the time they were losing got her hot and more than a little bothered.

Whenever they finally broke the connection, she held on to the new memory while waiting for the ache that rode with it to go away. As soon as it receded enough for her to move, she crawled into bed and waited for sleep to have pity on her.

Finally the day came for Jeanine to go to Oahu and begin the training. Now she had a second reason to look forward to it. Not only was she doing something that she had been so enthusiastic about, it also meant that the time was shorter until she and Chris would be together again. He had gone to a second conference in Los Angeles. *He'll be back in a week, but I'll still have two more weeks to go.* She frowned. *Three weeks without contact with him. The phone conversations had been no substitute for being able to physically touch each other, but even that seems desirable now that it's no longer possible.* She frowned. *Cut it out,* she told herself on the inter-island flight. *When we see each other again, the time apart will make it even sweeter.* She shook her head. *Not possible.* She didn't open the book she had in her purse. There was no way she could concentrate with Chris and the program swirling through her mind. *Maybe when he gets back we can manage to at least talk to each other.*

She arrived at the meeting site fifteen minutes early, but three of the other trainees were already there, and the last two showed up soon after. After quick introductions and before changing into new uniforms, they went outside police headquarters for a press conference.

Reporters filled the plaza in front of the building and spilled over onto the grass. It wasn't often that these pilots would be needed by the police, but when they were, lives would be at risk and the members of the media, as well as the public, knew it.

Jeanine stood with the five others and smiled for a group picture. Because she was the only female in the group this time and because of her recent accident, she received more attention than the others. Unwanted attention. One reporter in particular refused to allow her to be just one of the trainees. Jeanine managed to be pleasant when the woman's questions focused on her.

"No, I'm not afraid of flying again." She forced a smile rather than a glare when the reporter asked the same question that Jeanine had already answered for another reporter. "What happened was an accident. Accidents happen in all kinds of settings. I had an accident. An accident." *Why can't this woman let it go?*

"Do you think you can correct the mistake that caused yours so that the same thing won't happen again?" The reporter elbowed her way to the front of the group.

I need to sit her down and teach her the meaning of the word "accident."

Jeanine glanced at the other members of the press. They looked as if they were waiting for the biggest story of their careers. She forced a smile, put her hands into her pockets instead of around the woman's skinny neck, and looked at her. *It would not be wise to commit murder, no matter how justified, in front of the press, not to mention the police commissioner. No, not wise at all.*

The microphone wavered in the woman's hand and her smile trembled a little as Jeanine's answer to the last question was to pin her with a stare.

The others in the training group moved closer to Jeanine, and she relaxed a little. They had just met and already they were closing ranks to protect one of their own. *Great*, she thought as she prepared to answer the same question yet again.

Smile gone, she leaned toward the reporter and let the words ease out in slow motion. "It was an accident. An accident. Do you know the meaning of the word 'accident'?" *How long will it take for her to get it?*

"Thank you for your interest," the police commissioner said as he stepped in front of Jeanine before the reporter could respond. "If you'll excuse us, we have to get to work." He nodded to the program supervisor, who led the group into the building.

"Do you want something to throw?" One of the men asked Jeanine after they were inside the building and on their way to the conference room.

"It won't do her any good," another said before she could answer. "It's too late. The target has already slithered away."

Jeanine laughed as they walked to the conference room for the orientation.

SEVENTEEN

The next morning Hassan burst into the cabin hidden in a dense stand of trees. Although he had walked more than a mile from the bus stop, he had difficulty containing the energy that filled him.

"Look at this." He slammed the door and pounced into the room as if he were a predator whose last meal had been days before. "This!" He held out the morning newspaper as if it wouldn't be seen otherwise. "This is the same woman. The one who you said has nothing to do with anything." He stared at Abdul, who was leaning against the old desk. His stare lasted for a few seconds, then he marched back and forth across the floor, waving the newspaper in the air like a flag being carried into battle. The picture of six smiling trainees faced outward so the other two men in the room could see it. "I told you we should have taken care of her."

"This picture does not prove anything. There is a limited number of helicopter pilots. It is a coincidence. If she were important, why would they allow the publicity?"

"You are so gullible. How did you get to be in command?"

"Our leaders decide who is in command positions just as they make all important decisions." The older man pointed at him. "You will watch yourself when you speak to me. You will show proper respect."

"Respect must be earned." Hassan held up a finger. "She is everywhere. She is piloting a helicopter with a part that Ben Manto stole from us and sold to her company." Another finger joined the first. "We see her go with the government agents and she is with them for hours. I, myself, saw that." His eyes narrowed. "If she knows nothing, why was she with them for so long a time?" A third finger went up. "Now she is in this program working with the government." He tightened his hold on the newspaper and it crumpled. "For all we know, she was responsible for our people on Maui almost getting caught. But for the grace of Allah, the crop would have been harvested a day later, and they would all now be in a cage in Cuba. I tell you, we have got to do something about her. She is a threat to the cause."

"What happened on Maui was not out of the ordinary. Hikers often discover what are thought to be hidden crops. We are not the only ones using the excellent weather here to our advantage. We knew there was a possibility that the plants would be discovered. The men were prepared." Abdul stood straight. "Our people did *not* get caught. The mountains provide many places for growing. That is one reason why we are here. Already they have found another site and are in operation. The funds from the harvest of the last crop are already at work. For all these people know, greed is the only reason for growing poison for them to draw into their bodies. They have no idea that the money serves to further our cause."

"I still say that she has a connection in all of this. She is more than she seems." His voice rose as if hundreds of feet separated him and Abdul.

"I tell you, forget the woman. You will take no action against her." Abdul closed the space separating them until he was close enough for Hassan to feel Abdul's breath. "I repeat: you will take no action against her unless I tell you to do so. You will not chance bringing attention to us with your spontaneous behavior. The woman has nothing to do with us. Even Manto may have been no threat to us. Had you not been so rash in your actions, we would have questioned him and we would have known with a certainty the extent of his knowledge. He would have told us if there was more to the missing parts story. He would have told us if the government was involved. He would have told us if he had told them anything." He moved until only a scant few inches separated them. "But he had nothing to tell them except that he was a thief."

Hassan backed up a few feet, but he lifted his chin and glared at Abdul. "If he had stumbled across anything to tell anybody, you can be sure that we would now have such information ourselves. I would have extracted it from him."

"You did not have orders to act on the matter of Manto." Abdul repeated what he had said in the conversation they had when they last met.

"There was no time to wait for orders from you."

"There is always time to await orders unless you are told not to. You would do well to remember that. Do not be surprised if you receive orders to return home." Abdul's stare narrowed. "You must learn to follow orders. You must learn to heed your superiors. You are of no use to the cause if you cannot control your actions. You will bring attention to us. We can be sure that even though the death is gone from the news, officials are still investigating."

"The authorities will only think that he was killed during a robbery. Fortunately for us, such crimes are not rare even here in the islands. Occasionally, someone gets killed. I made sure that they will reach that conclusion in this case."

"You are not as clever as you think you are, and that is the danger. You might have put the operation in jeopardy. It is too important to place in danger. We do not need your impulsive actions to draw attention to us. Maybe your usefulness is at an end."

"And you are of no use to us if you have grown soft. Perhaps you have been here too long."

"Perhaps you need to remember who is in command."

"Perhaps that will change." Hassan folded his arms across his chest. "Perhaps it is you who will receive new orders when we notify our superiors of what has occurred with the woman."

"Stop!" The third man, Kareem, stood. "Enough! We need to remember that we work for a common good. Fighting among ourselves is of no use to us." He glanced out the window. Nothing moved that shouldn't. He turned back to them. "I will give my report now. Already we have been here too long. That alone could put everything we are doing in danger." He glared at Hassan, then looked away. "You use too much time telling us what you think. I will talk of what *is*. The laboratory is in operation, and they are on schedule. I will check with them again as has been planned. They will advise me when they have what is needed for the next phase. I will inform you, Abdul," glancing at Hassan, "as you are our superior. Our operatives are already in place for the next phase and waiting to hear from me." He allowed a slight smile to show for a few seconds.

"They say that they are sick of the coffee and they do not even drink it."

Abdul and Hassan laughed with him. It was one of the rare times when they were in agreement. Then, individually and with many minutes between departures, all three left.

Is this what boot camp is like? Jeanine wondered as she plopped onto her bed the third day.

The first two days had lulled her into thinking that the

three weeks wouldn't be very difficult. After all, she was in top physical condition. She wouldn't have any problem handling a little more of a workout. *Boy, was I wrong.*

She groaned and stretched her hands over her head, trying to work out the aches from muscles she hadn't paid much attention to before. She didn't need the clock to tell her that the day was nudging the night out of the way. *Why don't they extend the training a few days and let us get a normal night's sleep?*

This was the third day that they had started at dawn and she knew they wouldn't finish until midnight.

During the first two days they had reviewed general helicopter procedures, and Jeanine decided that, although she was learning nothing new, at least she had something to help the time pass while waiting to be with Chris again. Then the instructors moved to specific procedures to be followed in various rescue scenarios, and things got intense. Then it seemed to Jeanine as if a new trainee had suddenly joined the group: one well-known character named Murphy.

On day three, after finishing only one full day of intensive rescue training and with a lot more to go, one of the men had to leave because of a family emergency. Later that day, despite wearing protective gear, another trainee had a bad reaction to the chemicals used to extinguish chemical fires and had to be airlifted to the hospital from the rugged location where they were camping.

Jeanine thought that some variation of musical chairs must be in effect. She remembered an old Agatha Christie mystery titled *And Then There Were None*. She hoped it wasn't an appropriate title for the training program.

As if those two incidents weren't enough and Murphy couldn't find something else to upset, three and a half days into the program an accident happened.

EIGHTEEN

Midnight had come and gone so long ago that daylight was waking up. Engrossed in his paperwork at the desk in his hotel suite, Chris never noticed. The all-news television station provided background sound as he worked, but that held less than half of his attention. His focus was on the blueprint in front of him. The design he was working on as his final project was for an imaginary building complex; it would be torn apart at the nine A.M. workshop, but he wouldn't mind. Sometime in the future, he'd most likely take the plans from paper to concrete and metal, so he'd rather discover flaws while all the work was still on paper. Paper was cheap; building supplies weren't. He leaned back and stared at the empty coffee pot on the counter of the kitchenette in his Los Angeles hotel suite.

Any more of that liquid caffeine and I won't sleep for a week. He shook his head. *Not even halfway through my time away from Jeanine, and already it's doing a number on me. It feels as if we've been apart for months.* He frowned. *How did she get so deeply inside my mind so fast?* He smiled and folded his arms. *Two more weeks plus. I won't see her for another seventeen days.* He shook his head. *I need something to make me sleep the time away, not something to keep me awake. She's got me so mixed up, I'm talking to myself.* He sighed, closed his eyes, and remembered their last morning together.

Was it only a week and a half ago? Has it been such a short time since I held her? Since we woke up in each other's arms the morning I left? It hasn't been months since we joined together and visited that place that only the two of us know?

He opened his eyes. That wasn't helping. It was only allowing the ache to grow. *Force your mind away from her. Keep busy. Make the time go faster.* He shifted in the chair. *Yeah. And while you're at it, flip the real days the way you do calendar pages and stop at two weeks from now. Of course, you have to find some powerful magic to make that work.* He shifted in his seat as if that would help. *We have to find a way to get together when I get home. There has to be an evening, a meal—sometime when we can steal a few minutes to be together.*

He stared at the brightening sky outside the large window, but didn't see it. It was beautiful, but it was wasted on him. An ugly brick wall would have been just as good. He picked up the pencil and went back to work. Maybe he could learn something useful from the time spent away from Jeanine.

"We have just received this breaking news. During an evening exercise, an accident has occurred involving one of three remaining trainees in the Hawaiian Police Civilian Rescue Training Program."

The television was no longer merely background noise for Chris.

"No!" His pencil dropped to the desk. The papers in front of him were forgotten as he gave his full attention to the early morning broadcast. He swiveled his chair around to face the screen and concentrated on the reporter's words.

"No further details or the name of the trainee involved have been released pending notification of the family." The reporter gave background information about the program and the different ways that those who complete it help the police. What he didn't give was what Chris needed to hear.

The reporter continued and Chris listened, hoping that, when the name of the accident victim was given, he wouldn't recognize it.

"If this latest incident means that the trainee involved will have to leave the program, what started as six will leave three to finish. Since the beginning, this particular session has been plagued by mishaps." The reporter related the previous problems, then moved on to the next news item, but Chris didn't move with him.

He wasted no time trying to control his panic as he grabbed the phone and punched in the numbers needed to reach Nate. After what was only a few minutes but seemed like forever, the ringing stopped.

"Yeah?"

"Where were you?"

"Sleeping, man. Do you know what time it is here?"

"There's been an accident."

"Are you okay? What happened? Where are you? What do you need?"

"Not here. Not to me." He breathed deeply and wished the trembling rippling through him were due to the coffee. "When's the last time you heard from Jeanine?"

"I haven't. From what I hear, the sessions start before normal people are up and they don't stop until normal people are in bed. What's up?"

"The all-news television station reported an accident to one of the people in the training program. They didn't say who was involved."

"I'll see if I can find out something and give you a call back."

"Don't bother. I'm catching the first flight with a seat out of here. If they allow standees, I'll take that."

"What about the conference? You won't be able to help her if it is Jeanine. But I'm sure it wasn't," he hurriedly added before Chris could respond.

"Forget the conference. I'm coming home. Some things are more important. I know that now." He stopped long enough to take a deep breath. "I knew the program was dangerous. I told her not to go. I knew something was going to happen." He slapped a suitcase onto the bed and opened it.

"Chris . . ."

"Find out what you can, okay? Find out where they're training. When you do, call me. If you can't reach me, leave a message on my cell phone. I'm going directly to Oahu. Hopefully, by the time I land I'll have a message from you. If not, I—I guess I can try to find out for myself after I get there, but . . ."

"I'll get the information for you." Nate paused. "You know, she's not the only one in the program."

"Yeah." Chris put a stack of clothes into the suitcase. "But almost. Things have already happened to some of them. What kind of safety measures do those people follow? How could they let accidents happen to people trying to help them?"

"Chris, it's probably not Jeanine. If it is, it might not be much of anything. Every bit of news from the program would get a lot of attention even if it was a broken fingernail. They don't train very often. Besides, you know how it is here. The opening of that superstore was headline news."

"So you think it was Jeanine." He grabbed clothes from the closet, removed the hangers, and shoved his things into the suitcase.

"I didn't say that."

"A guy wouldn't care if the tips of his fingers were ripped off, and Jeanine is the only female in the program."

"I used a bad example."

"How competent is she?"

"She's the best pilot we have."

"But this training isn't just about flying." He emptied the last drawer and set the items in the suitcase. Then he swept everything from the top of the dresser and dumped them on top of the clothes. "I saw how dangerous a rescue operation can be, remember? I was being rescued. I remember how close they had to fly to the cliff. I remember the problem they had with the basket." He paused and ran his hand through his hair. "There are so many things that can go wrong—things that I don't even know about." He got the last of his possessions from the bathroom, dumped them into the suitcase, and zipped it. "She shouldn't be flying anyway."

"Chris, when you get to her and you see that there's nothing wrong with her, take it easy. Think before you say anything. Don't tell her that you left the conference because you heard about the accident." Nate paused. "Maybe you should let it go at, 'Hi. I came back early because I missed you.' Better yet, just kiss her. Don't say a word. If the kiss is good enough, it will be all the talking you need."

"I'm going to tell her how I feel about this. I have to let her know what the thought of her being hurt did to me. I need to let her know that I can't take this kind of stress, this not knowing." He ran his hand through his hair again. "If she's all right . . ."

"She's all right," Nate said. "Don't blow it, Big Brother. She's the best thing to come your way in forever."

"Don't you think I know that? That's why I can't stand the possibility of losing her." He squashed the fear of the unthinkable so he could do what he had to do. "I'll talk to you after I land."

Six hours later Chris was leaving the nearly empty plane in Honolulu. He rushed into the terminal and checked his voice mail. Then he nodded as he heard Nate's voice giving the training location. Nate hadn't learned the name of the person who was hurt, but the location was a start.

Chris went to get his luggage. Although he was grateful that there weren't many people on the flight and that the luggage came quickly, he still wasn't able to smile. Nate hadn't found out anything about the accident. It could be Jeanine.

He grabbed his bags and went to the car rental booth. Soon he was driving along Route 63. "I should have taken H3," he thought as he battled to keep from going over the speed limit. Then a truck carrying men in back pulled in front of him from a side road. They looked as if they were dressed for farm work, but as slowly as the truck was traveling, they weren't on any time clock. Chris clutched the steering wheel tighter. *No sense getting uptight,* he thought. *The way this road curves there is no way to go around them.* The frown that had been in place since he saw the broadcast in Los Angeles deepened. *You'll get there when you get there.* He had to struggle to accept that fact.

He reached Route 83, and the truck turned off the highway just as a second lane was added. *Now you leave,* he thought as he pushed the car to the speed limit. *She's okay. She's okay. She has to be okay* ran through his mind as he made his way to the training camp in the Kahuku area.

Why way up there? he asked himself as he passed a branch of Brigham Young University. *All right, Chris. You're almost there. Just a little bit farther. Hang on.*

He repeated those thoughts until he pulled into a parking spot in front of the local government offices more than an hour later. He dashed from the car and into the office.

"They're camped inland," the woman at the desk said and went to a map on the wall. She pointed to a narrow road. "If you follow this road, you'll come to a clearing. Park there and walk over the hill, and you'll see their tents." She smiled. "If they're practicing rescue techniques from the air, you'll hear the choppers first." She turned from the map. "If they're off, you'll have to wait for them to return. Drive carefully. That's not the best road in the islands."

"Have you . . ." Chris stopped. She stared at him, waiting. "Have you heard anything about the accident?"

"I think somebody broke something, but I haven't really heard any details."

"Was it serious?"

She shook her head and shrugged. "Sorry. I don't know. Probably not. If so, I would probably remember."

He remembered to thank her and got into his car. When he reached the small road, he made himself slow down. A broken axle wouldn't help him find Jeanine.

It seemed to take hours to reach the clearing that passed for a parking area, but finally he was there. He sprinted from the car, took the hill as if there were a pot of gold over the ridge, and stopped short.

Five tents were grouped around a clearing with a fire ring in the center. Except for a small pavilion with no walls, it resembled a small military camp. Chris looked for signs that anybody was there. He heard voices in the jungle before he could see who was talking. For the first time since he'd heard the broadcast, apprehension eased from him. *Jeanine! One of the voices was hers!* Laughter, followed by more talking, reached him. He found where the voices were coming from and waited. Three people emerged from the trees, strolling as if they had been on a casual outing.

"Chris?" Finally Jeanine was there, standing in front of him, looking as perfect as ever. She was frowning, but she was there.

"Are you all right?" He touched her arm as if he had to make sure she was really standing in front of him and it wasn't a cruel trick of his imagination.

"Sure, I'm all right. What are you doing here? I thought you had another half-week to go before your conference ended. What happened?"

"The conference isn't over." He glanced at the other two people, who made no attempt to pretend that they weren't listening.

"Well, why are you here? We're not supposed to have visitors unless it's an emergency." She frowned at him. "Are you okay? Is Nate okay?"

"I heard about the accident on the news."

"Accident? What accident?"

"Can we go somewhere and talk?" The others moved away, but not so far that they couldn't still hear the conversation. "Maybe we can talk in the car."

Jeanine looked at one of the men, who nodded to her. "Sure."

She let Chris take her hand and walked with him to the parking area. He tried not to notice that she wasn't holding his hand as tightly as he was holding hers. He worked at ignoring the little voice inside that was tugging at him. When they reached his car, she turned to face him before they could get inside.

"What's going on, Chris? Why are you here?"

"A television report said that a trainee in your program had an accident."

"You left your conference because of a news report?" She dropped his hand as if it had become uncomfortably hot.

"They didn't give the name of the person. I—I thought it was you."

"There were six trainees in the program, and you assumed that the one most likely to get hurt was me." She put more space between them than Chris would have liked. Still he plunged on.

"I don't *know* the others. I don't *care* about them." He lowered his voice. *No sense moving away from the others if I'm going to talk loud enough for them to hear.* "I don't want *anybody* to get hurt, but I . . ." He shook his head slightly. "But I thought it was *you*. You don't understand. They didn't say exactly what the accident was. If they broadcast something, especially as a special break, they ought to give the facts. They shouldn't leave people hanging." He frowned. "If they don't have the whole story, they shouldn't scare the public. I thought you had been hurt. Or worse. I thought I had lost you."

If they hadn't made it sound like the greatest disaster of all time, I wouldn't be in this mess. I'd be in Los Angeles concentrating on building instead of trying to justify my actions to Jeanine. He frowned. *Who isn't even glad to see me.*

"I'm fine. In spite of your obvious lack of confidence in my abilities, it wasn't me. Paul got careless and slammed against a cliff. He broke his shoulder. He's going to be fine, too. In fact, he'll come back and complete the training the next time they offer it."

"So you're going to stay here."

"Absolutely. I don't have any reason to leave." She folded her arms across her chest. "I wouldn't have started if I hadn't intended to finish."

"But it's dangerous. The next time it could be you." *Why is she being so stubborn? Doesn't she realize what that broadcast did to me? Why can't she understand my point? Why does she need to risk her life?*

"Life is dangerous, but we don't huddle in our houses, afraid to go out."

"First the helicopter accident. Now this. Maybe somebody is trying to send you a message."

" 'This,' as you called it, didn't involve me except for the fact that I helped carry Paul out."

"I think you should come home."

"Oh? You do?"

"Yes."

"And do what? Should I buy a few shapeless house-dresses and spend my days cooking and cleaning and waiting for you to come home? Would I be allowed to wear shoes, or would the barefoot part be in effect?" She leaned against her own car, putting more distance between them.

"Baby, you're being unreasonable. If you'll just be honest with yourself, you'll admit that this is dangerous." He ignored the closed look that she was giving him and went on. "As if you aren't at risk enough when you fly that fat thing, now you'll be involved in this. More danger. I don't know if you have a death wish or what. I do know that I don't want to wonder about whether or not you'll come back to me each time you go on a mission. It's bad enough worrying about you whenever you fly."

"We already had this conversation, remember?" Her words were quiet. "Flying is what I do and I enjoy it. I'm not thrill seeking. I'm doing an ordinary job that hundreds, maybe thousands, do all over the world every day. I am not pushing the imaginary envelope that you seem to envision." She shifted positions, which put her farther away from him. "Besides, I want this. *I* decided to be part of this training. *Me*. I still am the one who decides for me." Her look was more like Alaska than Hawaii. "I will *always* decide for me, remember? Just as you are the one who decides for you. I thought we were clear on that.

Evidently not." She stared a while longer. "Go back and salvage what you can of your conference." She sighed and shook her head. "This thing between us. It isn't going to work." She pushed off from the car. "Good-bye, Chris."

"Wait," he called when she turned to go. "How can you just leave like this? I thought you cared for me. I thought we had something going. How can you turn your back on it? How can you throw it away?"

"I thought so, too. I do care for you. I care a lot." She swallowed hard as if trying to keep her next words from coming out, but they did anyway. "More than I've ever cared about anybody before. But I can't go through this every time you feel insecure about my job. And it sounds as if that would be all the time. I couldn't live with the constant tension. I can't." She shook her head again. "Good-bye."

Chris watched as she left him. He searched through the entire vocabulary that he had stored in his mind, trying to find the magic words that would make her come back. He exhaled sharply and watched her move into the camp. *If there were such a thing as magic, I could replay this whole scene and start over.* He frowned. *And what? She's right. We did have this conversation before.* The crease between his eyebrows deepened. *It ended this same way then, too.* He frowned. *How can I change how I feel? How can I convince myself that she's perfectly safe when I feel so strongly that she's not? How can I make an impossible choice: lose her now or lose her later?*

He waited for a few minutes for her to return. Then he waited a few more just in case she needed more time. Then he got into his car and drove slowly away, as if hoping she would come after him and make things right and could reach him quickly.

By the time Chris reached the airport road, she still had not appeared. He parked along the side of the road. A steady stream of cars passed by. Finally he pulled out his phone and called Nate. *May as well get his "I told you so" out of the way.*

To Nate's credit, he never used those words. Chris wouldn't have minded if he had. He had lost Jeanine. Nothing else mattered now.

He sat a while longer, then continued to the airport. May as well return to the conference. He could do nothing more here. He had already done too much.

Chris checked into the hotel in Los Angeles and even got his old room back because he'd been gone a short time. It didn't matter. He had been gone long enough to mess up his life.

He managed to resume the conference schedule, but, his mind still on Oahu, nothing made any sense to him. He stayed because he had to be somewhere, and this was as good a place as any.

The conference ended and Chris went home. Two weeks earlier he had wondered how he would be able to stand being away from her. Now, if it had been two years, it wouldn't have mattered. *Jeanine. What is she doing now?*

Jeanine threw herself into activities. Today they were simulating an ocean rescue of passengers from a capsized boat far offshore. If she concentrated hard enough, maybe she could forget that this was the day that Chris was coming home. The ache in her chest was as real as a physical injury. *The heart really can hurt,* she thought while pain settled in and felt permanent.

The instructor called on her, and she forced her attention to him. It was her turn to play victim. *The problem is, there is no victim in our situation. Why are you so closed-minded, Chris?*

She got into the harness and held on as they lowered her to the so-called rescue site. Maybe the cool waters off the rugged coast would distract her. She doubted it, though. *What's he doing now?*

NINETEEN

Chris glanced at the calendar on his office wall, but he wasn't admiring the photograph of a perfect sunset. *I haven't seen her since I got back. Not for a week and a half.* He frowned. *If I hadn't come charging back and gone to the camp that day, would we have found a way to sneak some time together? Would she have gone against the rules for me?* His stare hardened into a glare. *Probably not.* He shook his head. *Definitely not. She wouldn't do anything to jeopardize her place in her precious program. Another week and she'll be finished. She'll be coming home.* He leaned back in his chair. *But not to me. She won't be coming back to me. If it weren't so painful, it would be funny. We worried about how we'd manage to survive being away from each other for four weeks. Neither of us considered the possibility that we'd never be close again.* A sigh escaped from him. He walked to the window.

What can I do to get us past this? I thought I had dealt with it. I thought I was okay with her flying. Then she pushes it further by entering that stupid program. He chewed on his bottom lip. *If she cared about me, she wouldn't do this. If she would try to understand how I feel, she'd be with me now.* He looked out the window, but he paid no attention to what was out there. *What can I do to fix this? There has to be a way. All I have to do is find it.*

The intercom buzzed just as his mind was trying to form an idea. He answered the phone and put his idea on hold. But he didn't dismiss it as ridiculous as he would have after their first argument.

The phone call over, Chris returned to the idea that had been cut off and let it finish forming. Then he made a phone call. After hanging up, his mind was clear. One plan in place, he was ready to work on the others on the paper in front of him.

"We just got a call," Jeanine's instructor, Captain Richards, said. "It looks like we get to see if you folks are ready to put our theories to work." He looked at each of them in turn, then focused on Jeanine. "Stewart. You got the highest marks on water rescue both on paper and in operation. We have a small boat capsized with four passengers aboard. It caught fire and they evacuated, but they sent a May Day before they did. No injuries. We got the call because they're in the water not far from here. It's a straight-up case. Go with Sergeant Bailey. He flies; you get wet." He fixed her with a steady look. "Think you can handle it?"

"Yes, sir." Jeanine was proud that her voice didn't show her apprehension.

"Any questions?"

"No, sir. I'm ready."

She smiled and ordered the quivers in her stomach to stop. *This is it. This is what you wanted. Now you get to see if you can do it.* She focused back on the captain. *Don't miss any last minute instructions.*

"Good." He nodded. "Remember your training. Use what you learned. I wouldn't send you if I didn't think you could handle it. Get going." He smiled slightly. "I'll expect you to give us a full report when you return."

Jeanine ran behind Sergeant Bailey to the chopper and strapped in. Despite the return of the quivers, her smile stayed in place.

Chris arrived at the small building a few miles from the airport an hour before his appointment on Tuesday morning. He parked his car, but he didn't get out. *I must be out of my mind. I've heard of crazy for love, but this is ludicrous. Or at least it would be if I weren't so scared.*

He thought about staying in the car until it was time to go inside, but he was afraid that if he didn't leave the car now, he'd change his mind and go back home. As it was, with every step he took toward the building, he had to fight the urge to turn around and retreat to the safety of home. The only thing that kept him from doing just that was the fact that Jeanine wasn't waiting for him and would never be if he didn't go through with this.

He swallowed hard and entered the building. He checked the directory, then went into the last office on the left. Nothing blocked the view of the airfield, but he did not look to see if the choppers were visible from this distance. He was afraid that they might be.

"I did it, I did it!" A dry Jeanine twirled around in front of her tent. If there was such a thing as a routine rescue, she had just finished participating in one. She hadn't been the pilot, but she had used the procedure she had learned. It worked just as it had in theory.

She took a deep breath, got herself under control and, after managing to adopt the appearance of one who had just completed a routine flight, went to join the others in the pavilion.

An hour later, after many questions, nothing except

smiling faces looked back at her. Captain Richards dismissed them for dinner. Pats on the back and a few high fives didn't make up for the fact that she'd never share her great experience with Chris. She swallowed hard. She'd never share anything with him again.

"You sure you want to eat with us lowly creatures?" One of the men asked as they left the mess line.

"Yeah. If you do see fit to honor us, sit at the head, Oh Great One." The second man bowed, then pulled out a chair for her. "Thereby you can share your wisdom with both of us equally."

"Cut it out, you guys." She sat and shared a meal that she didn't feel like eating and made herself take part in the gentle kidding that lasted through the meal. She wished she could be as enthusiastic about her experience as they were. She would be if something weren't missing from her life. The other two talked about how they planned to celebrate after they finished with the program. Jeanine was glad she didn't have to participate in the conversation. She had other things on her mind.

When I get home, I have to call him. We have to work this out. She frowned. *How? He objects to my flying, and I won't give it up. There has to be a way through this. I just have to find it.* She shook her head. *No,* we *have to find it. How do I approach him?*

The training period ended, and the three trainees rode the van to the airport. When they arrived, a crowd of reporters greeted them as it had before they left. This time any questions directed at Jeanine concerned her participation in the rescue. Only one reporter asked her to compare being on both sides of a rescue. After that, the questions were general or directed at the two men.

During both the press conference and the ceremony

awarding the certificates, Jeanine's gaze panned the audience several times, but it never found the person she was looking for. It never found Chris.

Chris sat behind the wheel of his car and leaned back. *That wasn't as hard as I thought it would be.* He smiled. *They say education can free you, and I guess that's right.* He frowned. *I never thought I'd even consider learning to fly, and here I am.* He sighed. *This comes under the category "The Things We Do For Love." And I do love her. I hope it's not too late to convince her of that.* He shook his head. *That's not the problem. The problem is to find a way to make her believe that we can make this work.*

Ironically, he had just completed his first week of classes in the basics of piloting two days after Jeanine finished her training. He hadn't decided whether to follow through and actually become a pilot. Aside from the fact that a lot of hours were needed, his motivation had not been to fly as anything other than a passenger. His sole purpose had been to simply understand the theory so that he could address his unease. His goal had been to believe that piloting was safe. Maybe it wasn't as safe as constructing a building, but nevertheless, it was a safe occupation. He thought about Jeanine.

When the rescue trainees returned to Hilo, pictures of the graduation ceremony had filled the front page of the newspapers, and the press conference for the event had made the news on all of the television stations.

Unlike the last time, when Chris rushed away from Los Angeles because of a news report, this news didn't make him want to act. This time it was definitely a happy story. Even if it had not been, he would have thought things through before racing to Jeanine.

He put the key in the ignition but didn't start the car. Instead his mind replayed the day.

He had been tempted to go to the ceremony instead of watching it on television. He had also been tempted to call her when he figured she had had enough time to get home. He had even been tempted to go there and surprise her, congratulate her. But he resisted all of those temptations.

This time his instinct told him to wait. He had to be further along in what he was doing before he faced her again. He knew that if she would talk to him at all, a heavy discussion would take place. He had to be sure that he could give her proof that he had changed, that his mindset was different from the pre-flight days. He smiled. *I think I'll see this through to the end. It must be a feeling of great power to control something so huge.* He nodded. *Yeah. I'm going to finish.* He started the car. *I have to go see her. How can I do it so she'll hear me out instead of slamming the door in my face?*

"See? She is here in the news again. I say . . ."

"I do not care what you say. We will not discuss her again. That is not what we are here for." Abdul turned to Kareem, who stepped forward and spoke.

"There has been a minor problem at the lab so our plans have been delayed. Someone chanced across the cabin." He looked at Hassan. "Before you ask, it was not her. The description did not fit." He turned his attention back to Abdul. "No one saw inside, but our people decided to move the operation."

"Are they certain that they were not compromised?"

"A group of hikers got close and asked for directions. Fortunately, one of our people was outside at the time and was able to send them away." His stare found Hassan again. "Had you been there, your behavior would have made the entire operation worthless."

"You do not know what I would do."

"All of us involved know what action you would have taken."

"You are not in charge." Hassan strode toward him and stopped only a scant foot away. "You have no right to speak to me that way."

"I am in charge and I concur with Kareem." Abdul watched Hassan a few seconds longer before turning back to Kareem. "Continue."

"They have moved farther toward the interior and onto a steep slope. No one should venture there even by accident. There is nothing of interest to anyone except us."

"How long a delay? They are getting impatient back home."

"Not long. It is just a matter of getting things set up again, and that will go quickly. In fact, they should be finished in three days, and then they can continue with the growth of the fungus. Then it is just a matter of waiting until it is ready. When it is, it will be a simple matter to distribute it to our men already on the farms."

"We will meet in a week. It will be too early for distribution, but we will know exactly when to put the next phase into operation. I trust that the news at that time will be good."

They left as they always did: one at a time and with long intervals between them.

"Hey, Nate. Miss me?" Jeanine stopped at the machine shop before she went inside.

"It has been so quiet around here these last three weeks that I thought I was dreaming."

"I missed having somebody to argue with, too." Her smile slipped. "How's the house coming along?"

"It's coming. It would probably be done if I hadn't kept having Chris make changes." He stared at her. "When you two gonna fix this rift?"

"Some things can't be fixed." She blinked hard several times.

"This isn't one of them."

"I—I have to go. I have a flight." She turned away.

"You coming to my open house?"

"I probably won't be able to make it." She never turned around. Nate shook his head as he watched her leave.

Jeanine, still trying to get her mind back on track and off Chris, picked up her flight plan and went to the field. It was a little difficult adjusting to regular flights after the intensity of what she had been through for three weeks. But not as difficult as accepting that she and Chris were through.

She pasted on a smile and waited for her passengers to arrive. Her smile dropped when she saw Chris coming toward her. Her heart leaped as if to meet him, but settled back to normal. *Don't get your hopes up. You'll only get hurt again. Nothing has changed.*

She stared at him. *Why couldn't he leave me alone?* She opened the folder to keep from having to took at him. *That's not what I want. The last thing I want is for him to leave me alone.* She breathed deeply. *But I don't want to be hurt again, either.*

"Hi, Jeanine."

She didn't think it was possible, but he looked better than ever as he came toward her. When he reached her, she tightened her hold on the folder as if she expected a hurricane-force wind to try to rip it from her hands. *I will not reach for him. I will not check to make sure that he's really here. I won't go through that pain again.*

"I—I have to go. I have a flight."

"I know. I'm your passenger."

"Oh." She frowned at the folder crumpled in her hand. *Why didn't I check the passenger list? Maybe I would have been more prepared for this.* "Do you need more pictures of your building site?"

"No." He shook his head slowly, but his gaze never left her. "To start with, I need to talk with you. After that, I'll share what else is on my Needs List." It was her turn to shake her head.

"There's nothing new for us to say. At the end, it will just come down to 'good-bye.' I can't go through that again."

"I paid for an hour and a half, and I want it."

"Okay." She sighed. "Get in." She led him to the chopper. It was hard to do, but she turned toward him. She opened the folder, glad to have somewhere to look instead of at him. "It says here that you said you don't want the usual flight, but it doesn't say where you want to go." She forced herself to look at him. "You just said that you don't need . . ." She stumbled on the word "need." Then she found her train of thought and went on. "You don't have to go over the site again. What do you want?"

"You."

"Chris, don't do this."

"I paid for the time. Let's spend it sitting in the chopper. Just give me one more chance."

"You don't want to go up?"

"I don't want to mess with your concentration."

"What?"

"Wait a minute." He held up both hands. "I'm not saying that you can't talk and fly at the same time. I know you can, remember? I'm only saying that I want your full attention. This is too important to give it anything less. This affects our future." He took a deep breath. "Please, Jeanine. Give us another chance."

She watched him as if waiting for him to give her an out. When he didn't, she shook her head slowly, but said, "There's no reason to sit in the chopper. My car will do. Let me turn off the engine and notify Hal of the change in plans." She inhaled deeply and then exhaled. *I hope I don't regret this.*

She climbed into the cockpit and shut down the engine, but she didn't get out right away. She spent a few seconds trying to prepare herself for the conversation that was to come. When she couldn't find anything else to do inside, she slowly returned to him.

Silently they walked to her car. They walked close to each other, but they didn't hold hands. They didn't even touch.

"Okay," she said after he slid into the passenger seat beside her. "What has changed?" She appeared to be talking to the windshield.

"Not what—who. I have."

"I know." She nodded. "You're sorry. You won't even hint, again, about me dumping my career. You also agree that decisions about my life are mine to make." The look she gave him held sadness mixed with resignation. "Did I leave anything out?"

"Yes." He hoped that what he had to say would erase what he was seeing in her eyes. "I'm taking flying lessons."

"You're what?"

"I'm taking . . ."

"Never mind repeating it. I heard what you said; I just have a hard time believing it." She frowned. "You don't even feel at ease as a passenger. How can you do this? Why are you doing it?"

At least the sadness was gone. He felt a little more optimistic. Surprise had taken over. That was a ton better than sorrow.

"It wasn't easy at first, but I hung in there. I've been taking classes since the week before you came back." Love filled the gaze that he fixed on her. "As for the why, you have to know the answer to that."

"But you're uncomfortable flying."

"You got that almost right. I was *afraid*. But I was more afraid of never having you in my life again." He dared to hold her hand. He relaxed a bit more when she didn't pull away. "You know, like that green eggs thing, I found that I like it." He smiled—the first smile he had used in a long time. Since the last time they had been together.

He told her about the classes and how he planned to continue. He talked until his throat was dry. A couple of times he gave her a chance to say something, but she didn't use it.

Finally he reached the previous day in his story. Then he had nothing left to try to convince her that he had changed. He tightened his hold on her hand and waited.

"I can't see you in the pilot's seat."

"A short while ago, I couldn't see me there, either."

"You really have been taking flying lessons?"

"Only the classroom part." He shook his head. "I can't begin to describe how much work it was to persuade myself that I could do it." He dared to touch the side of her face. "I intend to continue. I'm going to follow this to the end."

"You're going to leave your dangerous construction job and get a job flying?"

"Baby, I'm not going to go that far. But I will learn to get off the ground, fly around so that I'm convinced that being up there is scientifically feasible, and then safely land. I have read so many statistics about the number of helicopter flights on any given day. I have memorized charts that show how rare accidents are. I have even examined the insurance companies' tables and charts." He eased her against his side. "Do you know that the rates for many other professions are a lot higher than those for pilots in general? And those for helicopter pilots are even lower?"

"Oh, Chris." She leaned away so she could look into his face. "I missed you." She shook her head and smiled. "I can't believe that you did that for me. For us."

"Baby, I love you. I'd do anything to prove that to you."

"You know, I wasn't trying to push you into doing something as drastic as that. I wasn't trying to push you into anything." She swallowed hard. "I—I just didn't see how we were going to get over how you feel about my job."

"Felt. Past tense. I have to admit that it was almost impossible for me to walk into that building for the first class. Only the thought of never having you again made me go through with it. I was more scared of that." He smiled. "Then, gradually I began to understand the logistics and the theory of aerodynamics. The more I understood, the more comfortable I became with the idea." He rubbed his thumb along the back of her hand. I should have taken those lessons a long time ago." He brushed his lips across hers. Then he pulled back. "I have missed you something fierce."

"Not as much as I've missed you." She leaned her head against his chest. They sat like that for a long time.

"How many flights do you have today?" Chris kissed the top of her head.

"Too many." She stroked his chest. Then she glanced at her watch and groaned. "I have to go. My next flight is in twenty minutes, and I have to get the information from the office. I have one more after that."

"I should have paid for all three flights."

"Paying for flights with me and not taking them would not be a wise use of money."

"I don't know. It would let us get together sooner." He smiled and removed his arm and groaned. "I guess if you gotta go, you gotta go."

"Yeah. I guess so." Jeanine moved a few inches away from him. "Okay, we both get out of the car right now."

"Not on three?"

"If we wait for three, we might change our minds." She chuckled. "Okay. Now." Neither moved. "I know it's hard, but we can do this."

"Don't say 'hard.' Say 'difficult.' Just don't use the word 'hard.' Okay?"

"Most definitely." She touched his chest once more, then slid from the car. Slowly he did the same. He walked around to her side and gathered her into his arms.

"I have to go." She moved closer until the lengths of their bodies were touching.

"I know." He kissed her forehead, then her cheek, then her forehead again. "Your place or mine?" he asked as he moved away from her.

"Either." She grinned. "It doesn't matter."

"Your place. I'll bring dinner." He moved against her. "You can be dessert." He kissed her, then backed away. "Until tonight, sweetness." He winked, then turned and went to his car.

She didn't have much time, but she waited until his car disappeared before she went into the hangar.

"I didn't know what to wear so I could impress you," Jeanine said when she opened the door to Chris.

She turned around slowly after he stepped inside. The skirt of her red dress moved with her as she turned. Then it settled back into place. The slightly loose-fitting top moved a bit, too. She grinned at him and held out her arms. "You like?"

"I more than like." He pulled her close and took her with him as he set the bag he was carrying on the hall table. Then he turned and wrapped both arms around her. Soon they were lost in the kind of kiss that they both had hungered for since their breakup. He eased a few inched away. "The dress is beautiful, but what's underneath is more beautiful."

"Are you sure? It's been a long time since you've checked."

"Too long." He rubbed his hand along her back. "I know how we can find out." His hand brushed the sides of her breasts.

"You mean, like an experiment?" She felt as if someone had decided that she had used up her allotment of air.

"No." His hand found the fullness of one breast and stroked across the tip. "Not unless our goal is to prove what we know is true." He wrapped his hands around her hips and pulled her close. Her response was to wriggle against him. His response was to groan. She wrapped her hands around his shoulders and tugged him closer. Then she captured his mouth with hers and swallowed his moan.

He lifted her and carried her to her bedroom.

"I have missed you more than I can say." He unfastened her buttons and quickly slid her dress from her.

"Not any more than I have missed you." Her fingers worked quickly and soon his shirt joined her dress on the floor.

Working as if somebody were timing them, they helped each other remove the other barriers between them. No words were necessary. Chris lifted her onto the bed and quickly followed.

His mouth found her breast. Jeanine moaned and

pressed closer. She ran her hands along his hips and hung on as if afraid of falling.

His hand stroked her thigh, then moved to her front. His mouth moved to her other breast. He could feel that she was ready. He positioned himself between her thighs.

"Please," she breathed as he found the most sensitive part of her body.

"Yes, baby." He made himself enter her slowly when what he wanted was to hurry and find relief.

Soon they were trying to make up for the time they had been apart—trying to rush to the place that they could only reach together.

"Do you have to work today?" Chris stroked the leg that was draped over his.

"Not until this afternoon." Her hand found his waist and stayed there. "How about you?"

"I'm playing hooky." He kissed her gently.

"The perks of being the boss, huh?" She pressed her mouth to the flat button hiding within his chest hair. She brushed her tongue over it. Then she smiled as he groaned and his arousal pressed further against her.

"I guess we'd better take advantage of the time." He explored her body slowly and gently, pausing whenever she favored him with a gasp or a moan. Then they traveled to their private place again.

"I have an idea." Jeanine traced a finger down his face. "Let's pretend to be tourists."

"Tourists?" Chris drew her finger into his mouth and licked it.

"Stop."

"You want me to stop?" He ran a hand over her hair.

"Not really, but we have to leave this bed sometime."

"I don't know why." He pressed a kiss to her forehead.

"Change of pace." She squeezed his arm. "We have to take a break before we kill ourselves."

"Yeah, but what a way to go." They both laughed. "Okay." He shifted. "On three."

She laughed again. "Why is it always three?"

"Because two is not enough and four gives you too much time to think." He shifted all the way from her, then forced himself to stand. "Come on." He reached for her hand and pulled her up.

"Dibs on the shower first." Jeanine headed for the hall.

"We're not going to share?"

"Not this time. If we do we'll be having this same conversation again tomorrow." She winked at him. "We can share something better later."

"Promise?"

"You got it."

"Don't you mean I'll get it?"

Their laughter blended as she entered the bathroom.

TWENTY

"Are you ready?" Jeanine stood at the door of her bedroom.

"I guess so, if you insist on leaving right now." Chris walked slowly toward her. He stopped only when he was standing against her. "Seven o'clock in the morning is very early to be leaving for anything. I can think of better things to do this early."

"We had this conversation last night before we went to bed, and you showed me 'better things to do with my time.'" She smiled. "You showed me again during the night and yet again before daybreak, so don't expect any pity from me when I won't let you show me *again* right now." She stood on her toes and kissed his chin.

"You left out yesterday afternoon." As he closed his hands around her hips, she pulled away. "No, no, no. That kiss was just a preview of what's to come when we get back—if you're good."

"I thought I *was* good." He drew her against him again. "If I wasn't, we can practice right now, and you can tell me where I need to improve." He rubbed against her and nuzzled her cheek. "What do you say?"

"There is no room for improvement." She tried to frown, but the sparkle in her eyes gave her away. "I'm talking about appropriate behavior in public." She grabbed his hand and tugged him toward the front door.

"Oh. That." He overemphasized the sigh that he released. Jeanine giggled and shook her head. "Okay," he said. "Let's get this over with."

"This is not something to 'get over with.' We will enjoy the venture. We're merely tourists on our way to explore the farms and to sample the coffee for which Kona is famous." She grinned. "It's been a long time since I've been over to that side of the island," she said as they left the house. "Taking the tours will be worth the long drive ahead."

Chris opened the car door for her, and she slid in. Soon they were on Highway 11, making the long drive around the island to Kailua Kona and the many coffee farms in that area.

"We have tasted coffee mixed with every flavor that man could come up with," Chris said hours later. "I have even sampled chocolate-covered coffee beans." He grimaced. "Definitely not one of my favorites. We have so much caffeine floating through our systems that we won't be able to sleep for a week."

"We haven't been doing much sleeping since we got back together, anyway." Jeanine tapped his chest. "But okay. There's one more farm that I want to visit. We don't want them to feel neglected, do we?"

"I guess the answer is supposed to be 'no,' huh?"

"You are so smart." She wrapped her arm through his, and they walked back to the car. "Do you know what I want to do?"

"Make love under a coffee tree?"

"You have a one-track mind."

"But it's an interesting track."

"True. However, making love under the coffee trees is a good idea if we want an audience." She squeezed his arm. “But that’s not what I had in mind.” She put their latest gift-shop purchase into the trunk.

“We have to go back soon anyway.” Chris glanced into the trunk before he shut it. “The trunk is full.”

“We can’t stop at a farm and not buy something. It’s not right.” They walked around to the front and got into the car.

“It’s a good thing that there aren’t any diamond mines to tour.”

“Very funny. You changed the subject. I want to pick coffee beans.”

“You want to do what?”

“Don’t you think that would be fun?”

“We can ask the folks who try to make a living at it.” He drove out of the parking lot and headed for Highway 180.

“Well, if not fun, it would be interesting.”

“Maybe for the first ten or twenty beans.”

“Good. I’m glad you agree with me.”

“ ‘Communications gap’ does not begin to describe what we have here.” He glanced at her and smiled. Then he slowed and gave the sharp curves his full attention. Finally they were in the parking lot of the last farm.

“Aloha, folks. My name is Alan and I’ll be your tour guide. We have an orientation film about the industry.”

“I don’t think we need to watch it,” Chris said. “We’ve been visiting farms all day. We could probably give a tour ourselves.”

“I’d like to pick some coffee beans,” Jeanine said to Alan.

“A lot of tourists want to pick their own coffee. They don’t realize how many steps it takes before coffee is ready for drinking.” He laughed. “Neither do they realize how many beans it takes to make a pound of ground coffee.”

“I don’t want to pick enough for that.” Jeanine didn’t explain that they weren’t tourists. “I just want to see what it’s like.”

“I’ll take you to the section that we’re working today.

You have to stay out of the way of the workers, though. Each one is trying to pick about two hundred pounds."

"Two hundred pounds? In one day?"

"Some manage three hundred. Of course, some don't even come close. We have a few new pickers who are still trying to master the technique. And that's after they learn the difference between ripe and almost ripe. But if that's want you want, come on."

The rich coffee aroma became stronger as they walked several yards to the trees and then a few hundred yards more through the rows of trees. Finally Alan stopped and handed them small charts and aluminum pails.

"Here you are. That chart will show you what color the ripe beans are." He grinned. "When you get tired, come on back to the office. I'd give you a bag to dump the beans into, but I doubt if you'll be out here that long. Have fun."

"We will." After Alan left, Jeanine turned to Chris. "Okay. Where do we start?"

"I'm with you. I'm only here because you promised me a reward later."

"Chris, Chris, Chris. You are insatiable."

"Um hmm," he responded. Jeanine laughed and led the way.

She browsed along the rows as though waiting for a tree to identify itself as the one she was looking for. Finally she stopped at a tree that looked like all of the others. She glanced at the pickers a few feet away.

"Look how fast they pick. I don't see how they can work that fast and still pick the right color. I wonder how long they . . ." She gasped as her stare met that of one of the workers. Her pail tumbled to the ground, but she didn't bother to pick it up. She backed up a few feet, but her eyes stayed on the man. She would have backed up more, but Chris was blocking her way.

"What is it?" He glanced at the trees, at the men, then down at her.

"We have to get out of here." She grabbed his hand.

"What's the matter?" He followed her line of vision. "Do you know him?"

"Come on." She was still looking at the man. He stared at her as hard as she looked at him. Finally, she turned and pulled at Chris. She looked back once more and saw the man start walking toward them. "Let's go!" She dropped Chris's hand and ran toward the car.

"What's going on?"

"Get in! He's coming!" She jumped in the car and fastened her seatbelt. "Come on, Chris!"

He got behind the wheel and started the car. "Want to tell me what's going on?"

"We should have brought our cell phones." She looked back toward the trees. The man had stopped before stepping into the clearing. "Hurry!"

"You said you didn't want us to be interrupted. Remember?" He drove onto the highway. "And we can't hurry on this road. Not if we want to reach 180 safely."

"Find a phone. I have to call the police."

"Tell me what's going on." He glanced at her, but quickly gave his attention back to the road.

As they rode, Jeanine kept looking over her shoulder. Still, she managed to explain about the man at the cabin that she had chanced upon when she was hiking on Maui. It had happened months before, but her body trembled at the memory of the gun.

"I cannot reach Kareem so I called you." Elam leaned against a tree with his back to the other pickers. They were too far away to hear what he was saying on the cell phone, but he kept his voice low, anyway. "I'm not sure what to make of this. I have only seen her in pictures in the newspaper, but she seemed to recognize me."

"You did the right thing, Elam. He would just go to Abdul, but Abdul no longer makes wise decisions. Again he would say it is nothing." Hassan stood against the windowsill in his apartment and looked out on the alley. "You have the license number?" He nodded. "Good. I will take care of this." He quickly, but carefully, wrote down the string of letters and numbers.

"I will try to reach Kareem again."

"No. I will take care of this. You must leave that place in case she knows something about you. Follow them. If the opportunity is given to you . . ." Hassan paused. "The road is made of many sharp curves. Accidents happen. Perhaps you can help one occur." Again he stopped. "It is unfortunate that I am so far away. I would take care of this properly. Go. You are wasting time. Keep me informed."

Elam avoided the farmhouse and went directly to his car. He drove as fast as he could, grateful that the farm was at the end of the road and that he didn't have to wonder if he was going in the right direction. He glanced at the glove compartment and wondered if he would have a chance to take care of the woman and the man and get away. He shook his head. No matter. If he was successful with her, the rest did not matter. The man did not seem to know whatever it was that the woman knew. He increased his speed. First he would have to catch them.

Ten minutes later the horn of an oncoming car made Elam move completely to his own side of the road. Fifteen minutes after that he saw the car he was looking for near the curve ahead, following the edge of a cliff. He speeded up and tried to catch it. Soon. A truck's horn in the opposite lane made him swerve back to his side of the road. He gunned his motor, and his wheels tried to find traction in the soft dirt of the shoulder. He pushed the gas pedal as far down as it would go, but the soil still refused to hold. His car teetered on the sharp edge of road and slid to the rim of the cliff. He leaned forward as if that would help him get back on the road. Then he turned to look back. His rear wheels hung in the air, then tipped down as he moved. He turned back to face the front and leaned forward again, but it was too late. Still upright, the car began to slide slowly down the hill.

Elam loosened his hold on the steering wheel. It was a long way to the bottom, but if this was how it would be, he would be ready. Already he was planning how he would find the woman again and do what he must.

Then the car hit a rock that was large enough to give him hope that he would not have a long climb back to the road. In an instant he learned that it was too small to hold him. He leaned on the horn as if that would help and pushed the brake pedal down as far as it would go, but the car refused to obey. It left the ground, traveling through the air before it landed hundreds of yards below. His horn still sounded.

Above, tires screeched as vehicles from both directions stopped along the sides of the road. People rushed from them and peered over the side of the cliff.

When they heard the horn, Jeanine had looked out the rear window.

"Stop!" she said needlessly. Chris was already pulling off the road in front of another car. They raced back the few hundred yards to the scene of the accident.

"Maybe some of my first aid training will help," Jeanine said as she made her way to the front of the small crowd gathered around the tire scuff marks leading over the cliff edge. She looked down at the car.

"I don't think you'll get the chance." Chris held her

arm to prevent her from trying to reach the bottom. The danger was obvious.

"There's no way down. At least, not on foot." She scanned the crowd. "Did somebody call 911?"

"I did," a young woman said. "The operator told me a car was in the area. It should be here soon." She came over and stood beside Jeanine. "The car didn't turn over. Do you think the driver is all right?"

Only if it wasn't his time to go, Jeanine thought as she stared at the vehicle. It looked as if it had gone through the car-flattening machine at the recycling plant near the Philadelphia Airport.

Elam, eyes closed, sat strapped behind the wheel, but he was not aware of the commotion above or the fact that there was no road out of where he was. He was not aware of anything.

The contents of the glove compartment were scattered on the seat beside him. It looked as if somebody had flung his papers into the air like large pieces of confetti. As if his gun were playing a game and waiting for someone to find it, it lay almost hidden under the papers.

TWENTY-ONE

"He was tearing along this road like he had to be somewheres yesterday," the truck driver said. "I blew my horn. I had to. He was headed right at me." He glanced at his truck. "No way his little car coulda come out okay from that." He took a step closer to the edge and peered over the side. "Don't look like he done too well as it is. Maybe I shouldn't've blown at him. But what else could I do? He was way into my lane. It was like he thought this was a one-way road and he was going the right way." He stretched a little farther. "I didn't have no place to move over. As it was, I scraped the cliff." He glanced around at the others in the crowd. "What else could I do?"

"Nothing." A woman came closer. "I was in front of him until he passed me on the wrong side. He almost ran me into the cliff, too." She gazed over the edge. "Look where speeding got him."

The agreeing murmurs of the crowd mingled as Jeanine and Chris stared at the car with the others. They watched as members of the rescue team took out equipment and walked from where they were parked on the narrow service road below the wrecked car.

The climb to reach the site covered many steep yards from the dirt road, and they had to maneuver over loose rocks and soil. Jeanine felt her body tense as if doing so would help the rescuers carry the awkward stretcher and unwieldy equipment up the rough hillside. She and the others watched intensely as the crew tried to use the jaws-of-life equipment to pry open the door. When that didn't work, they lit a torch. Slowly, with sparks flying and then disappearing, they worked to cut open the side of the car.

If it's that bad, how could anybody survive? Jeanine thought as the team finally peeled back the metal. *What would make somebody speed on this kind of road?* she wondered. A nagging idea tugged at her, but she ignored it as if giving the rescue her full attention would make their efforts more successful.

One of the crew climbed in and took the board that another handed him. She couldn't see it, but Jeanine knew they were strapping the driver to a body board. She watched as, as slowly as he'd gone in, the rescuer inside and one of the others eased the board out.

"He's alive?" The truck driver asked as they all saw that the sheet was pulled up only to a man's neck. The crowd clapped. Jeanine tightened her hold on Chris's arm.

"Must not have been his time," Chris murmured as he put his arm around her waist. Standing close, they watched as the two men slowly carried the stretcher down to the waiting ambulance.

"I don't know how he survived," Jeanine said. "Even so, the impact must have done major damage, especially to the spinal cord." She exhaled heavily. "We may as well leave. We can't do anything here."

Slowly, the crowd drifted apart. Just as slowly, one by one, the motors started and everybody drove away.

The quiet in the car with Jeanine and Chris was heavier than any words could be. Chris drove more slowly than he had been driving before.

Jeanine's nagging thought returned, but she didn't share it with Chris. Neither one spoke until they reached the police station, although their hands remained grasped together during the entire ride. They were still holding hands when they walked inside the small building and told the man at the desk about the call they had made.

"They're here," he said into the intercom. Then he looked at them. "The chief will be out in a few seconds.

"I checked with Detective Hagasi on Maui, and he filled me in," the man who identified himself as Chief Green told them. "Hagasi said that the description that you gave him was . . ." He hesitated.

"Vague," Jeanine finished his sentence. "That's true, but I know that the man I saw today at the farm was the same man."

"Do you think you can give us a description?"

"I'm sure of it. Today he didn't have his gun to distract me."

"Let's give it a try." Green led them to a small office near the back.

"Lieutenant Clark will work with you." He left them.

"Please sit down." Lieutenant Clark opened the small loose-leaf book on the table in front of them. Chris squeezed her hand, then sat in a chair against the wall.

"We'll start with the shape of his face and then move to his features. Okay?"

Jeanine nodded and looked at the face outlines as the lieutenant slowly turned the book's pages.

"Nothing?" he asked when he reached the end of the section.

"I'm sorry." She frowned. "I never realized that there were so many different shapes."

"That's okay. We'll go through them again. You don't have to get it perfect. Stop me if you think one comes close. Don't think about it. Go with your first impression. We'll add the hair later, but if you'll think in relation to his hairline, it might help. If you decide later that you didn't pick the right one, we'll try again. Okay?"

Jeanine nodded and took a deep breath. *How can I be so sure that I'll recognize him if I'm not even sure of the shape of his face?* She glanced at Chris. He smiled and nodded encouragement.

"Okay. Here we go." Clark turned to the first page and started again.

"I think that's it," Jeanine said when he had almost reached the last one. She sighed. "But I'm not positive."

"That's okay. We'll work with this one and see how it goes. Next we try for the hair." He smiled at her. "He did have hair, didn't he?"

"Yeah. Nothing extreme, just a normal hair style. I'll bet you have a lot of so-called normal hairstyles in your book right?"

"We also have some not so normal ones. Let's get started."

They didn't get far before Green came in with another man.

"This is Agent Dillard. His agency has assigned him to this case."

"Any relation to Agents Monroe and Sullivan?" Jeanine asked.

Agent Dillard's face remained stoic. "We work together."

"I hope you have better manners than Monroe does."

"These are tough times." Dillard turned to Clark. "Thank you. I'll take it from here."

"You can't be related to them," Jeanine said after Clark and Green had left. "The words 'thank you' are foreign to them."

A quick knock sounded on the door before Dillard responded. Green entered the room again.

"Could the man have been following you?"

"I don't know. Why? Do you want me to look at a lineup?"

"If it's who I have in mind, he won't be in a lineup."

"The man in the car that went over?" Jeanine stood.

"Possibly."

"I thought about that, but I didn't want it to be true. He was guarding a field of marijuana. What's he doing here?" She frowned. "That man didn't see me. He couldn't have. He—he would have killed me if he had."

"I don't know. Did you say anything to him?"

"You mean like, 'I saw you with a big gun when you were guarding that pot crop on Maui'?" She shook her head. "Of course I didn't say anything to him."

"Maybe it's not the same man."

"But she did react." Chris moved closer to Jeanine. "Baby, you had that shocked look as you backed away from him."

"Oh, man." She nodded. "I know I did. But I couldn't help it. I never expected to see him again. Certainly not doing something as innocuous as picking coffee beans after holding that huge gun. Besides, he was on Maui."

"Excuse me." Dillard walked over to Green. "Can I talk to you in the hall?"

Jeanine and Chris watched as the door closed.

"I guess he is related to the other two. At least a little." Chris glanced at the door.

"Yeah. He left us, but he said, 'Excuse me.' "

"And he asked instead of ordering."

"Do you think the accident victim is the same man?"

"If it is, you don't have to worry about him bothering you for a long time, if ever."

Sounds seeped in from the hall, and several times footsteps seemed to pause outside the door, but nobody came in. Chris had his hand on the doorknob when the door opened.

"I have a picture for you to look at," Dillard said, but he made no move to give it to her. "Remember, he was in a terrible accident." He shrugged. "You know that. You were there. Anyway, he looks real rough. They cleaned him up as best they could, but considering . . ." He stared at her. "Anyway, here it is. You might want to sit down."

"Is he still alive?"

"At least for now."

Jeanine took a deep breath, but she didn't sit. Slowly, she took the photograph from him and turned it over.

The victim's eyes were closed as if he was just asleep. The fact that both eyes were black and bruises covered the rest of the swollen face showed that it was more than that. An oxygen mask covered the mouth and nose.

"I know it's difficult considering the condition of his face," Dillard said. "I asked them if they could remove the mask just long enough for a photograph, but they said that they couldn't. They took this before taking him into the operating room so they could try to find his next of kin. He didn't have any identification on him." He watched Jeanine, who was looking at the picture. "That alone is enough to hold our attention. I'm sure he doesn't look the way he usually does. If necessary, you can try again after the swelling goes down—if he survives that long."

"We don't need to wait. This is the same man." Jeanine was surprised at how calm her voice was. Fear and questions and the unreality of it all skipped through her, yet she managed to sound as if she were talking about a man whom she just happened to pass on the street and who had been handing out advertisements.

"You're sure?"

"Positive." She handed the picture back. "Now what?"

"We take it from here," Dillard called over his shoulder as he pulled out his cellular phone and left the room. "We got a match," he said as he closed the door.

Chris and Jeanine looked at the door and then at each

other. They were still wondering what to do when Green came in.

"So. It's the same man?"

"Yes. What is he doing here?"

"I'm sure Agent Dillard will find out." He smiled at her. "He's probably trying to decide if I'm worthy of sharing his information." He shook his head. "I hope we don't get into a territorial struggle over this. It's my accident case until he tells me different." He held out his hand. "Thank you for coming in. I wish I could tell you that I'll keep you posted, but I have a feeling that I'm going to have to fight to stay in the loop myself." He opened the door for them.

As Jeanine and Chris left the building, they turned over in their minds what had just happened.

"What do you think is going on?" Jeanine asked, once they were on the way home.

"I have no idea. What's the connection between a pot crop on Maui and a coffee farm here?"

Although they knew that they wouldn't come up with answers, that didn't stop them from trying to.

TWENTY-TWO

"I did what needed to be done." Hassan didn't look at Abdul as he spoke. Instead, he stared at the screen of the small television in his apartment.

The face of a badly battered Elam filled the screen, but Hassan was unconcerned as the reporter pleaded for information about the accident patient. Those who knew Elam would never come forward.

"Look what you have done." Abdul drew Hassan's attention, and he turned to Abdul.

"I do not know why you are worried. No one will tell, and there is no way to trace him to us. He should have been more careful. He will not survive the next hour if he is not already dead." He shrugged. "He knew the risks. When he volunteered he was prepared to give his life to further our cause."

"The order to follow the woman was not yours to give." Abdul kept a distance between them, but his voice reached across it.

"Elam called me because he could not reach you." Hassan turned off the television. "Or perhaps he did not try very hard. Perhaps he knew that, if he had spoken to you, you would not have given the correct order. That woman can do us damage."

"Still, Elam did not succeed, so the woman is still out there. It was for nothing. He has brought attention upon himself and possibly us for nothing." He took a step closer. "What does she know? That a man picking coffee beans startled her."

"Elam suspects that she saw him with the crops on Maui. He said that is the only explanation for the way she acted. She is most likely the reason why the site was discovered."

"We do not know that. Even if it is true, what harm can it do us? Laborers move from one island to the next all the time. She still would only know that a man with the marijuana crop was also working on a coffee farm. It still is not traceable to us." Again he moved closer. "Again you have overstepped your position."

"Again I have taken action that needed to be taken."

"Have you considered that Elam will survive? If he does, he will talk. He is not as strong as others. That is why he was put in that position. He does not know much, but he knows enough to arouse suspicion. *He* is the one with information that can hurt us. *He* is the one who can link the two crops. If he reveals what little he knows, the entire assignment will fail, and it will be your fault. If you had not given him orders, the situation would be thus: a woman who may or may not have seen Elam with the crop on Maui saw him on the coffee farm in Kona. That is all they would have known. Elam could have disappeared. I could have sent him home. Now, look."

"Elam knows what to do."

"If he is able. He could have gone home and worked for us on another project." Abdul's glare was harsh enough to make Hassan falter. "I am awaiting orders regarding you. I have told them what you have done. You will report to the cabin this evening. I will have new instructions by then." For once Hassan didn't answer. His response was to show resentment on his face. Abdul continued to glare.

"I will see you this evening at the usual time. Do not be late." He glared a few seconds longer, then left.

Hassan looked out the window and watched Abdul cross the narrow street. He continued to look out long after Abdul had caught the bus. The view did not hold his attention. His mind was busy forming and discarding various plans.

"Sure we can't put this off?" Chris nuzzled Jeanine's ear and moved his hand slowly from her knee to her hip.

"Um hmm." She moved her head slightly to allow him access to more of her neck. His hand moved up to her breast and stroked along the side. She shifted to make it easier for him to find the waiting tip.

"Is that a yes or a no?" Chris allowed his finger to skim across the tip. Then he gently turned her to face him.

"It's . . ." She moaned as he tugged on the tip. "I can't think straight."

"Don't try. Just feel."

"That's why I can't think straight." Reluctantly, she stilled his hand, but she let it stay on her breast. She moved a little away from him, but her hand brushed along his hip. "We have to go." Her hand kept moving as if it didn't agree with her words. She pressed her lips to his jaw. "Look at it this way: the sooner we go, the sooner we can come back."

"But if we don't go, we can finish what we've just started."

"It will be that much sweeter if we put it off."

"Impossible. Hey," he protested when she swung out of the bed. "What happened to 'on three'?"

"You know that never works with us." She grinned down at him.

"So you really want to leave."

"Absolutely not." She sighed. "But we have to. You are coming with me, aren't you?"

"Absolutely yes." He sat up. "I can't let you face those androids alone. Even the Tin Man had more heart." He sighed. "Okay. I know sharing is out of the question, so you pick a shower, and I'll use the other one. I'd suggest that we synchronize our watches, but we seem to have lost them along with our clothes." He grinned. "You'd better hurry and leave before I try to entice you back into this bed."

"It wouldn't take much." She looked at him a few seconds longer, then left the bedroom.

Twenty minutes later they were both dressed.

"I still don't see why you have to go to the hospital to identify that man. You've already identified him by looking at the photograph." Chris stood in Jeanine's front hall with her. "If that wasn't good enough, why did they even bother showing it to you?"

"Who knows?" Jeanine shrugged. "Maybe they want to make sure. If I'd said that the picture wasn't the right man, they wouldn't need me to do this."

"I guess." Chris opened the door. "Let's get this over with. Aside from the fact that we have some unfinished business, whatever this mess is, I want you out of it ASAP."

"Not any more than I do." She wrapped her arm through his.

"You know," she said, after they were on their way, "I hope they give us some answers. This whole situation is really weird."

"His condition is stable." The doctor looked at Agents Dillard, Sullivan and Monroe. "That's the best I can say."

"Can we talk to him?"

"He's still unconscious."

"When will he wake up?"

"I can't answer that."

"We need to get him to a more secure facility."

"If you move him, I can guarantee that he won't survive."

"How soon can he be moved?"

"Agent Monroe, I appreciate that there seems to be an urgency about this man and this situation, but what you want and the reality are far apart." He shook his head. "You want to move him and question him, and I still can't promise that he will survive even if he stays here. It's a miracle that he's alive right now."

"It's vital that we question him."

"Tell that to God." The doctor fixed his eyes on Monroe. "It's in His hands, now." He walked away and left the men standing in the hall.

"First thing we find another room for him," Monroe said after the doctor moved far enough away so he couldn't hear them. "One away from the end of the corridor. Meanwhile, we need more manpower. The three of us can't do this alone."

"You believe the woman?"

"She seemed pretty sure of herself when she gave the description and worked with Lieutenant Clark. Then she identified the photograph as a probable match. We'll see if she can identify him in person." He shook his head. "That's gonna be difficult. The way he looked when he came out of surgery, even his mother would have had trouble with that. I doubt if he looks any better now." He frowned. "What's the connection between pot and coffee?"

He took out his phone and walked to the elevator that would bring the victim down from the recovery room. He took a position beside it while Dillard moved to one end of the corridor and Sullivan took a position at the other.

***

By the time Jeanine and Chris got to the hospital, Elam was in his room.

"Miss Stewart." Monroe met they as soon as the doors opening into the hospital slid apart. "This way."

"Good evening, Agent Monroe. I'm fine. And how are you this beautiful evening?"

He looked back at her. "Busy," he finally answered. "This way." He led them to one of the elevators. It was supposed to be self-service, but a man was operating the controls.

"Wow," she said as she and Chris got off the elevator. Uniformed police officers were positioned along the entire hall. She turned to Monroe. "So you think it's the same man that I saw on Maui and on the coffee farm?"

"We went with that assumption. You seemed so certain. We just need your confirmation." He started toward the room, then turned back. "He's pretty banged up. He won't look like he did when you saw him before."

"I saw the accident scene. I don't expect him to look as he did in the coffee field." She frowned, but continued to face Monroe. "I expected to have to identify a corpse." She took a deep breath. "Can we get this over with?"

He nodded, walked to a room, and opened the door.

Jeanine thought she was prepared until she stepped inside the room. Machines wheezed and throbbed; others pinged and blipped. Wires and tubes were attached to various places on the man lying so still. She took another deep breath and stepped closer to the bed.

"We know you have to make allowances for the current condition of his face, so there might be some uncertainty, but if you'll . . ."

"It's him." She nodded. "It's the man from the coffee farm. And from Maui." She spoke to Agent Monroe, but she continued to stare at the patient. His chest rose and fell as if he were taking the kind of deep breaths that follow heavy exercise, but Jeanine could see that the movement was synchronized with one of the machines that was hooked up to him. Finally she managed to shift her gaze from him and to the agent. "He looks to be in such bad condition. Who is he? Will he live?"

She was unsure that she wanted to hear the answer. The accident had not been her fault. He had followed her; had most likely meant to harm her. Still she felt a twinge of guilt.

"I don't get it. What's the connection between his guarding the marijuana crop and picking coffee beans? What's going on?"

"Thank you for coming down. We appreciate it. This no longer concerns you."

"Wait a minute." Chris stepped forward. "Just like that? This man came after her. He wasn't coming to say 'hi.' He planned to hurt Jeanine. Probably try to kill her. How do we know somebody else won't try to do the same thing?"

"Miss Stewart is safe, now. There's no reason for anyone to come after her. Whatever is going on, when this man followed her, he put the attention on himself instead of her."

"I am standing right here. Quit acting as if I'm not."

"Sorry, baby." Chris squeezed her closer to him. Then he continued to talk to Monroe. "Is he going to live? You didn't answer that. Will he go to jail? How can charges of carrying a gun and growing pot be worth his risking his life?"

"We don't have those answers. Even if we did . . ."

"Yeah, I know." Jeanine said. " 'Need to know,' 'classified information,' and all that stuff." She was angry. "I'll bet when you were a little boy, . . . if you ever were, you played Spy and CIA while the other kids played Cops and Robbers and Superhero and Bad Guys."

"Thank you for your cooperation. We won't need you again."

"I'd say it's been a pleasure, but I'm not going to lie."

Monroe just looked at her. Then he turned and walked back to the elevator.

"Wonder what he'd do if we refused to leave until we got answers."

"You want to stay here with him?"

"Sure. He's as much fun as my favorite team losing the Superbowl." She laughed as she took Chris's hand and strolled to the elevator.

Instead of meeting with Abdul that evening, Hassan decided to follow his own plan. *Who knows what Abdul told them at home?* he thought. *Whatever he reported, it was told in a way to make himself look good. I will fix things as he should have.*

Hassan rode the bus to the hospital, still deciding on the details of his plan.

Once inside, he went to the emergency room. *Good,* he thought as he looked around. Nearly every seat was taken. On the other side of the small room, a woman tried to comfort a crying baby. Another struggled with a small child who kept trying to get down and join two children who were playing a chasing game.

Hassan glanced at the large sign directing people to the window to give their information to the receptionist behind the desk and take a number. She was busy talking to a man who stood in front of her, arguing. A siren came closer, and an ambulance, its red light flashing through the glass door, stopped directly outside. The receptionist glanced from the man to the door as it opened. Then she directed the team wheeling the gurney to a room to the right. One of the children decided to use the newcomers as a barrier in the game of tag. Two women shouted at the children at the same time.

Hassan left his spot beside the front door and slipped into the chair closest to the door leading to the interior of the hospital. He looked through the glass panels and tried to decide on his next move. A man dressed in an orderly's uniform and pushing a large cart caught Hassan's attention. He hesitated, then approached him.

"Hi," Hassan said, reading the man's name tag. "Don, I have a question for you."

"Okay, but I have to get this to the laundry room."

"I'll come with you." Hassan took one side of the cart and pushed.

Deep in conversation with his new acquaintance, Hassan accompanied him into the main section of the hospital. He hesitated when he saw a security guard at the front desk, but relaxed when the guard, involved in conversation with the receptionist there, merely nodded to them.

Hassan smiled as he followed Don to the sign-in sheet. *What good is this procedure if nobody pays attention to it?* Hassan thought, but he didn't complain. Instead he followed Don to the service elevator, asking questions about working at the hospital. They had reached the basement before Hassan asked the question he had been waiting to ask.

"Have you seen the man whose face was on the news?"

"The accident victim?" Don laughed. "I did, but they really gave me a hard time. They act like they're guarding all the money in the world. I gave them attitude right back. I told them that maybe they wanted to do the job themselves." He laughed again. "You better believe they let me in." He glanced at his watch. "I gotta go up there in fifteen minutes. I'm only working the emergency room tonight because somebody called in sick."

As they turned the corner, Hassan continued to ask questions. He learned that Elam was expected to live.

"Man, if it was me hooked up to all those machines,

when I came to and saw them, I'd pass out again." Don stopped halfway down the hall. "Why you ask so many questions?"

"Just curious."

Don looked at Hassan a bit longer, shrugged, then continued down the hall. By the time he unlocked the laundry room door, Hassan knew Elam's floor, his room number, and the routine for servicing the room.

"Where you going?" Don asked as Hassan followed him inside. "What are you doing, man?" He asked as Hassan closed the door. "Who are you?" he asked when his first two questions were ignored.

TWENTY-THREE

Again it is up to me to fix things, to make sure that nothing goes wrong.

Hassan adjusted the name tag on the uniform that he had just buttoned. He tugged at the uniform to keep it from looking too big. Then he glanced once more at the cart spilling dirty linen. He tamped it down. Then he shoved it behind two others that were full. *I'll be gone before they process that one.* He pulled an empty cart toward him, glanced back at the far cart one last time, and left the laundry room.

He was alone in the service elevator as he rode to the third floor, and he used the time to consider several plans.

Perhaps there is more information I should have gotten from Don, he thought. *No. What I have will have to suffice.* The elevator door opened and he slowly left, scanning all around him.

It took no more than a second to see which room he wanted. A metal detector stood in such a position that everyone who left the elevator had to go through it, and guards were posted at regular intervals along the entire hall. But only one room had men posted on each side and a uniformed man sitting in a chair outside the door.

So many guards and such security. All for an unidentified accident victim? Apprehension bubbled inside him. *Did Elam awake? Was he not in as bad a condition as I thought? What do these people know? Why are there so many guards? What did Elam tell them?* His face hardened. *That woman did this. She is next.*

Hassan forced his face to relax, took a deep breath, and started forward. He'd gone a scant foot when the metal detector archway sounded just as he had expected it to. *Further proof that I am on the correct floor. Also proof that they know something.* He exhaled slowly. *Or they think they know something.*

He stood as still as he would have during the scanning routine at an airport. He held his place and smiled when a guard came forward to wave the detector rod over his body and then examined the empty cart inside and out. He remained relaxed, knowing the rod would remain silent. *I am smarter than that.* He watched as the guard tipped the cart on its side and examined the bottom. Finally satisfied, the uniformed man stepped back.

"They've got to come up with something else," he said as he motioned Hassan through. "Metal sets that thing off every time. It doesn't know weapons from carts and beds and wheelchairs. Sorry you always have to go through the procedure."

"It is all right. I understand the need for such things."

"You're in a better mood than some of the others who come through here. It ain't like I enjoy doing this."

"Some understand better than others."

The guard frowned slightly, but motioned Hassan along.

Hassan kept his smile and made himself push the cart slowly down the hall. *I am so close to making sure.*

"What are you doing?" a guard standing against the wall pushed away from it as Hassan peeked into a room.

"Just making sure that they did not put a patient in there and forget to tell me about it." He forced himself to keep smiling. "They do such things and then I am to blame if I do not provide service to the room." The guard failed to return the smile.

"The only room occupied is down there." He pointed toward the guard farther down the hall. Hassan proceeded toward his objective.

"How are you doing?" he asked the guard sitting in the chair outside the door and forced a smile.

"Still in one piece." The man glanced at the name tag as he answered. His hesitation was so slight before he stood that Hassan decided that it was because of the circumstances. "How about you, brother?" The guard fixed Hassan with a stare.

For a second Hassan hesitated and his eyes widened. Then he realized that the man was merely using slang. "I'm good to go." He used a term that he had heard several times. Again he smiled and the guard nodded.

"Let me get the door for you, brother." The guard eased past Hassan and the cart. He reached toward the door, but suddenly grabbed Hassan's arm instead. Before Hassan realized what had happened, he was shoved against the wall and held there with both hands over his head.

Another guard dragged the cart away and shoved it down the hall so hard that it hit the fire door at the end, opposite the elevator. So many men surrounded Hassan that he was barely visible.

"What is the matter?" he managed to ask.

"How's Maggie, Mr. Don Carlen?"

"Maggie?"

"Yeah. You know. Your sister. The one I graduated from high school with? A year after you did?"

"We'll take it from here." Monroe and Sullivan came from the room across the hall and took Hassan from the guard. They turned him to face them and pulled him down the hall, away from the room. There they patted him down.

"Open your mouth," Monroe demanded.

Hassan looked straight ahead as if the men were not there. He took a deep breath, bit down hard, and swallowed.

"He's dead," said the doctor whom Monroe had summoned. "If he used the same stuff that they usually use, he was probably dead before he slumped forward."

Monroe would have been surprised if that were not the case. He stared at the body in the room four doors from Elam's. After again stressing to the doctor the importance of not revealing the situation, Monroe let him go.

"Further proof that we have someone of importance in there." Monroe nodded toward Elam's room. "It is no coincidence that we now have two men with no identification and that one followed the other here."

"How did he know to come?"

"It is impossible to keep information like that secret in a place this size. Too many people are involved. Remember, he came in as an ordinary accident victim." He walked to the door. "We have to move him out of here. The doctor has to get his condition stabilized. My gut tells me that we don't have much time to find out what's going on." He scowled. "My gut is never wrong."

Half an hour later, Hassan had been processed as a deceased patient and taken to the morgue. Fifteen minutes after that, Monroe was arguing with Elam's doctor.

"If we don't move him now, we might not get the opportunity later. We don't know how many others are involved."

"Just because he's holding his own doesn't mean that he's out of danger."

"I understand that, but he's in more danger here than if we move him."

"He needs more time to regain his strength."

"I don't think we have more time. We have to get him to safety."

"Since you've gone over my head, I can't stop you." The doctor glared at him. "But I won't take the responsibility for what happens, either." He walked away, and Monroe got on the phone.

An agent took Elam's place in the hospital bed. For the charts, his condition had been upgraded and all machines were disconnected. The agent's problem was to act as if he were recovering from a horrible accident and to fight the boredom of supposedly not being well enough to watch television. Special personnel had been called in to take over his "care" so no hospital employees would need to be involved. His job was to wait in case the accident victim had more visitors.

At three o'clock in the morning, a minivan, configured as an ambulance, pulled away from the hospital service entrance. Sullivan drove while a doctor associated with the agency rode in back. Agents Monroe and Dillard followed the vehicle to an isolated cabin partway up a rutted dirt road.

"Now what?" Sullivan asked Monroe after Elam was again connected to machines and his condition had been stabilized once again.

"Now we wait to see what our people in the field uncover and pray they find something soon. Real soon."

"This man worked for you?"

Agent Novak stood in the small office of the farm manager, Kyle Loki, and handed Elam's picture to him. Loki held it almost against his nose, moved it farther away, then held it close again as if waiting for it to get clearer. Finally he handed it back.

"That looks like Elam, but it's hard to tell. Is he going to be okay?"

"Didn't you see this picture on the news? Why didn't you call the police and tell them who he is?"

"I don't watch the news. Too depressing." He shrugged.

"None of your other workers mentioned seeing his picture on the news?"

"If they even got televisions, I doubt they watch the news." He shrugged again. "When Elam didn't show up for work, I figured he just took off. They do it all the time. Of course, new guys show up looking for work all the time, too, so it balances out."

"Did you hire anybody else the same day you hired him?"

"No." He shook his head. "Just him."

"How about a few days before or after?"

"Yeah." He nodded. "I did. One man two days before and another two days after." He frowned. "I usually don't get new pickers so close together. These men aren't very good, and they don't seem to be getting any better, but they show up. They get paid according to what they pick so we don't lose any money on them." He shook his head. "As slow as they are, I don't see how they can live on what they make."

"I need all the information you have on them."

"Sure. What did they do?" He opened a file drawer crammed with folders. He looked embarrassed as he slipped his hand inside the drawer to free a stuck folder. "With the turnover we have here, it makes for a lot of paperwork. Some stay only long enough to get a paycheck, then they're gone. Yet we got to report it all to the IRS. We still keep good records." He pulled out another folder and held it up. "Here's the proof," he said as opened it and took three sheets of paper from near the top. "Here you are. Elam's application is there, too."

"Are the other two men here today?"

"Yeah. They're both here. They show up every day.

Sorry I don't have pictures for you. Want me to take you to them? What'd they do, anyway?"

"No. What I need is for you to make copies of these for me." He looked at the man for a few seconds, then shook his head. "We need to put two of our men out here. Can you assign them to work with those two without it looking suspicious?"

"I can do that." Loki nodded and walked over to the copy machine.

"I can't stress how important this is." Novak's look was even more intense than before. "We also need you to stay away from them."

"I wouldn't tell them anything." He handed him the copies, put the file away, and pushed the drawer shut.

"I believe that. But sometimes we have a hard time controlling reactions. We don't want them to know we have them under surveillance. Do you think you can do this for us?"

"I can."

"And can you not mention it to anybody? I can't tell you how important this is. I wish I could give you more information, but I can't. I know I'm a stranger, but we need your cooperation."

"Are those guys involved in some of that terrorist stuff that's going on all over?"

"Mr. Loki, we're investigating suspected illegal activity. We need you to trust us."

Loki stared at Novak for a few seconds before speaking. "I lost my granddaddy at Pearl. I won't ask you any more questions. You got my cooperation. Let me know if you need anything else from me."

"Will do. We appreciate it."

Novak left, frowning. *I don't like involving civilians. I don't like unknown factors.*

He sat in his car in the parking lot and made a phone

call to Agent Monroe. As they talked, he checked the papers he had gotten from Loki and shared what little information they contained. When he was finished, they still didn't know much about the men, but they did have one useful tidbit. They had addresses. Novak broke the connection and waited at the farm as he had been instructed to do.

"I need you two in action yesterday," Monroe said into the phone after giving a field agent the two addresses. "If you learn anything, I'll be more than surprised. I don't need to tell you how to handle this." He rubbed his midsection. "When they show up, follow them. I'll have two men on them when they leave the farm. If we're lucky, they'll all end up at the next rung of their ladder." He clicked the connection off, then made another call. As soon as he gave his report, he clicked the phone shut and paced to the window. *Now comes the hard part. I can't do anything else here except wait to hear from somebody and pray that they have good news.*

Novak was still sitting in his car twenty minutes and five tourist cars later when another car parked beside him. It looked as if it should have been put out of its misery many thousands of miles before. The two men who got out were dressed as if they were glad to have any car at all, but Novak recognized them.

He brought them up-to-date, then watched them go inside the farmhouse. As soon as they could, they'd use their picture phones to send photos of the men to Monroe. Novak's job was to keep waiting.

He sat up when two more cars pulled into the lot ten minutes later, but leaned back when tourists got out of both. They went into the shop discussing coffee. *Hurry up and wait.*

His phone rang fifteen minutes later, and he smiled slightly. Monroe had received the photos. *Our guys are good.*

As soon as the tails for the two men came, he could leave. *Four agents on two guys, so far. How many more will it take?* He had caught Monroe's sense of urgency. *What had Miss Stewart stumbled into? What was going on?*

"Do you think we are really and truly finished with Agent Monroe and company?" Jeanine took one final look in the mirror.

"You look fine, baby. It's a wonder your mirror doesn't tell you so." Chris wrapped his arms around her. "To answer your question, I certainly hope so." He rubbed one hand along her arm, then placed both hands around her waist. "How many flights do you have today?"

"I won't know until I get there." She smiled at him in the mirror as he nuzzled her neck. "Are you going through with your lesson today?"

"You best believe it. I'm sticking with it until I'm controlling one of those birds by myself."

"You don't have to do that, you know."

"Sure, I do. How else can I challenge you to a race?"

She laughed. "I have never heard of racing choppers before."

"Maybe we'll start something new."

"I hope not. That would not be a pretty sight. Neither would it be anything I'd want to hear." They walked from the house. "What do you have planned for today?"

"Do you mean before or after we get together after dinner?"

"I know what your plans are for then." She grinned. "I mean before."

"I have to check on Nate's house. It won't be long before it's finished. Once he quit making changes, things went faster than I expected." He opened her car door. "I also have to work on the plans for the new development."

"Busy, busy, busy."

"Yeah, but not too busy to miss you."

"I'll bet you say that to all of the girls."

"Only the one I'm in love with."

"That must be catching." She looked into his eyes. "Because I love you, too."

They stood as if waiting for something—as if both had forgotten what to do next.

"We'll have to see what we can do about that," he finally said and kissed her forehead. "We'd better leave while we can."

He watched her drive away before he started his car. *I know exactly what to do, and I'm pretty sure she'll go along with it.*

TWENTY-FOUR

Agent Monroe was watching Elam. *At least we have his name.* It's probably phony, but it's more than we had before.

"What are you doing here, Elam?"

The man's eyes flickered.

"I pick coffee."

"And you grow pot. Pretty versatile crops."

Elam stared straight ahead and drew a deep breath from the oxygen coming through the nose clips, but he didn't respond. "Why are you here?"

"I pick coffee."

"We have your buddy. He was planning to kill you."

"You have Hassan?" A larger portion of oxygen entered his body.

Monroe smiled. *Another name to add to our list.*

"What did Hassan do? He didn't pick coffee with you." They had shown the picture at all of the farms. Hassan had not picked coffee anywhere on the island.

"Ask him to tell you." Elam still refused to make eye contact.

"Did the people taking care of you tell you that the little pill you had hidden in your mouth was removed? Did they tell you that the rest of your life will be spent in a bed like that one? That you will never walk again? Never even sit up? You'll have to depend on somebody to feed you.

Wipe your nose. You're what—about twenty? This is the rest of your life."

Elam swallowed hard, as if he had found the pill that Monroe claimed to have removed. He did not answer.

"Where are you from? Why are you here?" Elam acted as if he had not heard him. "Perhaps your buddies from the farm will be more cooperative." Elam gasped as best he could since he was dependent on the oxygen.

"You will learn nothing." The words struggled out. "We are prepared for such situations." His head lifted a bit, but the rest of his body stayed in place. "You will learn nothing. Nothing."

Monroe stared down at him for a second. Under other circumstances he might feel a little sorry for somebody in Elam's situation. Under other circumstances. He left the room.

Back to waiting. Not for long I hope, he thought as he entered the narrow hall. *We don't have long.*

"I'm not complaining, but why the change in plans?" Jeanine smiled at Chris across the table in the restaurant. Their plates had been cleared and Chris was waiting for the waiter to bring back his credit card. It was a weekday, but almost every table in Hattie's was taken.

"I'm going to do something that I swore I'd never do."

"What's that?" Jeanine frowned at him.

"You are about to witness a grown man making a complete fool of himself." He stood and walked around the table to her.

Jeanine gasped as he got down on one knee next to her. Her mouth was still open when he took her hand from the table and held it.

"Jeanine Stewart, I love you more than I thought I

could ever love somebody. Will you do me the honor of marrying me?"

Jeanine sat as if glued in place and she had forgotten how to close her mouth.

"You gonna leave me hanging? Or rather kneeling?"

"No. No." She grinned at him. Then she knelt beside him. She cupped both of her hands around his face. "Of—of course I will." She laughed. "I love you more than I thought possible, too." She leaned in and kissed him.

"Okay," Chris said as he allowed a little space between them. "Now, can we stand? This is not the most comfortable position. My knees are protesting big time." They both laughed.

He stood and helped her up with him. Then he pulled her close and covered her mouth with his. They were lost in the kiss until the clapping and shouts surrounding them made them separate. Holding hands, Jeanine and Chris looked around. Everybody from every table in the restaurant was on their feet, cheering.

"Way to go!" somebody yelled.

"How sweet," an older woman at the table next to them said. Her husband took her hand from the table and squeezed it.

"Oh, I almost forgot." Chris pulled a small red velvet box from his pocket and opened it. A square-cut diamond flanked by three smaller diamonds on each side winked at them.

"Oh," Jeanine gasped as he removed the ring.

"If you don't like it, they will exchange it for us."

"Like it? Don't you dare try to get this away from me." She wrapped her arms around him. "It's the most beautiful ring I have ever seen." Her eyes glistened. "I love you so much," she whispered before she pulled his mouth to hers.

When they separated, Chris wrapped one arm around her waist. They started to leave the restaurant.

"Hey, man, don't forget your credit card. Weddings are expensive." Chuckles sounded as Chris accepted the card and slipped it into his pocket. The applause started again and followed them to the door.

"Did you really say 'yes'?" Chris dared to ask when they reached the car.

"I really said 'yes.'"

"You weren't just trying to keep me from looking more like a fool?"

"You did not look like a fool. My fiancé could never look like a fool." She squeezed his arm. "I like the sound of that. My fiancé." She kissed him before she got into the car.

"It sounds okay, but not as nice as 'my wife.'" He slipped behind the wheel.

"Or 'my husband.'" Jeanine reached over and took his hand in hers. "I had no idea you were going to do that."

"I wanted you to have something to tell our children."

"Children?"

"Yeah. You know; little people who look like us." He glanced at her as he pulled onto the highway. "You do want children, don't you?" A serious look replaced the grin.

"Of course I do. I'd love to have a little Chris to go with my big Chris." She giggled.

"Then, I have to have a little Jeanine to go with my bigger Jeanine."

"Good. We agree." She shook her head. "I can't believe it."

"Why not? You know I love you."

"Yes. I do." She smiled at him, then held up her hand so her ring twinkled in the light coming from outside the car. "Engaged. I'm going to get married."

"*We're* engaged. *We're* going to get married," he corrected her.

"I stand corrected. We're in this together."

"For the rest of our lives." He squeezed her hand and held it the rest of the ride to her house.

"What have you got?" Agent Monroe didn't bother with 'hello' as he answered the phone. "Where?" He nodded and wrote as he listened. "Stay on him. One of them has to take us to the next level. This isn't about a bunch of guys working coffee farms." He hung up.

Marijuana and coffee farms. He frowned. *That phrase has been running around in my mind since Miss Stewart connected Elam with both.* What do the two have in common? He paced the office so many times that, had the floor been dirt, he would have worn a path. Still he moved. From time to time he switched directions, but he kept pacing.

After about the tenth circuit, he sat.

Coffee and marijuana. Marijuana and coffee. He covered the top page of the pad in front of him with the two words. Then he began drawing lines around them. Suddenly he put the pen down and stared at the paper. *What if the importance isn't a connection? What if the reason for the first is the same reason that most growers have? Money.* He drew dollar signs around each word. *That leaves coffee. Why coffee farms? Why put their guys on all of the coffee farms? What are they planning?*

New agents had been sent to the island and had followed Elam's associates until another man met with each of them separately. The same man. Another link. Another link up the chain. For Monroe it felt as if there were more agents on the island that tourists.

This was the second day they had been following all of

the first group as well as the new man to see where he went. So far he had led them nowhere but back to one of the others. The surveillance equipment had picked up nothing.

Monroe continued staring at the paper, but he wasn't seeing his notes. His mind was trying to find a link.

Coffee farms. Coffee. It was all connected to the coffee farms. The farms were legitimate businesses. Many were family owned. None of them had changed hands in years. *Coffee farms,* he doodled around what was left of the edges of the paper. *Coffee. Not the farms? The coffee?* He underlined the word three times. *Coffee.*

He hit a button on his phone and stood. For the few seconds it took for his call to be answered, he stared at the word.

"I need something checked ASAP. We need somebody who knows coffee, and I don't mean the thousand and one varieties sold to consumers. Yeah." He nodded. "I said coffee. These guys are on every coffee farm on the island. Check with our guys and see if they can come up with a reason. Maybe a chemist. Put a rush on it. Something is about to go down. We need to stop it. Meanwhile we'll stay on them at this end."

Monroe paced in front of the window. Each time he passed the desk he looked at the phone as if that would make it ring. On what seemed like his hundredth turn, he was rewarded.

TWENTY-FIVE

"Who is this? Tell me you got something for me," Agent Monroe demanded into the phone. As he listened, some of the tension left him.

"A lab? The guy led you to a lab?" He squeezed the phone in frustration. "Look. We need more than a shop for processing pot. This has got to be bigger than that. Too many people are involved." He nodded. "Oh. So you think it's more than just a cabin? Can't you see inside any better? I know you're a long distance away, but our equipment should be able to read the date on a coin in the pocket of a guy inside." He shook his head. "No. Don't go in. Hold your position. I'm on my way. If he leaves before I get there, you know what to do with him and how to do it."

His car squealed out of the driveway. As he raced to the mountain, he hoped he would not be stopped by a police officer. He could explain things, but it would take time. Time he thought he could not afford to waste. He put on his headset and hoped for a call from Washington that would give them the missing puzzle piece.

Just before he reached the site, the phone rang. For the first time in what seemed like years, he showed a slight smile. A chemist had theorized a possible reason for the interest in the coffee crops and was on a private jet from Los Angeles. Monroe instructed Agent Dillard to be there when it landed. *Another hurry-up-and-wait scenario*, he thought. *Not quite. This time we're moving forward.*

He parked far away from the road and under trees, thankful for the rich vegetation. Then he walked several hundred yards inland.

"Nothing yet." They were nowhere near hearing distance, yet Agent Sullivan's voice was barely a whisper. "Our guys in the trees say they seem to be packaging something, but they can't tell what. They have to rely on what they can see through a small window. I'm surprised it wasn't covered."

"They're probably sure that they are safe." Monroe exhaled sharply. "Thank God for small miracles. What else you got for me?"

"We followed six men here, and we don't know how many were already inside. Our men are scattered around. Nobody will get past us." Sullivan glanced at Monroe then back in the direction of the cabin. "What do you think is going on?"

"We got a lab guy on the way. I hope he'll be able to tell us." His eyes stayed on the cabin. "Whatever it is, it looks like we caught it in time." His face tightened. "Now we wait some more.

"Heads up, guys," Monroe said half an hour later into the microphone linking him to the other agents. Through binoculars he watched the cabin door open, but he stayed in place. "We've got some action. You know the drill. Give them time to get well away from the cabin before you grab them. We don't want to warn the others still inside. If they follow their usual procedure, you'll have plenty of time to take one before the next one comes out. Forget about trying to get the man you followed. Take the one who comes closest to you. I don't need to say it, but I will: keep them quiet and make sure they stay with us. We need answers. Bodies won't give them to us." He paused. "This first guy is carrying a package. Handle it carefully until we get HAZMAT equipment up here."

Monroe watched as, ten minutes later, another man came out carrying a similar package. At the same intervals, the other five left the cabin. Monroe heard nothing, but he wasn't worried. He wasn't supposed to be, and his men were good.

An hour later he motioned to the men with him. Slowly and quietly they reached the cabin and waited on all sides. Two voices were murmuring inside. Quiet laughter mixed with words that the men outside didn't understand.

"Close in," Monroe ordered quietly. The jungle seemed alive with more men moving from it to surround the cabin. Monroe took a deep breath and crept to the door. "Now!" he shouted as he kicked in the door. At the same time agents climbed through the windows and entered the back door. "No!" he yelled and grabbed the man closest to him. He forced his mouth open and removed the man's escape pill. At the same time other agents were doing the same thing to their prisoners. It was obvious that one agent had been too slow when one prisoner slumped to the floor.

It was over in less than ten minutes. The six men who had been followed were sitting on the floor and against the wall. Two men in white coats sat beside them. White masks hung loosely around their necks.

"I don't mind telling you that this place makes me nervous. Those masks and plastic gloves don't soothe my nerves." Sullivan looked around the small cabin. Every inch was in use.

A long table stretched along one side of the room with

fluorescent lamps hung low over it. Another, in the far, dark half of the room and separated from the other table by tall metal padlocked cabinets, almost touched the wall. Covered glass lab dishes filled one end of it while the other end was empty. Empty petri dishes were stacked in the gray concrete sink.

"What were they messing with?" Sullivan voiced what Monroe was wondering himself. Monroe walked over to the padded stool next to a small table.

A lighted microscope sat on the table as if waiting for company. Test tubes stood in holders to the side. Other lab equipment was set in an orderly fashion beside them. Monroe recognized some of the things from his college science classes. Most, however, he had never seen before.

Where's that scientist? Monroe glanced at his watch. *It's too soon, but somehow I don't think we're under as tight a time frame as before.* He watched as the prisoners were taken away. *Maybe somebody will talk. Maybe not.* He shrugged. *We got the lab. One point for us.* He waited in the cabin for Dillard to bring the scientist. Several other agents were back in place in the trees and hiding throughout the area, just in case. From the outside, the cabin looked as it had before the agents came. Monroe nodded. *That's how it should be.*

When Dillard arrived with the scientist, Monroe took a few minutes to brief him. Then he moved out of the way and let the man go to work.

Late evening; early morning to most. The scientist called Monroe. He came from the almost comfortable spot where he had camped out.

"Fungus," the scientist announced as he turned from the table.

"Fungus? As in mushrooms?" Monroe asked.

"Not quite." He beckoned to him. "Look." He pointed to the microscope. "This is nothing as simple as a mushroom. These spores are specialized; they're picky. They only like coffee."

"Coffee?"

"As in beans. The fungus is engineered to attack coffee beans as they grow. If it were released on the farms, the crop would be destroyed. That would mean economic disaster to one of the major sources of income in the state. Factor in the domino effect on employment, stores, shipping companies, and you have a slice of disaster. If this had worked, they probably would have moved on, possibly to the mainland. Maybe releasing blight on wheat crops?" He shook his head. "Good you uncovered them when you did."

"We had help." Monroe thought of Jeanine.

"Make sure you say your prayers tonight." He packed his lab coat into the small bag on the floor. "And don't think of what might have happened." He picked up the bag and started for the door. "That kind of imagining can shove you over the edge."

"You're right about that." Monroe rubbed his midsection, a nervous habit. "Dillard will take you to the airport."

"I hope I won't see you again."

"So do I." The scientist nodded and left.

Monroe watched the door until the sound of the motor disappeared. Then he took one last look around before leaving. Once outside, he nodded to a man standing in the shadows. Without looking back, he got into his car and left.

The cabin would be watched constantly in case someone returned to it. As for Monroe, his part was over.

Too bad I can't let Miss Stewart know what her obser-

vation led to. Too bad she would never know what happened. He smiled. A real smile. *Or what didn't happen. This one goes into the win column.*

TWENTY-SIX

"What do you think happened with that stuff with Monroe?" Jeanine stood with Chris on his lanai. She leaned back against him as they watched the sun making its last appearance before it retired for the night.

"I don't think we'll ever find out." He tightened his arms around her and kissed her cheek. "Maybe that's a good thing."

"Yes." She nodded. "This is truly an example of no news being good news." She tilted her head to the side, and he pressed his lips to her neck. "Still, I wonder what it was all about. What was that man doing on the coffee farm after guarding the pot? And what happened to him? After that first news release, we haven't seen or heard anything else about him. Did he die? Did he give an explanation?" She sighed. "I hate loose ends."

"Usually I do too, but you and I have other things to worry about."

"Oh yeah?"

"Yes. How are we going to exist apart for four long days?" He stroked her arms. "And four even longer nights."

"You'll get no sympathy from me. You should have thought of that before you decided to meet with that corporation in Los Angeles."

"I know, but this came up and I was afraid to turn down

the opportunity to design that new complex on Maui." He ran his hands from her waist to her hips and back up. "After all, in exactly four days and eight and a half hours, I'll be a married man with responsibilities."

"Acquiring a ball and chain, huh?"

"Marrying the most beautiful woman to ever walk the Earth."

"Wow. I hope you feel that way years from now."

"For ever and ever, baby."

"Amen," she added as she rested her hands on his, around her waist.

They stood staring at the horizon until there was only a pink and gray sliver of light, and then nothing. They went inside.

"We have four days of loving to stock up on." Chris turned her to face him.

"I guess we'd better get started, huh?" Jeanine stretched up and met Chris's mouth. Soon they were lost in each other as if they believed stocking up on love were possible.

"I'll see you on Friday evening." Chris and Jeanine stood on the sidewalk outside the airport terminal door early the next morning.

"Friday is a long way off."

"You'll have Trent and Angela and your nephew, Dan, to take your mind off me."

"You know nothing could do that."

"More than a good answer." He pulled her close for a final kiss. "I am going to miss you like crazy."

"Concentrate on your presentation. That will take your mind off me."

"To quote a wise and beautiful woman: 'You know

nothing could do that.' " He stepped away. "Gotta go." He gave her one quick kiss and walked into the terminal.

Jeanine watched him go to the desk. He turned around, and she gave him one last wave. Then she drove to the other side of the airport. She had a flight before she picked up Trent and his family.

It will be so good to see him. She smiled as she thought about her brother. *It will be so good to see all of them. It's been too long.* She shook her head. *Little Dan will have to get to know me all over again.* She shrugged and went to report in and get her itinerary.

"Hey, Nate." Jeanine walked into the open hangar on her way to the field. "Have you recovered from your open house last Saturday?" She grinned at her soon-to-be brother-in-law.

"That was days ago. It's old news. And it was not an open house. Guys don't have such a thing."

"What do you call it, then?"

"I call it having my friends over to see my new house."

"All of your friends at the same time?"

"Yeah."

"With a caterer and all the trimmings."

"When folks come to visit you have to offer them something to eat. It's only hospitable."

"New vocabulary book?"

"I hope my big brother realizes what he's getting into."

"Trust me." Her grin widened. "He does."

"You all set?"

"I have everything except my passengers." She looked at him. "Does Lisa like the house?" Jeanine could swear that Nate blushed although she knew he would deny it from now until forever.

"Yes," he mumbled and frowned at the ground.

"She's a nice woman, don't you think?"

"Yeah." He scowled at her. "I checked out your bird."

"You always do."

"Yeah."

"When you going to see her again?"

"Here comes your party."

"Saved by the passengers, huh?" She squeezed his arm. "Being in the same family will be very interesting, don't you think?"

"You should have learned a long time ago that it's not nice to tease."

"But it's so easy with you." She giggled. "See you later."

Three hours later Jeanine was waiting outside the Arriving Flights section of the airport. She didn't have long to wait.

"Over here." She waved at Trent, who was pushing a heaping luggage cart. Angela walked beside him, trying to keep Dan from pulling loose and running ahead.

"I am so happy to see you," Jeanine said when they reached her. She dropped a lei over Angela's head and kissed her cheek. Then she did the same for Trent.

"I thought this ritual was supposed to be performed for females by a handsome young man wearing an aloha shirt and a winning smile," Angela said.

"My sister knew better than to put some innocent man's life in danger." Trent smiled at Angela and gave her a quick kiss.

"My brother is so territorial." Jeanine laughed.

"Yeah, but he's so cute." Angela hugged Trent.

"Hi, Dan." Jeanine stooped down to the toddler who was hiding behind his mother's skirt. "Remember your Aunt Jeanine?"

"All of a sudden he's shy. And still. We should have had

you with us on the plane." Angela eased Dan from behind her and picked him up. They followed Jeanine the few feet to her car.

"How was the flight?"

"Long." Trent and Angela answered together. Then the three laughed.

"Can you imagine how it would have been if you hadn't spent three days in Los Angeles first?" Jeanine opened her car's trunk.

"I don't want to even think about that," Trent said as he put the largest suitcase in first. "Mercifully, Dan slept for a long time during the flight. I think he's still on East Coast time."

"We did the sightseeing bit, too, in L.A., so that probably had something to do with tiring him out," Angela added. "I don't care what the reason is, I'm just thankful for it."

"The flights didn't bother your leg?" Jeanine looked up at Trent, who paused before putting another suitcase in.

"The kinks will work out as they always do. What do you think?" He pointed to the rest of the luggage. "Mission impossible or do-able?"

Jeanine shook her head. "It's a good thing I didn't bring the stroller you asked me to rent."

"You don't know what it's like to travel with a little kid," Angela said.

"He has more stuff that the two of us together," Trent added as he placed the two carry-on bags in.

"I hope I won't have to wait too long to find out." The softness in Jeanine's voice made Trent and Angela pause.

"You won't," Trent said.

"Then I'll remind you of this moment," Angela added as she put Dan down, but held onto his hand. They laughed as he tried to pull her toward the sidewalk.

"The first thing we do when we get to your place is turn him loose until he falls down from exhaustion."

"I'm afraid we might fall down first." Trent leaned toward Angela for a kiss, but Dan picked that second to try to get away again. "Later," he said as Angela lifted Dan back into her arms.

"I'll hold you to that promise." The love in Angela's eyes looked as if it came from a newlywed.

Jeanine glanced from one to the other. *That's what I want.* She smiled. *In a few days, I'll be on my way to having it.*

"You are as ready as you're ever going to be." Lisa patted the veil pinned to the back of Jeanine's head. She lightly smoothed the satin skirt of the long, fitted wedding gown, then adjusted the lace-trimmed scooped neckline so it was perfectly centered. She stepped away, then back and tugged slightly on first one sleeve, then the other.

"Enough already." Jeanine pulled at her shoulder.

"Don't do that. You'll mess it up." Lisa smacked the bride's hand, then adjusted the shoulder seam back into place. She stepped back and smiled. "Perfect." She shook her head slightly. "Too bad Kalele couldn't be here." She swallowed hard.

"I'll send her some pictures by e-mail, but it won't be the same thing." Jeanine blinked rapidly. "I miss her."

"I do, too, but don't cry." Lisa daubed at Jeanine's eyes. "You'll mess up your make-up." She smiled. "At least I won't have to fight her for the bouquet." She grinned and stepped back again. "I know Chris would wait forever, but let's not make him do that, okay?" She handed Jeanine the bouquet of pale orchids and pink plumerias.

"Okay." Jeanine took a deep breath and gave Lisa a quick hug. "Let's go."

Jeanine stood in the middle of a tall archway covered with greenery and pink and white plumerias. Jasmine blossoms, fastened among the other flowers, released their perfume into the air as if not to be outdone. The room had been transformed into a fairy-tale chapel. It was beyond beautiful, but Jeanine didn't notice.

Their friends and family members filled the seats on both sides of the aisle, and everybody stood. It was all lost on her. She started forward.

The reactions of the guests as she passed on her way to meet Chris went unnoticed, too. The only thing she was aware of was Chris, standing so handsome in his white tuxedo next to Nate; Chris, who was waiting for her. Chris, with whom she would spend the rest of her life. Her Chris. Her smile widened as she got closer to him.

Finally she reached him and Lisa took the bouquet from her. Jeanine was unaware of it. She wasn't aware of anything except Chris. The two of them looked at each other as if they were the only ones in the room, in the universe.

Reverend Grant cleared his throat. "I understand that you've written your own vows?" His voice made them look at him.

"Yes," Chris answered first. The minister nodded, and Chris held Jeanine's hand and took a deep breath. "Jeanine, I spent my life looking for you. Before I met you I was nothing. I cannot believe that you agreed to be the bride of somebody as pig headed as I am. I will spend the rest of my life trying to make you happy. My heart holds more love than I thought was possible. I want to grow old with you."

"Chris, until I met you, there was a piece missing from my life. You complete me. I am so thankful that I found you. I never knew that my heart could hold so much love. I want to watch every sunset from now on with you. I want to spend the rest of my days trying to make you happy." She squeezed his hand, and they faced the minister once more.

Reverend Grant finished the ceremony, but the only way that Jeanine and Chris knew that was from the applause of the guests. They each took one step toward each other. Their lips met in a kiss that sealed their promises to each other. Slowly, they parted.

"Ladies and gentlemen," the minister said, "may I present Mr. and Mrs. Harris." The applause grew louder as Jeanine and Chris walked hand in hand to stand at the back of the room.

The line of guests moved past them, and Jeanine hoped she said the appropriate thing to each one.

Chris and I are married, kept skipping through her mind. She felt her grin widen. *I am Mrs. Christopher Harris.* She shook her head. *I hope nobody pinches me. If I'm asleep, I don't want to wake up.*

Finally the last guest greeted them and followed the others into the adjoining room for the reception, where hot and cold hors d'oeuvres were being offered by the wait staff circulating among the guests.

Chris and Jeanine remained behind and allowed a photographer to direct them. Then they went to the lobby and out to the garden.

"Enough," Jeanine said. "Our guests will think we took off."

"You have enough pictures, don't you?" Chris wrapped one hand around Jeanine's waist.

"A photographer never has enough pictures." He raised his camera. "Just one more. I promise that this is the last one."

When Jeanine and Chris appeared in the doorway of the reception room, the band began to play an upbeat version of "Here Comes the Bride." The couple grinned all the way to their seats. A meal was about to be served.

The bride and groom were still grinning when the meal was over. They had stopped grinning only long enough to share the many kisses triggered by the tinkling of glasses and the many toasts offered.

The band started with traditional dances and then began serious get-down music.

"I know it's supposed to be bad manners to ask, but I'm curious. Where do people who live in Hawaii go for a honeymoon?" Trent stood in front of them as they left the dance floor.

"A different island. Where else?"

"You aren't going anywhere?"

"Sure we are. We're going over to Maui, but don't tell anybody else. We don't want to be bothered."

"Sure." Trent shrugged. "If you spend your honeymoon the way we spent ours, it won't matter where you are." He chuckled and went back inside.

"Let's go finish with tradition. I'll toss my bouquet, and you can throw my garter. Then we can leave."

"We'll take care of those two things." He pulled her close and looked down into her eyes. "But we won't be finished with all of the traditions."

"No," she agreed.

"We'll have one very important one left." He placed his hands on her hips and pulled her against him. "We still have the wedding night." He kissed her.

"I doubt if we'll wait until the night."

"Some traditions benefit from adjustment."

"It's okay if we're both willing." She kissed him again.

"We're both more than willing." They stood pressed against each other. Chris kissed each of her eyelids. Then her cheek. He kissed his way to her mouth. A deep kiss was followed by an even deeper one.

Their kisses were filled with hope and promises for their future together. Promises of happily ever after.

To the Readers

I hope you enjoyed Jeanine and Chris's story. Jeanine is the sister of Trent, the hero in *Escape to Love*. Because of her career, I decided that a strong woman deserved her own story. I also hope you enjoyed my venture into Hawaii. Words cannot do it justice. If you have never been to Hawaii, go. Forget the long airplane ride. I still sigh as I remember sitting at the table with my laptop and being able to look out at a spectacular view. There are no ugly nature scenes there. It truly is a paradise on Earth.

I decided to address a very real, ugly subject rather than give you a complete escape from the cares of the world, but I also gave you an upbeat ending.

As always, keep reading, and I'll keep writing.

Please visit my website:
www.alicewootson.net

You can reach me at the following:
Alice Wootson
P.O. Box 18832
Philadelphia, PA 19119
or
agwwriter@email.com